HARDLY A LADY

Frances M. Strickler

RABBIT HOUSE PRESS
Versailles, KY 40383

Edited by: Erin Chandler
Cover & Interior Design: Daphne Vorel

Published in the United States by Rabbit House Press
Printed in the United States of America

ISBN: 979-8-9907833-7-9

Dedication

Goldie Droege Strickler

1916 - 2013

Hardly a Lady

Chapter One

Engagement Party

2010

It is the 10ᵗʰ of July. I'm tired. My bones ache in places I didn't know I had bones. I will admit, though, I am happy. Very happy, I think. I thought happiness was beyond me at this point in my life. What a surprise it is that I feel the rush of excitement and delight I firmly believed was gone forever. I'm attending a reception to celebrate my granddaughter's engagement. I am 94 years old. I never believed I'd make it this long. Some days, I believe my long life is a punishment for past sins instead of a gift.

For this special event, I'm wearing a lovely watered-silk purple dress with flutter sleeves and a V neck. It is the most exquisite dress I have ever worn. Of all the beautiful dresses I have bought or made, I think this is, unquestionably, the most elegant. At my throat, I wear a pear-shaped amethyst necklace anchored to the chain by a 3-karat diamond, which my daughters believe is fake. I've watched them snicker and nod as they shift it around in my jewelry box. They glance at each other and shake their heads. Their tight smiles say, "Now who the hell is going to have to deal with this gaudy thing after she's gone?"

I smile and nod to myself because I know it isn't fake. The matching earrings have diamonds which are quite small. The clip-ons pinch more than they used to, and they leave little dimpled indentations in my ears which seem to have grown larger and coarser than when

I was young. My granddaughter, lovely girl, will inherit this piece of jewelry. She can appreciate it or sell it. I don't know which, but at any rate, it will make a valuable gift.

I don't take a deep drag on my cigarette, pull off my earrings, and stick them in my purse for safe keeping as I once would have done at a reception. Come to think of it, I didn't have a cocktail either. Someone handed me a plastic glass of some frozen lemonade punch that lacked a kick. Nasty tasting stuff. Heaven only knows what the expressions would have been if I had pulled a cigarette out of my tiny clutch purse. This purse is so small it can hold no more than a packet of sen-sen (the breath perfume of choice in my younger days), a linen hanky, and maybe one small hand-rolled cigarette or a Lucky Strike even. I gaze at the purple shimmering fabric and notice the edges have grown a bit frayed at the edges. It is a treasured reminder of times and people of the past.

Oh, for the days when I could ask the adorable young man sitting next to me for a light and to run along and fetch me a martini, classic or dirty, preferably dirty. Would he look at me, grin just enough to let his dimples show, light my cigarette, fingers softly wrapped around mine, and unwrap his elegant long body out of the dinky little chair and run off to do my bidding?

Gasp! Shock! What? There is no smoking allowed here and no Granny drinking. Maybe I could pull it off were I to sneak outside, but how does one sneak outside in a wheelchair? All in all, it seems this is the best party I have ever attended. I've gone to wonderful parties in my lifetime and have worn gorgeous dresses, but this time I have had the best of both. Funny, isn't it, how your kids and grandkids see you as sweet little old granny? My older daughter comes to me and offers to put a blanket over my lap and asks if I am feeling chilly. "No thank you, dear," I say, trying to divert her from hovering. My younger daughter comes over and speaks loudly into my face assuming I cannot hear her and asks if I have taken my pills. "Yes, dear," I tell her. "Every damn one of them." I need to be kind. They are trying to be helpful, but instead, seem quite annoying. I may be old, but I am not frail or helpless.

One of their friends comes over, sits down beside me, and pats me on the hand. She chatters mindlessly about the party and then she leans into my face and asks me, "Now, can I ask you how old you are, Mrs. Raisch?"

I answer her with a whisper as I lean toward her, "Can you keep a secret?"

"Oh, of course," she tittered.

"So, can I," I responded as I turned and wheeled away. I giggle to myself because I was not always nice, not always old, and hardly ever a lady. My goal as a girl and woman was to design and make beautiful dresses for the stars. Well, sometimes, your dreams can take a bit of a twist. I intended to sew for the stars but ended up getting involved with the mob. It's hard to explain this to these well-meaning but ignorant young people, who are certain they have all the answers to all the questions. The truth lies in my journals. I tried to be honest and faithful in them over the years.

My first journal was given to me by my Momma and Poppa for Christmas, 1929. I shake my head when I think of it, all those years ago. Looking back in time, I wonder how I could have ever been that innocent or naive?

Chapter Two

Josie

1930

J*anuary 1*

Dear Journal, my name is Josie Kassemier. I am fourteen years old, almost. I got you from Momma and Poppa for Christmas, 1929. I am going to fill you with everyday facts and events of my life for this year. Poppa told me it was important to keep facts, events, and the important things in the world in writing. Momma told me to write about things that happen to my everyday self. I won't put everything that happens to me in here, and I probably won't write in you every day, but I will try and remember the more important things.

Important facts of my life are that I live in California, Kentucky. I am 5 feet 7 inches, I wear size 5 1/2 shoes, size 9 1/2 stockings, and size 8 gloves. My best friend in the whole world is Jenny Mae Aldrich. She is small, blonde, and pretty. She has huge blue eyes, and all the boys like her. She is also smart. She plans to go to the University in Lexington one day. She lives in Alexandria, Kentucky, and even though our mail comes to California, Kentucky, I can walk to her house.

I am tall and thin with brown eyes. Although I am a good student, I'm not quite as good as Jenny Mae. My special talent is sewing. I can sew, make clothes, and embroider. Now, I make most of my clothes with Momma's help, but someday I want to make and design a catalog of perfect clothes. So, this is where I will begin this year. I will try to keep up with the best stuff.

Turning the yellowing pages of my journals, I think about this person. As a young girl, when I saw beautiful clothes, silks, tweed suits, saucy little flounces and frills, heads covered with cute berets or maybe a tilt hat, I could certainly see myself creating these types of fashions. I thought maybe with Momma's help and that of my teacher, who was a wonderful mentor, I could do this. The picture in my mind was of my grown-up self as this glamourous woman sweeping through a crowded room leaving a trail of luscious scent wafting behind me. I pictured the men in the room all gazing after me trying to identify who I was and what my last movie had been. Of course, I would be the one who designed and modeled these clothes for the stars, but how would they know?

In fact, most of the things I did during the day were about school. When I was at school, I helped by washing dishes and helping the teachers pass out paper and pens. At home, I helped feed calves and pigs, put up hay and worked in the garden. I cooked, cleaned, canned, and sewed, sewed, sewed. I sewed clothes, curtains, dishcloths, and worked on rugs all around the house. The activities I enjoyed, other than sewing, were church and Sunday School, choir, and revivals. The thing I loved most was going to basketball games. I didn't play basketball even though I was tall, and everybody seemed to think I should. They didn't realize how my feet seemed to run into each other, or how uncoordinated I could be. If they had, they would have known that playing basketball wasn't for me. This miserable lack of coordination would stay with me for the rest of my life.

January 28

We are planning to start out to a ballgame, but our Tin Lizzie (our car, which most around here call their machines) has frozen up, so we can't go.

During all this cold, Tin Lizzie sat in the driveway frozen up most of the time. It was frustrating to try to plan anything. Darn. Horses were much more reliable. Poppa was still firm about raising and training his horses. There was definitely a need here. Most of the neighbors had been looking at and buying cars, and Poppa didn't want to be left behind. Still, Poppa knew cars weren't being used to plow our fields. He loved and cared for his horses, but this love wouldn't last forever.

February 14

I got 30 Valentines on Valentine's Day.

April 8

Twelve baby chicks and 10 new beagle puppies were born on the farm today. Momma made me make a list for making custard. I'll have to remember how to make this:

¼ teaspoon salt to 1 quart milk for custards

1 teaspoon flavoring for 1 quart custard or cream

6-8 eggs to 1 quart milk for custard to be turned in a mold

4 eggs to 1 quart milk for plain custard.

2/3 cup sugar, or less, to a quart milk for custard.

April 26

My birthday. I got a new dress that was store bought from Momma and Poppa. I was so happy about the dress. Money is hard to come by. I saw the love and laughter in their faces as I opened the box. Poppa with a proud smile. Momma with her beaming eyes. I got a box of letter paper. I made my birthday cake. It was chocolate with caramel icing. I am now 15 years old. The pups' eyes are open. Cutest little things you ever saw.

May 9

My friend, Rose Riley was sent home from school today with Scarlet Fever. Lots of children die with this disease, I've heard. Hope she doesn't die. Hope I don't get it.

May 12

I woke up this morning feeling awful. I ached all over. My throat was sore and my tongue felt like it had swollen up to twice its size overnight. I sat on the edge of my bed for a moment and then plunked back down. Since it's Saturday, I didn't miss school. The doctor came over and said I have Scarlet Fever. Guess I caught it from Rose?

With this sickness, I didn't feel as sick as I imagined I might be. However, I wasn't allowed to go out to see my friends, so I might as well have felt terrible. Boring! What was I supposed to do staying at home all day? It was finally spring. The sun was shining, the flowers blooming, and I was stuck in the house. Was I stuck doing my embroidery all day? Phew. Even worse, we were told that we had to have a red sign tacked on the door that said I had scarlet fever. I took all this quite lightly, not realizing at the time how serious Scarlet Fever could be.

It would be days before I could get up and out. Jenny Mae's fellow, Bob, brought my schoolbooks home to me. I couldn't let him get too close because he could have gotten scarlet fever too. He was Jenny Mae's fellow, but he always seemed to be finding reasons to talk to me. So cute with his blond hair and green eyes. I wouldn't hurt Jenny Mae for anything, but I didn't know if she liked him as a boyfriend or not. Looking back, I wonder why on earth I didn't come right out and ask Jenny Mae if he was her beau or not, but I never did.

On Thursday, I felt I had to get out of the house. Jenny Mae and I decided to go down to the store and see if they had any licorice. How sneaky this felt, running around this way. Since I didn't have any spots left, and I wasn't itching, I thought I must be well. I felt skittish from all that sitting around the house.

On Saturday, since Thursday had gone well, I thought I would meet up with Jenny and a couple of the other girls to go to the drugstore and get a soda. The very minute I got home, though, Poppa told me he ran into the doctor while he was in town, and the doctor said that I could get out of the house. "Did you tell him that I had already been up and running around for at least a couple of days," I asked Poppa.

"No, I didn't want to ruin the surprise if he was to catch you doing just that." His face crinkled into a big grin. Wonder if he was hoping I would have. Poppa seemed to think that was funny. I didn't. Poppa was never mean, but he could be a prankster at times.

June 27

It is a sweltering hot day. Every time I go outside, I feel hot and sweaty. These little drips of perspiration, not supposed to call them sweat, are under the arms of my blouse. That is perfectly fine because I need to stay inside and work on my new summer dress.

I loved this dress. It was a soft blue cotton print dress with wide shoulders, puffy sleeves, and a simple neckline. Poppa would have had a fit if it had been low cut. It had a belted waistline and a mid-calf flared hem. I could hardly wait for someplace special to wear it. I couldn't get the hem quite right, so I decided to hop on the bus to go see if my cousin, Velma, could help me.

Finished it, thank goodness, and it was as lovely as the design in my teacher, Mrs. Parker's, pattern book. We had a grand visit. The next day we picked dewberries. It was tough trying to get back on that bus carrying a basket of dewberries and my beautiful new dress. Getting off that was the real problem. As I stepped off the bus, I dropped my basket of dewberries. The berries went slipping and sliding in all directions, and so did I. My foot stepped down on a bunch of berries, and I went down in a heap. I did manage to hold my dress above my head to keep it safe. Harold, the driver, and the remaining passengers chuckled and sniggered. I felt foolish, but my dress was safe. Guess I had to remember what was important, and my pride needed to take second place. I kept telling myself that as the flush ran up my neck and into my cheeks as I wiped clinging dewberries off my rear end.

July 7

This afternoon I was so excited. Mrs. Parker, my teacher, took me to Cincinnati to get material for a dress and a slip to make for the 4-H show at the county fair. This will be a big adventure for me as I hoped to do well enough to compete in the state fair next year.

I got the material in lavender. I wanted to make a fitted dress with capped sleeves and the hem just above the knees. The slip would be more of an underskirt with the top of the dress floating over the top.

Mrs. Parker looked at the material I had chosen and the pattern. "Don't you think this is a little daring for a teenage girl?" She fingered the soft folds of the material. I wanted to shrug with impatience. I knew how it would look. It would be daring and brave, not the sort of dress that looked like a house dress. I wanted it to be a dress that a movie star would wear to a county fair.

We settled on the fabric I had selected but changed the style to one with a drop waist and the hem a bit below the knees. I wasn't sure how the judges at the fair would look at it, but I knew how I would design that dress for me. After the competition, I would change it into my design. In the future, I would call my designs "Josie's Jewels," and people would come from near and far to buy one of my creations. But not yet. I had to get out of high school first. I guess I would have to be a grown up to see my creations come to life. Someday, I thought, I would have a shop in Cincinnati and have beautiful models wearing my clothes. I dreamed I would go to New York or Hollywood and design clothes for the stars.

July 14

I worked all day cutting out my dress and slip. It is going to take more work than I thought it would. I finally finished cutting out the dress and sewed on it. Momma wasn't feeling well, so I went out and helped dig potatoes.

It seemed that so much of what I did during that month was work on the dress. I wondered that if I worked this hard on a Campbell County fair dress, how much work would I have to do for a state fair dress. When I sewed and designed for the stars, I wondered, would I ever be able to get it all done? I knew the solution would be to have lots of helpers. I could just design, draw, and boss people around. I found that I would have to give up my dreams for the county fair that year. I had to set my heart on next. Momma was not feeling well. She seemed to get tired easily and felt dizzy. She also seemed to have a bit of numbness in her arm. Since Poppa was afraid she would fall and hurt herself, I was going to have to spend a good bit of my time helping Poppa on the farm. It didn't seem right that Momma wouldn't be working alongside me and Poppa in our closely woven group of three. She had had Scarlet Fever the year before, and I remembered that the doctor thought this might have been the culprit. Some mention of a heart involvement, maybe.

We had tobacco to cut and corn to shock and shuck. I knew we would have neighbors to help and pitch in, but Poppa would expect me to help where I could. I would be expected to pick up tobacco leaves, work with the corn where I was needed, and of course, to cook for the workers. I knew that the farm was our life, but I was almost sick to my stomach when I thought of giving up my contest dreams. All that work! The hem taken out, the sleeves reworked, and the buttons changed seemed like time wasted. Dreams are just that, I decided. For the time being, matters on the farm needed to take priority.

September 23

We had corn shucking yesterday. It was fun, but not as much as last year. I did get to dance with David Taylor, but then after a couple of dances with me, he went on over to Flossie Lou Alford, ate dinner with her, and took her home after. I ate dinner with Jenny Mae and Rose, my friend, who gave me Scarlet Fever.

During tobacco and corn harvest, at dinner, we set out a big trestle table. I cooked and put out the lima beans, fried chicken, ham steaks, biscuits, and pies. Of course, Aunt Flossie helped, and Momma did what she could if she was sitting down. The year before, we had the most fun with the shucking. We piled most of the corn in a big pile and Uncle Oliver put a big jug of liquor down in the center. Then, we piled more corn on top. One of the men grumbled about it being prohibition time, and Grandpa Herbert said that didn't make any difference when you made your own. Everybody shucked as hard as he could, old, young, and in-between, to get to that jug. The person that uncovered the jug first won it. Grandpa Herbert had the best technique since he had done this for years. I watched his hands flying. We knew we would be at it for quite a while. There were cobs flying left and right. Grandpa Herbert was getting close I could tell. Then, little Jimmy Jones, a tow-headed eight-year-old, reached in and hauled out the jug. Imagine what an eight-year-old was to do with that jug. His Poppa pulled it right away from him with a hug and a grin. I hoped that Jimmy would get more reward than that.

Later, after the jug was won and corn was done, we danced. We danced until the sun went down, the moon came up, and all the stars glittered. We had a big bonfire and lots of good food put out. There was good music too. Lots of banjos, harmonicas, and fiddles. Uncle Oliver played a potato bug. The potato bug was a type of mandolin that he had played since he could walk. It looked like a ladybug in shape, but I thought the tone was pure heaven. Would the shucking make up for me losing my chance at the county fair this year? No, it didn't, but it was a lot of fun.

I also spent a good bit of time on hog killing. Some of the neighbors slaughtered by the moon, but not Poppa. He always said to slaughter when it was cold enough. Poppa would kill the hogs by hitting them on the back of their heads with an axe head. Then, we would put the hog in a big tub set in a stone furnace. The tub would be filled with water, and then a fire was lit in the furnace. My job was to work with getting the water heated almost to boiling, so the hair on the hog would scrape off easy. Then one of the men would add hot rocks in the tub. The rocks in the bottom would keep the water hot longer in order to soften the hog's skin. I worked on canning sausage and cutting lard for the most part. I had always helped with this before, but now, I had to do more of the work. I had to cut up the ribs and backbone to can, as well as slice up the bacon to salt. So much of what we needed to do to eat had to come from our hog products. Momma felt bad, I know, since she couldn't do what she had always done, but there was no another choice.

One thing about my Poppa, he made sure the hogs didn't suffer. He was gifted that way. I couldn't watch the killing. I would shut my eyes when they brought the carcass to the water, when they pulled it out, and when they scraped the hair off. I left and went about other chores when they hung the hog to gut. I knew we had to eat, but I looked forward to the day when I left the farm and would be a grown woman living in the city making my dresses. While all the killing and cutting were happening, my escape was to pull myself away to another place in my mind where everything was beautiful and gentle.

December 23rd

Jenny Mae and my friend Hazel came up. We went sleigh riding. Decorated the church for Christmas. It was so pretty. I was certainly proud of all the decorations. We had a little Nativity scene with the cutest baby Jesus in a feed trough manger. Went home and wrapped gifts.

Chapter Three

The Competition

1931

January 1

I am now in the 10th grade. For Christmas, Momma and Poppa gave me permission to get material for a new dress for the 4-H competition this year. I know money is hard to come by, so I will have to work hard to make a nice dress for very little money. I think I can do that.

February 2

I have made a good start on the dress for the competition. Momma and Poppa took me to Cincinnati, and I used my Christmas money to buy an end piece of material to make it. I am so proud to be a careful shopper. The fabric is a lovely color, a peachy apricot, and so soft. Momma and Mrs. Parker will want to help me, I'm sure, but it needs to be my work. I can't wait to see how it will turn out.

April 7

A perfect spring day. Played ball at school today. As usual, I fell, skinned my knee, and sprained my ankle.

April 9

Today as I was going to school, I sprained my other ankle. Now, I can hardly walk. This is the very reason I don't try to play basketball.

Gracious, it made my life so hard to be clumsy, but my sewing teacher told me it was because I grew so fast. In my mind, I thought she saw me as one of Poppa's colts, an ungainly creature at best. At least, she gave me credit for being good with needles and thread. I was making slow but steady progress on my competition outfit. The cuffs were deep and white. They were hard to sew just right. I had to rework them a couple of times, but I thought they were getting better. I was proud, scared, and excited all at the same time. I knew I had to have a special outfit if I wanted to win the county competition.

August 12

I competed in the County fair. I won in my division. I am so excited. I will be able to go to Louisville in September to compete in the state fair. The competition will be fierce at the state level, I know. I expect most of the county winners will be competing. That is, if all the counties have complete costume competitors. At least, it isn't beef judging.

September 19

I won my division in Louisville this week, and so did Jenny Mae. Jenny Mae won for her wonderful canning skills, and I won first place in the complete costume exhibit. Yippee! This makes me the state clothing champion. My outfit was the lovely apricot colored skirt and jacket I had been working on most of the year. The skirt swished and swirled around the calves of my legs just the way I hoped it would. I thought I looked so glamorous. The look of it reminded me of soft summer flowers.

I made a matching jacket with the white cuffs that I had so much trouble sewing and with the draping at the neck. I made my outfit, undergarments, and a purse made from scraps for a total cost of $20.93. The limit for the complete outfit was $25.00, and I was well under that limit. We were named in the Junior Hall of Fame at the University of Kentucky. Part of our prize is a trip to Chicago. We won't be heading there until November, but I can hardly wait. Only two more months before the trip.

I could hardly get a lick of work done around the farm because I was so excited about the trip. Still, I knew I needed to work hard because Momma and Poppa had given up a lot to help me. Momma was still not strong, so I'd been trying to help more with the chickens and milking the cows. It seemed we had lots of extra schoolwork to do, and I knew I needed to keep my mind on my business. I was still excited.

November 21

Poppa took me and Jenny Mae to the 4-H banquet which was held as a celebration for our county winners and those who won at the state level before we headed off to Chicago. It is so hard for me to believe that this trip is a part of my prize. We had the best time.

November 27

Today is Friday. Went to town this afternoon. I got my hair marcelled, but I call it curled. It looks so nice. The waves in my hair look perfect. I am so excited about my trip. Yesterday was Thanksgiving, but I couldn't even think about enjoying Thanksgiving, not even the least little bit. Momma didn't feel like fixing a big dinner, and I was too excited to worry about what we had for dinner. Dinner was taken care of, though. We went to Jenny Mae's house for a good meal.

We planned to ride to Chicago with Mrs. Parker, and her husband, our principal. They were so nice. They would drive us in their car, and we would stay at a swanky hotel. Jenny Mae and I made up all sorts of tales about what our trip would be like every time we got together. None of our wildest stories came close to the real experience.

I got up 15 minutes before 5:00 on November 28th. It was way too early for me. My eyes wouldn't even open. I think they must have been glued together. I feel sleepy and excited all at the same time. Poppa took me and Jenny Mae uptown to meet Mr. and Mrs. Parker, and we started for Chicago at 6:30. We got along fine until we were about 82 miles from Chicago, and then the car broke down. I could hear the engine cough, cough, chunk. Plunk. Done. We had to pull the car over to the side of the road. Mr. Parker got out and examined the car. He had his nice clothes on, so he didn't want to crawl under the car and get all dirty and greasy. There was steam coming out of the front. Mr. Parker said he thought, maybe, the fan belt had broken. The steam was from the radiator. He stood and looked at the car. We sat and looked at him.

Up the road, we saw a milk truck coming back down on the opposite side. The driver pulled over when he saw the four of us with a broken-down car filled with bags. "Hey, folks," he hollered out. "What you all got going on down here."
"Looks like we have a broken-down car and two young ladies trying to get to Chicago," Mr. Parker answered.

"Well, we have a little shop down the road. He won't open until later today, but I could take you in and let you wait and talk to him. Your passengers could take the bus. The bus comes every couple of hours, so they wouldn't have to wait all that long. Then, you could go later in your car once it gets fixed, or if you don't want to wait, hop on another bus, whichever works out for you."

Mr. Parker looked delighted. We wouldn't be late checking in, and he could get his car taken care of. I was surprised since Mr. Parker, our principal, hardly ever smiled. This Mr. Parker had a face so lit up, it looked shiny. We pulled all our luggage out of the car and waited for the bus to come. Mr. Parker flagged it down when we saw it chugging down the road. The bus driver said yes, he was going to Chicago, so we piled all our luggage on. We waved goodbye to Mr. Parker and the milk man and climbed aboard. When we got to the bus station, we took a taxi to the Hotel la Salle. A few hours later, Mr. Parker arrived on a later bus.

This hotel is the most famous of Chicago's Loop hotels, or at least that is what they said. The brochure that I picked up at the front desk said that there were 1,026 rooms here, and I simply couldn't wrap my mind around that. Imagine! I don't think there are that many rooms in our whole town. I stood in the lobby and stared off in all directions. I had never seen a room so large. It had a marble floor with a carpet so long, I could barely see the end. The crowning jewel of this room was a gigantic elevator. We had to walk, carrying our luggage all the way down the hall. As I walked, my head swiveled in all directions. I felt like one of those ducks at the carnival.

Getting on that elevator took all the grit I could muster. It was a scary looking contraption for sure. There was this nice elderly gentleman who held the door open and helped us in with our luggage. Inside was a large golden panel at the inner edge of the door beside a little stool where he sat. He asked us what floor we were on. I blurted out that the man at the desk said I was in room #542. The operator smiled at us and said, "Are all of you on the 5th floor then?" Mrs. Parker said we were. The operator looked at us and smiled as he lowered a large lever and closed us up in this metal box. I shut my eyes as the box rattled and shook as it took us to the 5th floor. When the door opened and we set our feet into the hallway, I gave an enormous sigh of relief. I was so glad to get back to firm land again even if was a carpeted hallway.

Jenny Mae and I shared a room which had a bath for just us. Not like at home where baths were in the kitchen for everybody. Our room had two twin beds. I bounced on mine a time or two. Jenny Mae looked at me, and her look said that I better be careful lest I break something. Not sure if she was worried about me or the bed.

At the banquet, before the main events unfolded, I went with two girls who competed in my category from other states. My beautiful Spanish Tile dress had nature inspired details of flowers and leaves in a tile-like pattern. I designed and made this myself using lovely cotton voile material in shades of soft blue. It was in a tiered style that came almost to my ankles, including tassel accented ties that I could wear open or tied at the neck. It felt so special.

November 30

The excitement is building! We got up early and had our breakfast in the Louis XVI Room. The room is glorious. The ceiling is a lovely blue that feels *like it could be part of the sky. Hanging in the room are four crystal chandeliers with teardrop crystals. All the trim is golden. My mouth dropped open. I couldn't imagine trying to eat with my mouth closed in this room. Imagine, it costs $.60 to eat breakfast here. I haven't the slightest memory of what I ate, and that was only a few hours ago.*

After breakfast, we went to the International Livestock Exposition, and we rode on an elevated train. Took my breath away. I was a little scared at being up in the air so high, especially on a moving train. In the evening, we went to Wilson & Company where they had a certified bacon slicing room downstairs. Upstairs they had a restaurant and meeting rooms. We heard Richard E. Byrd give a talk about his trip to Little America or as they now call it, Antarctica. What an exciting adventure that must have been. I wanted to have exciting adventures in my life, but I didn't want to have to go to Antarctica to have them. Something else, please, I simply wanted excitement.

The second morning, I was allowed to have the $.75 breakfast. Mrs. Parker said that since this was a truly special trip for us that we might as well splurge a little. After breakfast, we went to the Chicago Lighting Institute, where we learned all about how lights could be used. I guessed this must be the end for kerosene lamps. Poppa would be so surprised to see these lights. He would never believe people could simply flick a switch, and the lights would come on. There was a little demonstration switch by the door. When we left the room, I reached around Jenny Mae and flicked it on and off a time or two. Our guide rushed around to see who was doing that. When he got close to us, I quickly masked my face to look innocent. Jenny Mae gave me the look.

We went on to the Art Institute. I had never seen so many beautiful pictures, with so many naked people. Well maybe in an art book at school. Gracious. I was certainly glad Poppa and Momma weren't here to see this. For lunch, we ate at the Chicago Mail Room.

Such a good meal. We were served Grapefruit supreme, Chicken a la King, Jello Salad, Mashed Potatoes, and June peas. Ice cream and cake were then passed around for dessert. After all this food, we watched a fashion show displaying all the beautiful clothes that any young lady would want to wear. They were called Style Queen clothes which were inexpensive and affordable according to the brochure we were given. Instructions were also provided in the brochure as to how we could purchase them. I certainly took my time to look, but only to see if I could decide how to make them for myself and my friends. I only had a few dollars to spend, and these dollars were to be used in the best possible way.

The last place we visited was the Alder Planetarium. The tour guide told us that this was the first Planetarium in the Western Hemisphere. I couldn't believe my eyes. He also demonstrated the instruments they had to measure the sky, the stars. The guide showed us a vision of the night sky on an enormous ceiling with all the stars, the moon, clouds. I thought to myself that when I got home and looked out at the stars at night, how could I look at them in the same way? I was impressed. I had my head bent back so far, I had a crick in it for the rest of the day. Not to say I wasn't having a wonderful time, but I preferred my sky at home. That is where I could have Poppa explain to me with one arm around my shoulders about the big and little dippers and all the other constellations.

We had breakfast at Montgomery Ward and Company, followed by shopping at Marshall Fields. We ate dinner at the hotel ballroom, the Blue Fountain room. The show sponsors asked me to model some outfits at the dinner. I was plenty shocked about that, let me tell you. Still, it was pleasing to wear several outfits and a raincoat with a cap, swirling around like ladies do at the movies. One of the men in charge came up after and told me in a deep whiskey voice that I might want to do this for a living someday. What? I was destined to design and sew clothes for glamourous and exotic people.

When it was time to go home on December 4th, we got up early and ate our breakfast. A taxi took us to the train station, and we boarded a train for the 82-mile trip from Chicago. No bus this time. We exited the train in the town where Mr. Parker needed to retrieve his car from the repair garage. Once Mr. Parker settled his bill, we all piled into the Parker's car and came home. It was raining and snowing when we left Chicago. I was more than glad to get back home.

Chapter Four

The Star Quilt

1932

January 14

It was 48 degrees above today. Started to rain tonight. I got a star quilt from Momma today as a belated Christmas gift for our 4H achievements. Didn't know a thing about it. The quilt is so beautiful. Blue and white. The quilt was so warm and cozy on my bed. Star quilts are given to mark important life events, like graduation. For some Indians the star quilt represents honor and generosity. My mother certainly was generous, and I appreciated her recognition of my 4-H achievements, but the most important event I could remember about this time was that my semester exams were over. Yippee!

February 14

I think I am supposed to be in love because this is the day. It was a nice bright sunshiny day today, and I got a Valentine with Guess Who? written in big bold letters. I bet it was Bill Hofacker who sent this to me. He is cute, but not that cute. He has a big gap between his teeth, but he is a good basketball player. The baker was here today to bring flour. I will be baking cakes again soon.

February 15

Well, yesterday was Valentine's Day, but I think I may have seen my true love today, who knows. This morning, Momma and I went to Miss White's funeral. I saw Bill Johnson there.

I didn't want to tell my journal who Bill Johnson was, but at that time I thought he was the cutest guy ever. A cousin of Mrs. White's, I think. He tipped his head to the side and gave me a slow wink. I liked to have totally forgotten I was at a funeral. I hope he thought I looked nice. I didn't wear black, but I had a lovely bombazine chocolate brown dress. Too bad it wasn't a snazzy orange. I wanted him to be impressed. My beige pumps were a little higher than usual with adorable bows. I wore a warm shawl to keep out the cold.

It was 30 above the morning of February 15th and I had a sore throat. I got Valentines from Hellen, Lillian, and Lelia. After dinner, I had a fever and a headache, and I thought maybe it was the hog that caused it. We planned to kill the hog that day, well several hogs, but mine was in the group. Pee Doodle was his name, at least it was my name for him. We'd been feeding them corn, so they'd have more lard. I loved that little guy. I would scratch his back where the hair was all bristly. He would lean up against me and wiggle so cute. I went into the house when they started to boil the water to loosen the hair. Thought maybe they would forget about him since we usually killed in November when it turned good and cold. Guess they didn't.

As I lay on my bed, the pain and fever rolled over me. In my mind, I could hear Pee Doodle screaming for his life, while casting his head around looking futilely for my gentle hand. I heard the metal clank of the hinge as Poppa came in the front door. I was lying in the bed shaking now with chills. Poppa covered me over with the quilt. I looked up at him, and I said, "Poppa, will I have to help with lard tomorrow?" He looked down at me and shook his head.

"Don't know what happened to that little hog of yours. Couldn't find him no place," Poppa said with a sideways grin. "Looked in all those places you normally hid him but couldn't find him. Forgot to look under those hay bales in the lean to. I reckon he might have hidden up there but guess now it is too durned late."

Poppa smoothed my covers with his calloused hand. "Got to wait till next fall, I guess. Don't know, though, he has a pretty color and nice stocky build. We might need him to bring more good porkers onto this farm for the next few years." Poppa brushed my face with his two fingers and turned down the light. "You go on to sleep now and feel better, baby girl." The heat I felt was warm and pure. Not like fever hot.

March 17

Momma is not feeling so well. Our phone line is out, so I went up to Aunt Flossie's and called the doctor. The doctor finally got here. Momma had a light stroke. Jenny Mae and her aunt came after some eggs. Hope Momma will be all right.

March 29

It was Momma's birthday. I made her a beautiful cake. Poppa and I gave her a store-bought dress. She seemed so happy. Her face lit right up.

April 26

It is my 16th birthday. It was cloudy early, and then it rained. Got a birthday card from Momma and Poppa. They got me a pair of beads and two pairs of hose. Got them when they were in town last.

The 4-H trip to Lexington was different from the state fair. I didn't have all that sewing to do. I could just participate with my friends and have fun. We were going for a singing presentation, and I really wanted to see Lexington. Jenny Mae talked about Lexington all the time since she was going to college there. We went to town to get some things for our trip. I got a new pair of tennis shoes, slippers, a new hat, and a dress. Poppa sold a couple of hogs to pay for my new clothes. I hated for him to do that, but he was determined that his girl was going to perform in style.

I got up early to get ready. Poppa took Jenny Mae and me up town. Mr. Parker took Mrs. Parker, Jenny Mae, and me to Covington where Mrs. Parker and I got on a bus for Lexington. Jenny Mae and Edward, one of the boys in our group, went on the train. Mrs. Parker and I got to Lexington at 11:10 slow time. We all gathered at the

Agricultural Building at the University when we arrived in Lexington. In the afternoon, Mrs. Parker, Jenny Mae, and I went shopping and then to a show. We went to the Strand Theater and saw Robert Montgomery in "Lovers Courageous." Don't know if Momma and Poppa wanted me to see that movie but it sure was romantic, that Robert Montgomery was so good looking. Jenny Mae and I grabbed each other and squealed, not too loudly, as Mr. Mongomery stared at us from the screen.

We stayed at Patterson Hall, a women's dormitory at the University of Kentucky. At least, Mrs. Parker, Jenny Mae, and I did. There were lots of other girls from other counties. I wondered at the time what it would be like if I was able to go to college here. This beautiful building with a large veranda and two wings of four stories jutting out on each side. Glorious. After supper, we had vespers in the open-air theater at the Memorial Building. We saw more moving pictures. Not as exciting as the one in town, and not nearly as much action and romance. On Thursday, we had our recital. We did really well and received a $5.00 cash prize.

After all the excitement of our trip, the rest of June and July went slow. Garden work, canning, cleaning, and sewing things for around the house, tea towels, curtains, aprons, some quilting, but nothing special. It seems I had more of these things to do because Momma wasn't able to do all the things she had always done. I don't think she went back to town after she and Poppa shopped for my birthday gifts.

August 12

Harry Raymond treated me to a bottle of Coca Cola at the Campbell County Celebration when the trotting horse competition ran today. I got to shake hands with Gov. Laffoon. Goes by name of Ruby Laffoon. Seems an odd name for a man.

I was so glad to go to the celebration. All the horses were beautiful. I started out with Bob and Jenny Mae, but Harry joined us. He was certainly a nice boy. In all the crowd and the noise, we got separated from the others. I was hot and thirsty. My throat felt as if it would simply crack from the heat. Harry asked if I wanted to sit at an outdoor table outside the stands and have a coke. I thought that was a wonderful idea. That cold drink slid down my throat and cooled me all the way down to my toes.

I kept looking at him and playing with the straw in my drink. I couldn't decide if I wanted him for a boyfriend or not. I thought at least he did buy me a drink, and he seemed thoughtful and kind, but his hair stuck up funny on his head. So, as far as a boyfriend, I guess not. Today, as I remember Harry, I thought if he had a better haircut, he would have had a better chance with me as a boyfriend. But with that hair… No.

I remember we had a total eclipse of the sun later in August. Frightening for me. The whole day seemed to turn to night. Only a whisper of red around the edge of the sun. I was scared to look and scared not to. I sat on a quilt in the grass to look at it. Momma and Poppa sat on wooden stools. Momma patted me on the arm, and I don't know if she wanted to comfort me or herself. I was relieved when it was over, but glad that I saw it too.

Chapter Five

Momma

1933

January 2

I had to do a good bit of the cleaning and housework since Momma seemed to be feeling worse. She was so quiet and had a hard time getting around. Her breath was labored, but she excused it saying she had gotten up out of her chair too fast or moved too quickly. She also said it bothered her to go up and down the steps. Laughed and said she was getting too old and fat. I didn't think she was either old or fat.

I didn't want her to know it, but I could hardly get through a day without cold dread creeping throughout my body. I was irritable and restless pacing mindless through my tasks.

March 14

Momma isn't feeling well again today. Our line is out of order again, so I walked up to Aunt Flossie's to call the doctor. I worried even more about Momma. She seemed worse with every passing day. I hoped she would feel better in the spring. Poppa and I had been doing more and more of what she normally had done. She had always milked one cow in the morning, while I milked the other. She got Rose, who could be a little ornery, and I milked Jasmine, who was pretty and sweet. Jasmine always gave good milk. Rose did too, but she tried to kick the can over if you weren't paying attention. She would kick you too if you didn't watch her. There was nothing that hurt more than a cow kick.

March 15

It's Saturday. The doctor was here this morning. Said Momma could sit up and eat some ice cream. She enjoyed that. He told us that the Scarlet Fever she had earlier may have damaged part of her heart, but he couldn't say for certain.

April 21

Momma is still not her best. Today is Tuesday, and she has been in bed since church on Sunday.

April 26

I am 17 years old. Momma got out of bed this morning and made me a special birthday cake. It is chocolate with chocolate icing, and it has little curls and flower designs in the frosting. She went to bed right after, but she held my hand and told me it was a special cake for her special girl. This evening at about 6 o'clock Momma passed away.

Had a lot of people here tonight. Poppa gave me a card that he and Momma had made for me. I could barely bring myself to look at the card. I knew that Momma was alive when she wrote it, and when I read it, she wasn't. It felt strange and sad. In the morning, I went out and milked both cows without Poppa even having to ask me.

It was hard to believe that my birthday started out so nice, and then, suddenly, things went all wrong, "The Lord Giveth, and the Lord Taketh away." I didn't understand why he took away my Momma. I was only 17, and I needed more time. A person was supposed to be old when her Momma went. I should have been all of 30.

The days after Momma died felt like eternity. Poppa and I went to the cemetery. There were lots of people there. Aunt Flossie was a big help, getting things cleaned out since I didn't feel much like doing all that. Jenny Mae brought me a pair of stockings for my birthday. Momma's funeral was at 11:00 in the morning at 6 Mile Church. All the uncles and aunts came for dinner. They brought lots of food with them.

It was a good thing people brought food because I didn't feel like cooking. I did have some pies I'd made and canned beans in the pantry that Aunt Flossie helped me put out. It felt like Momma should have been here to help arrange and serve the food and to talk to relatives and friends. I didn't want to talk to all these people. I just wanted to cry. I went to my room to hide out from the noise and bluster. I felt hot, sweaty, and cold, all at the same time. I arranged the new star quilt on my bed thinking I was glad to have a quilt to remember the better times with my Momma. I grabbed up one corner of the quilt and twisted it around in my hand. Then I straightened it out and sat staring at the beautiful stitches she had made. I could see her soft gentle hands moving over the squares, and somehow, I felt a sense of comfort to know she was here with me when I was cold and lonely. Poppa opened the door softly and stuck his head inside. "Baby girl, are you ready to come back and join us?" Poppa asked. "Some of the cousins are asking where you have gotten yourself off to."

I remember this as vividly as if it were yesterday. I also remember my gratitude that Poppa was there with me, "yes, Poppa," I said, as I ran my hands over the soft fabric once more. With a sigh, I pushed myself to my feet and stood up. I felt a little shaky, but I knew Momma would want me to do the right thing and be there for all the relatives and neighbors.

"More people will be on their way soon," he consoled me. "I know it isn't easy for you right now." He didn't have to say anything about my birthday because he and I both knew that from now on every time I had a birthday, I would remember the death of my Momma. The rest of the year was a blur.

Chapter Six

The Flame and Glo Club

1934

January 8

Jenny Mae left for the University this morning. Over the weekend, I finished the dress I cut out last summer and never made. I fitted it for Jenny Mae. It looked like a dream.

August 7

I went with some of my friends to Cumminsville, a part of Cincinnati, to see about a job in a sewing factory. They told me I could start work on Thursday. I came back to Cincinnati and got my Social Security number. Social Security. Imagine, me thinking about an old age pension. I wished I could go to college like Jenny Mae, but with Momma gone, I needed to stay close to home to help Poppa. Although he didn't say much about it, I thought he needed the cash money I could bring in to help pay some of the bills.

I got up early and went to work. I thought I would like it just fine. I met a nice girl who worked there named Helga Raisch. She had wavy blonde hair parted on the left side. In my mind, she looked a lot like Jean Harlow in the movies. She had a round face with a big dimple in her chin. She had one of those what I have heard described as 'a cupid's bow' mouth. She was shorter than me, but full of energy and chatter. "Here, you go, Miss Josie," Helga said as she marched me over to the machine I would operate. "You can just set here between me and momma, and we can let you know what to do with the shirts we're sewing."

I was a little scared and nervous even though I was certainly good at sewing. I wanted these new ladies to think I could do this job. The machines were set in long rows with a chair in front and a lamp overhead. It was a little hard to breathe with all the lint floating in the air, but I knew I would have to get used to it. It seemed awkward because I didn't know exactly where to put my hands or my feet. This wasn't at all like Momma's machine at home. My machine here was big and heavy, and I was afraid I would press the needle into my fingers. It ran faster than I was used to, but I thought I would get to where I could control the speed, or at least hoped I could.

Helga's momma, Bertha, sat on the other side of me. Didn't look like they were related, not a bit alike. Her momma was a stocky little lady with short brown hair allowing a few gray strands to sneak through. She had few words but looked at you like all your words were important. Both were good, hard workers. Helga told me as she sewed and worked that her momma used to bake bread and pretzels in her home when they first came to this country. The Raisch family came here in 1908 after the panic in Germany in 1907. At least her parents came then, Helga and her brother were both born here.

I looked at Helga and nodded my head. I had no idea about panics in Germany or whatever she was talking about. In the midst of her chatter, I understood that they lived in a walk-up apartment a short bus ride away. Her momma started working with Helga in the shirt factory even though it was easier to stay at home and bake because Helga laughingly told her stories about the brewery boys who rode on her bus.

"I know Momma thought the stories were as funny as I did until Graham told her all about what really goes on in those 'rowdy breweries.' Now, let me tell you that if those boys get out of line, I can handle them," she added with a pout. "Graham told Momma the boys are pretty rough. They don't care what they do or say when they get off the job. I know I can handle the rowdy brewery boys now that they are limited to 12-14 glasses of beer each day." She giggled and tucked her chin down. Her little pointed chin sunk into the marshmallow of her face.

I thought to myself, good heavens, were these big glasses or little ones? I didn't know any of my neighbors who could drink more than a glass or two of beer, at best. If they tried to drink 14 glasses, they couldn't stand, much less ride on a bus.

"That Graham, he is as bad as Momma, maybe worse. He says I have no business trying to take care of any rough, tough brewery men." Helga pushed out her bottom lip in exasperation. I asked her who Graham was. "He is my big brother," Helga let out a small soft sigh. "He's taken the best care of us since our father died. That happened about two years ago not long after father started working at the brewery," her bright lively expression faded. I gasped in shock. I knew how I would feel if it were my Poppa. She went on, "only six months after he started, he was crushed by barrels that rolled off a broken rack." The words dropped from her mouth like tiny stones. She continued with a look of grit and determination in her eyes. "Again, though, we have Graham, our apartment, and each other, so we can get by better than many." She turned away to shut off further conversation. I knew she needed to move away from that time of hurt and pain.

We stopped at 12:00 to eat our lunch. I brought an apple, a piece of cold chicken wrapped in a cloth, and a bottle of milk. Bertha saw my meager lunch and handed me a big pone of cornbread, that was a rich golden brown in color. I took it from her, and it lay soft and moist, in my hands. It tasted delicious, light and buttery. She also gave me a piece of Streuselkuchen, she called it. Helga noted my quizzical look at her mother and mouthed with a wink, "Crumb Cake. This is my brother's favorite kind of cake," Helga said. "Momma always makes it when Graham comes home. I do think you might want to meet Graham. Most girls think he is a real dream, but he hasn't settled down to one yet."

"Where is he coming home from?" I asked Helga. She didn't answer my question straight on.

"Oh, he is over on the Kentucky side," she said. She made no mention of what kind of work he did, and I thought it was best to wait until I knew her better.

September 20th

I made plans to go see Jenny Mae at the University. Imagine Jenny has only been at the University for a few months, and already, the guys have awarded her the Harvest Queen award.

A crowning ceremony was planned on Saturday afternoon with a big party on Saturday night. I wasn't able to ride down on the bus until Saturday morning because of work, but at least I could attend the party on Saturday night. Jenny said all kinds of fancy rich folks would be there at the party, and she and Winston, her new guy, had a guy picked out for me.

I was still a bit smitten with her old guy, Bob, but he faded out of the picture when she met Winston. Winston was a senior at the college. Jenny Mae acted as if he were truly special. There wasn't anyone blown away with me just yet. I had fellows ask me to have a coke and simple meetings like that but I suppose when you stay close to home, you don't have a chance to meet new people. Poppa told me with a wink and a grin that I would be falling for a fellow and leaving him for good before I knew it. Maybe I would find the fellow, but I wouldn't be happy to leave Poppa.

When I boarded the bus to Lexington, I wore a nice warm brown shearling coat with a cute fur collar. I carried a tapestry valise with bone handles that used to belong to Momma. It looked quite fancy. Somehow, when I carried it, I felt I was taking Momma with me into this new adventure. I wanted to look as elegant as I could when the new harvest queen and her escort picked me up at the station.

Jenny Mae and Winston were right there. I saw them when my bus pulled in. My bus was a bit late, but I made it in time. I stayed in Lexington with Jenny Mae who had a nice room at the college, even if it was a little small. However, it had big open windows and a wonderful view of the university grounds. I could see beautiful brick buildings and trees full of gold and red fall foliage in the distance. There was a gentle breeze floating through the windows carrying a trace of woodsmoke. Still, I didn't have time to appreciate the view. I had only a short time to freshen up before I met the person who would escort me.

I was proud of my lovely new claret-colored dress, that is the color that Mrs. Parker called it, with a bit of a daring drop at the back. It had a hem that flared and swished around my ankles. So stylish. Jenny Mae seemed to think I would be quite the 'looker' at the party. Jenny Mae led me out the door to meet my date. I got a glimpse of him standing by his car talking to Winston. From what I could hear, it sounded like football talk. He turned and looked at me as we strolled down the sidewalk. Whew! He was a fancy fellow. I knew his name was Jimmy Lee Reilly. He was slim and elegant with copper-colored hair and a trim mustache to match. I looked past him to the car that Winston had discussed at length. It was a 1933 Pontiac Eight Convertible. It was red with black fenders, a running board, red-spoked wheels, and two chrome horns, chrome headlights and a chrome grill. I didn't know all that at first glimpse, but I knew these details from Winston. Hadn't been told much about the guy... just about the car.

Winston told me that Jimmy Lee had a job in Newport keeping accounts for one of the clubs there. He came down to Lexington every few weeks to look at and/or purchase cars for the partners who owned the club. Winston said the club was called the "Hey-Ho." That part was a little sketchy. I planned to check it out when I got back home and to work. Whenever we had talked about Newport at work, Helga would shake her head and grin. Bertha would look grim and say, "Bad things happen in Newport." She would continue with, "Graham tells me that bad things go on in those 'day houses' and 'night houses.'" I wondered what day and night houses were. It was a puzzle. I hadn't met Graham yet, but they acted like his word was the final say on everything.

Seemed like Graham did some sort of police work, but I didn't know exactly what. Helga told me she thought it was some sort of government police work, but it was unclear to me how the government did that. Helga appeared more concerned that her momma paced the apartment and stared out the windows until she heard him come home at night. She said her momma was even more fearful when he had to be gone for a spell. I wasn't sure how long a 'spell' was supposed to be, but I guessed it was more than a day or two. I knew from my work experience that the bus ran to Cincinnati on Monmouth Street and back to Newport on York. I had seen some fancy looking places as we went through in both directions, but I didn't know which was the one where Jimmy Lee worked, or even if he did. Lots to discover. I found it all so exciting!

What I discovered when I strolled down the sidewalk to meet Jimmy Lee was that he had a way to charm. His beautiful wavy copper hair was worn parted in the middle. Just a bit of pomade seemed to hold it in place. His full mustache was the exact color of his hair when I had a chance to see him close. He wasn't tall, but he was taller than me, thank goodness. That way, I was able to wear my open-toed sandals with a heel and not tower over him as I did most guys back home. He looked straight into my eyes. His eyes were wide, fully framed with long black eyelashes, and were yellow brown in color. Tiger eyes, I would have called them, if he were my cat.

He greeted me after we were introduced as if he had waited his whole life for this special experience. His gaze made me feel that even though Jenny Mae was the Harvest Queen, I was the queen of his night. My heart fluttered in a way that I thought everyone could hear. I was so glad I had a small hanky in my purse because I knew my hands would be sweaty if I touched him.

Jenny Mae and Winston climbed into the back, and Jimmy Lee gallantly opened the front passenger door and guided me into the seat. He carefully arranged the folds of my dress before he closed the door, and we moved on to the banquet. When we arrived, everyone greeted Jenny Mae with warm greetings and praise. Lovely young men in fancy dress suits came up and spoke to her. Several were very shy and awkward, some polished and smooth. One, in a rush of greeting, nearly knocked her small tiara off her head. We finally entered the banquet hall and made our way to a special table where we were supposed to sit. It was a table for the four of us, but so many people kept coming up that I wondered if we would ever get a chance to eat.

The dinner was spectacular. We had a beautiful Waldorf Salad with apples and nuts in a creamy mayonnaise sauce, a wonderful clear soup, rare roast beef with potatoes and peas, and a choice of peach or apple pie with ice cream. I ordered the peach. I don't know when I've had a better meal even though my stomach felt a bit fluttery with all the excitement. I thought the best part was that I didn't have to cook it myself. Poor Jenny Mae. I don't think she got very much to eat. I dug right in. I was starving. It didn't keep me from noticing that Jimmy Lee had long slender fingers which handled his knife and fork with grace and elegance. A small scattering of fine red hairs sprinkled the back of his hands which added a touch of masculinity to his tapering fingers. You could tell he came from fine stock just looking at his hands.

After dinner was finished and the plates were cleared away, one tall, slim gentleman came to the front of the room, and we all grew silent. It was as if we all started with a large inhale, and none bothered to exhale. It was that kind of moment. He introduced himself and then acknowledged all the distinguished guests who were in attendance. I didn't know who any of them were, but I assumed they were college officials and benefactors of the College of Agriculture. Then, he naturally acknowledged Jenny Mae, and everyone clapped and roared their approval. She rose gracefully and addressed the assembled group with a wide smile, as she waved to one side of the room and then the other. I was so proud of my beautiful friend.

At length, the introductions and speeches ended, thank goodness, and the space at the front of the room was cleared for the dance floor. It was a spacious area for dancing with a shiny parquet floor and a small band at the perimeter. Now, I must tell you, I had not had a lot of experience at dancing, but with Jimmy Lee, it was a marvelous experience. Jimmy Lee took me by the hand and led me onto the dance floor. He tugged my hand a little more tightly than I would like, which didn't give me much choice but to follow him. The band played a waltz which I thought would be easy, but Jimmy held me tight. I felt as if I could hardly breathe, but I soon relaxed and moved into the rhythm of the dance.

It was fun. I felt wild and free for the first time in my life. I had no job, no responsibility, only a timeless movement with his body and the movement of the dance. When the band shifted to a more animated style, my body responded to the rhythm. Jimmy Lee swung me in all directions, dipping me toward him and then away. I felt flushed and out of breath, but I could not stop my feet from moving. It was as if they had a life of their own.

At last, we took a break and went back to the table. I certainly needed to rest a bit. Jimmy squeezed my hand and gave me a smile. His eyes were still locked on mine. He told me that he would get me a drink as I looked especially parched, and he said he was as well. I looked around in the crowd to see if I could see Jenny Mae and Winston, but all I could see was a flash of her golden hair as tall men in suits mingled around her. I thought to myself that she may have been the queen, but I was the lucky one.

I pulled out my hanky and dabbed at the bead of perspiration above my lip. It wouldn't do to look disheveled when Jimmy Lee came back. When he returned, he was carrying a frosted glass of something that looked like lemonade. I was so glad to have something cold to drink. He set the drink on a small napkin in front of me and pulled out his chair to sit down. I was so ungracious. I simply grabbed up the drink and took a large gulp. This was not lemonade. I choked as the drink burned down my throat. He gave me a small smile, but then cut it off before I became offended. He sipped his drink slowly which is what I should have done, but dumb me, I just didn't know. When Jimmy got up to refresh his drink, he brought me back a flute of water. He set it down with a grin. "No bourbon in this one," he chuckled. Was he making fun of me? No, he looked sincere and concerned. I was still flushed and flustered after that first drink. I didn't say a word but picked up the water and drank it down. I remember thinking that I had never had hard liquor before and didn't know if I ever wanted it again.

When we returned to Jenny Mae's dormitory after the end of that spectacular evening, Jimmy Lee led me to the door as if he were returning a jewel to its box. The soft glow of the porch lights lent a look of liquid gold to the entryway. Holding my hand, he said to me, "Miss Josie, I don't know when I've had a more wonderful evening. I am certainly glad my friend Winston was able to introduce me to such a special person." I looked down, a bit embarrassed, but pleased as punch that he said what he did. "Miss Josie, would it be appropriate if I were to call on you when you and I return home?"

"I would like it if you were to do that," I said. "I work in Cumminsville during the week, but I'm at home on Saturday afternoons and Sundays. You might come to my house. I just got off a full day today since I was coming here."

September 22

Journal, I am so excited to be on my way home on the bus. I can't wait to see Poppa and tell him all about my adventures in the big city. Poppa will probably be at church when I get home, but I can hardly sit still in my seat. My leg is just bouncing. I am so excited thinking of how I will tell Poppa all about the trip. Well, maybe not everything, but the basics: how the dinner went, how

It looked like Poppa was home, the lamps were still lit in the living room. It looked like, the best I could make out, that the mare was still in the lot. Poppa had been driving her more. Didn't know if it was for training her or because the machine was too darn picky. Poppa stepped out on the porch, gave me a wave and a grin, then came on down the steps to take my valise. "Well, how was your trip young lady?"

"Fine," I said. "Oh, Poppa, you wouldn't believe how wonderful this trip was. Jenny Mae looked so lovely. I had such a grand time. The fellow that was my escort was a special person, and so nice." I went on and on until I had to pause for breath. I wanted to let Poppa know how excited I was about the trip, but still, I wasn't about to tell him more than the basics. Not too much about Jimmy Lee. "So how come you weren't at church tonight," I asked.

"Oh, Uncle Verner came over for a kraut cutter, Poppa said. "And by the time I pulled it out for him, I was afraid I'd be running too late."

We sat down for a cup of buttermilk and cornbread. We talked about the bus ride, how Jenny Mae had handled her honor, how wonderful the dinner was, and about the important people who were there. Then, I gave a big yawn, and Poppa started rubbing the bridge of his nose as he did when he was tired. We knew it was time we started on our separate ways to make ready for bed. Since we each had a long day ahead for us, we thought it best to turn in. As I walked out of the room, I turned to Poppa and said, "Oh by the way, the fellow who was my escort wants to come call on me."

Poppa looked at me for a long minute and then nodded his head and said with a smile tugging at the corner of his mouth, "I expect if he made a good impression and seems an honorable sort to you, I guess I would be obliged to honor your wishes. However, I think he should have asked me in person." I was so glad that Poppa was not displeased. I stood, gave him a quick kiss on the cheek, and went on up to bed.

I thought I would be worn out from my trip, but even snuggled under my blanket and quilt, I was too excited to sleep. I turned to one side, then the other, and finally flopping over on my back. Knowing full well that I had a long busy day coming up. I tried to calm my breathing and sink into the mattress. Then, I got myself all excited thinking about telling Helga and Bertha about my trip. I hadn't said much about it before, but now I wanted to share all the details with them.

On Monday morning, I was all in a dither about what to tell Bertha and Helga. I told them about the dinner, what I wore, what Jenny Mae wore, how grand the event was and how lovely the room looked with the crystal chandeliers and the silver serving sets. They asked me about my escort, and I told him that he was a friend of Jenny Mae's beau. I started rushing my words in excitement as I struggled to describe his good looks, the elegance and beauty of his car, his lovely manners, how he treated me, and that he might come to call on me.

Bertha asked who his people were and did he live nearby. I said I really didn't know, but I hoped to learn soon. I did mention that I thought that he worked in Newport in a place called the Hey-Ho. Bertha's face closed, and her words seemed forced from her lips. "What sort of work is he doing in a place in Newport? It isn't one of those 'tiger blind' places, is it?" she asked. Helga broke in and assured her mother that most people referred to those places as 'speakeasies' and now that prohibition has ended, that wasn't something people worried about. Selling liquor was no longer illegal. "Listen, das Mädchen," Bertha reminded her, "I know what goes on in those places. It isn't all just the drink. It is the women, the cards, all of the evils. You better ask Graham more about these things."

I knew I needed to interrupt before something went further than just the words. "I think he works with their accounts and some of the money details," I stumbled awkwardly over this part as I truly wasn't sure, and somehow, I felt that no matter what I said, it wouldn't be right.

"Hmm, does this have to do with some of the payoffs for gambling debts and such?" Bertha asked. I couldn't believe what I was hearing. Payoffs for gambling debts? Why would she think such a thing? Did I say something that would make her believe that?

"I don't know exactly what it is he does," I said. "But he goes around with good people, so I'm sure he is a nice guy who does honest work. I know Jenny Mae and Winston wouldn't be his friend unless he was trustworthy.

"Well, I guess we'll just have to see about that," Bertha said, a dark look staining her face.

We finally got down to work and were soon in the rhythm of our machines and the numbers of shirts we were making. It seemed that the conversation was forgotten. When I got home, I kept my eye and ear on the phone hoping I would hear something. Nothing. To keep me busy until supper, I went over to our neighbor, Ollie, to have her wash and set my hair as well as to pick up some wheat.

At work on Tuesday, I was a bit grumpy. I thought Jimmy Lee would get right on to getting in touch with me. I guess he wasn't as smitten as I thought, or at least, I had hoped. On Wednesday, even Helga noticed that I was a bit out of sorts. She gave me a cheery grin, "I don't suppose you have heard from Mr. Wonderful, yet, hmm? Well, don't you fret one bit, you haven't met our Graham yet, and he will wow you away," she said. "That Mr. Jimmy fellow will look pale next to our Graham." Helga took her time getting back to work. Whenever I would look over at her, she would be nodding and tilting her head. With that expression, she looked as if she were thinking deep long thoughts.

When we got to break, she snapped her fingers, and her face lit up. "I know what we can do," she said with her voice rising in excitement. "Maybe on Saturday after work, you could come to our house instead of catching the bus back home and come to dinner. It won't be a lot, but I think Graham is coming in on Saturday morning, and you can get to meet him."

"Well, I guess that would work," I said. I was a bit doubtful, but I wanted to please my friend.

"Okay, then, it's settled," Helga said, a smile of satisfaction on her face.

After work on Saturday, the three of us rode on the bus to the Raisch home. They lived at the top of a long flight of dark steps, but the apartment at the top was spacious and airy. What a surprise. In the kitchen, a tall, lean man stirred a pot of soup. I was shocked when I saw a man cooking with an apron around his waist. Maybe it was just a towel, but it looked like an apron to me. Hmm. So, this was the wonderful Graham? He was hardly a man of interest to me.

Bertha smiled and walked over to him, her eyes almost closed as she savored the warm soup smells and yeasty fragrance coming from the oven. "What are we having, dear?" She asked as she patted the man on the shoulder as far up as she could reach. Even though Bertha was small, this young man made her look tiny. She looked up at him with an adoring smile.

"Potato soup, bratwurst, and nice fresh bread, if this oven works like it needs to," he answered, giving the oven door somewhat of an exasperated shake. "Oh, I also have some Quark pudding."

"We will get it all taken care of," Bertha said pulling off her coat and hanging it on the coat rack. Helga and I did likewise. I felt a bit awkward since the marvelous Graham seemed more vexed than happy to have visitors. Of course, I didn't know how men were supposed to act when they were the ones doing the cooking. Bertha put her arm around my shoulder and drew me toward the kitchen. "Son, I want you to meet our lovely new co-worker, Josie," she said.

Oh, my goodness. What an experience. I was definitely not used to looking up to a man. That is, if you figure distance upward. My eyes landed somewhat around his collarbones which was not the normal view I had of most men. I'll have to say he wasn't a bad looking sort when you got past the sour look on his face. He looked more like a carving of a man with all hard planes and angles. His hair was thick and brown and fell forward onto his forehead. He had nice eyes though, but still a bit stern looking. They were deep and brown and seemed to be looking through me rather than at me which gave me a strange feeling.

"Hello, Josie," he said. Then abruptly turned back to the stove. I knew I had been dismissed in a very, what I thought to be, rude manner.

"Can I help do something?" I asked.

"Oh no, I can manage," Helga said. In her fast lively way, she pulled out some mats to spread on the oilcloth covering the table. Thick heavy cutlery was in a tall glass in the center of the table so that left me with nothing to do except think to myself what the heck was 'Quark' pudding. I knew what bratwurst was because Momma served that at home, but I had never heard of the pudding.

The meal smelled delicious, and the butter fairly dripped off the thick slices of warm brown bread. I was too nervous to eat, even though I thought I was hungry. We sat down and wished one another "Guten Appetit" and began to eat. All I could do was feel self-conscious and awkward. The bratwurst was some of the best I had had in a good while, crispy and warm. A cabbage salad appeared which had been tucked away in an icebox. I think I was somewhat disappointed that the Quark pudding was only a mixture of cheese and fruit dessert. It wasn't sweet at all. Not like the cakes and pies I fixed. I could make a prettier tablecloth, too, if I thought we were having guests. I was just too aware of this strange tall man. He was nice looking, I'll admit that, but not one to my liking. He didn't speak much, and he acted as if he hardly knew I was there. He ate slowly and methodically like this was a chore he had to finish.

After lunch, I was more than happy to help Helga clean up and wash dishes until it was time to meet my bus. I had to walk down the street a couple of blocks to catch the ride back home, but I was glad to get out in the fresh air and go home. I wanted to feel a breeze on my face to help me sort out my thoughts and feelings. "Graham will walk you to your stop," Bertha told me.

"Oh no," I said quickly. I didn't know if I could handle more of Graham just yet. "I won't need an escort. I can go on by myself. It's only a few blocks away."

"It isn't seemly for a young lady to be walking by herself," Bertha replied, not allowing any room for argument. "Graham will go." He made no reply as to yes or no. He simply rose from his chair and headed for the door expecting me to follow like the silly goose I imagined he thought I was. No manners at all. Making our way out of the apartment, we stepped out into a gust of strong wind. There was a light mist in the air which I knew would make my hair a frizzy ball, that is if the wind didn't do it first. We made our way slowly down the street battling the gusts trying to push us back. He touched my elbow lightly to guide me around trash and mud decorating the brick sidewalk. Even then, it was a light, brief guiding touch, not at all personal. It was clear that this was a duty to him, and he was going to do it. I wonder what would happen if I stuck the toe of my buckled Oxford shoe in front of his not at all stylish boot? Would he trip and fall, or just move on in the determined steady way he was moving?

I guess I had expected way too much of the wonderful son and brother of my co-workers. At least, he was a good cook. I could say that for him. Not much else, to be sure. In my head, I remembered the wonderful way that Jimmy Lee Reilly looked at me. He seemed to consider me a treasure, while this man seemed to consider me a nuisance. Then I grimaced at the thought that maybe Jimmy Lee didn't care as much as I thought. After all, he didn't seem too eager to get back in touch with me. I suppose I was so caught up in all my thoughts and imagining, I tripped for real. Graham's arm shot out in front of me and blocked my forward movement. His arm felt as strong as steel, and I had to admit he almost knocked the breath clean out of me. No sprained ankle to be had, thankfully. If I had sprained it, I wonder what he would have done.

Then, maybe for the first time, he seemed to be looking at me. Maybe, not quite at me, but penetrating through me. His eyes were so dark, they appeared black. They seemed to drill a hole through my body. Gracious! I felt breathless for real. "Are you all right?" he asked, appearing genuine in his concern.

"Oh, I am fine," I answered, trying to act confident and self-assured. Actually, my foot was beginning to ache a little, but I didn't want to let him know how bumble footed I could be. When my bus arrived, I felt exhausted from all the twists and turns of the day. I would be glad to be back at home, settled in my own room, and in my own bed.

Poppa was inside tending to the fire since it had turned off cool. He looked around at me as I opened the door to come in. "Missed seeing that guy you spoke of from Lexington." He turned back to the fire and poked the logs around a bit.

"What?" I exclaimed.

"Well, I guess he understood that you didn't work on Saturday afternoon, so he brought himself over in that dinged danged fancy machine of his." I could tell that Poppa didn't seem too impressed. Maybe it would have been that way with any guy I took up with. I don't know. Poppa continued, "he said he tried to call, but the phone line was down again, so he brought himself up to the house. Guess he must have asked where we lived down at the store."

"What did you think of him, Poppa?" I asked, hoping for the answer I wanted to hear.

"He has a dad-gummed fancy machine, and he dressed too fancy for here," Poppa said.

"How fancy would that be?" I asked.

"Oh, I don't know. Fancy black and white shoes. One of them trench coats with a belt pulled around. Don't know where he thought he was going to. Looked like one of them Chicago types from the newsreels."

"Oh, Poppa," I was so disappointed and stressed. I was sorry that I missed Jimmy Lee and doubly sorry that Poppa didn't seem to like him one little bit. Wonder what he would have thought about Graham. "Where did you tell him I was?" I asked.

"I said you were flittin' around with some of your work pals," Poppa said with a slight grin. "He seemed a little angry about that. Wanted to know who and where. I told him that you were invited to a smart afternoon affair with some city types."

"Oh Poppa, you didn't say that did you?"

"Yep, and he got all red-faced and sputtery. Asked me when would be the best time to call? I thought about saying never, but I said he might come by tomorrow after dinner or next Saturday. He turned away after that and pitched some kind of plant he brought you onto the seat of that car and took off." Poppa seemed too pleased with himself to suit me. I was put out with him for sure. I just set about canning some lima beans, five quarts to be exact, but I had no more conversation with Poppa. Well, to be honest, I had to ask him about his pants that I needed to mend, but nothing more than that.

On Sunday, we went to church but came straight home. After dinner, we heard a machine pulling up the driveway. I went to the door, and there it was, Jimmy Lee's beautiful car. Not so beautiful with the road dust on it, but still quite nice.

September 30

Journal, I want to tell you that even though Jimmy Lee looked a bit ruffled and rumpled, he still managed to greet me nicely. He wanted to know all

We drove down by the river and got out, walked around a bit, took some pictures with my camera. When we came back to the house, we had cake, ice cream, pie, and real lemonade. I saw Jimmy Lee give a saucy grin when we started to drink the lemonade. He didn't say anything, though, and Poppa never suspected a single thing. I didn't think. I told him that I had to go to Camp Meeting in a little while and asked if he wanted to stay. He said he couldn't this time because he needed to be heading back. Maybe I would allow him to come back again next Saturday afternoon. I felt all tingly inside when he said that. I was wrapped up in my long sweater with pockets. I kept rubbing my fingers together, so I could hide how nervous I was.

"Tell you what," he said. "Maybe you could get a bit dolled up, and I could take you to dinner at the Flame and Glo Club in Newport. It is the sister club to the one where I work. They have delicious fried chicken, and their fried peach pies are the best. There can even be a little dancing there if you'd like."

"That sounds wonderful," I said. "I can't stay out too late. Remember, I have Sunday School and church early on Sunday morning. Poppa would throw a fit if I was to stay out late."

As I said that, Jimmy Lee's full lips tightened to almost a straight line. He raised one eyebrow, a trick I never learned to do, and said to me, "well, if it isn't something that you care to do, we just won't do it."

I caught my breath and answered quickly before he could change his mind, "oh no, I have a new dress I've been working on. I need someplace to wear it. It's a little daring for church and such, but I need someplace away to show it off." It was a beautiful seafoam green, calf-length dress, nice and warm but soft as a whisper with plenty of buttons and bows. I was so proud of that dress. Jenny Mae had helped me start it, but since it was a bit heavy for warm weather, I thought I would wait for the proper cooler time to wear it. Now, the time seemed perfect.

Jimmy Lee broke into my thoughts, "what time shall I come pick you up? Would 7:00 be agreeable? That will give us time for dinner and maybe a bit of dancing."

October 3

Journal, I am so nervous. What will I tell Poppa? Would he even allow me to go to a place in Newport. Does Poppa know about the Flame and Glo Club? I can say Jimmy Lee is taking me to a nice restaurant for supper. I might get by without saying where.

As it turned out, this was a problem that didn't need a solution. Poppa mentioned after supper on Sunday that he needed to go away next weekend to see about buying some colts. He and his brother would head out early in the morning to the horse auction. Since the auction would end late, and they didn't want to bring young horses back to a dark barn and lot, they would stay the night and return after dinner on Sunday.

"Will you be all right, and can you manage to feed and take care of everything by yourself?" Since I didn't exactly want to tell Poppa a bald-faced lie, I just said that Jimmy Lee Reilly had plans to take me to dinner on Saturday night, but I would clean up first and make pies for Sunday. That gave me time to feed and water the calves, pigs, and horses before we left. All Poppa said was, "be home and in bed in time so you don't oversleep for Sunday School and Church. Those slick city boys don't think about people who work for a living."

"Poppa, he does work for a living. He works with money and numbers instead of with his hands and back." I hoped Poppa didn't think I was making light of his farm work or that he wasn't a smart working man. Poppa gave me a grumpy stare as he tapped his spoon on the table. He didn't say anything more. Shrugging his shoulders, he shoved back his chair, stood up from the table, and started out the door to go feed the calves. Pausing as he opened the door, he stopped and turned back to look at me.

"I want you to remember your manners and make sure this man remembers his. I don't want him treating you like some of those trollops he no doubt meets in that work of his."

"Oh, Poppa, I know he is a nice man and an honest one. Do you think that Jenny Mae and her Winston would be likely to introduce me to a con man or anyone of that sort?"

"I suppose not," Poppa said. He shook his head and turned back toward the door. In my heart, I knew that Poppa didn't quite believe me.

On Saturday morning, we woke up to a hard rain. When I peeked out the front door, I saw streams of rainwater gushing down the hill making small gulleys in front of our house. I worried about Poppa setting out in the near dark to go to the auction. I hated hearing him start up the old Ford truck and wondered if he would have any trouble picking up his brother, Calvin, who lived at the end of a pitted pockmarked dirt road. Still, I felt better knowing he had someone with him, especially when green colts were involved.

The day yawned endlessly, making me plenty nervous waiting for 7:00 in the evening to come around. To occupy my time, I baked a new kind of cake and did a lot of cleaning. Listening to the rain caused me to worry about my new dress getting all wet and spotted. We had umbrellas by the door, but that wouldn't protect my shoes from getting mired down in the mud. I could have worn my rubber boots, but I didn't want Jimmy Lee to see me in those ugly old-fashioned things with their hideous metal clasps. Heavens! What would he think of me appearing in those? Mercifully, the sun came out about noon, warming and drying the ground. I hoped I could find the dry parts in the grass to make my way to the car, so I wouldn't damage my cute little pair of heels.

When Jimmy Lee came for me, it was too dark to see where the wet and dry places were. I wrapped myself in a cape to keep dry and warm, but I feared for my shoes. Jimmy Lee fixed that. He simply knelt and picked me up in his arms. When we got to the bottom of the porch steps, he carried me straight to the car. Gracious, I felt like a queen for certain.

Riding in his car made me feel like a goddess in her chariot. The soft luxury of the leather seats enfolded me like a smooth well-worn glove. Even the scent was rich and luxurious. The top was up because of the threat of rain, but I imagined how it would feel with the breeze tumbling your hair. Maybe you would have a brightly colored scarf draped over your hair and around your neck. It would be wonderful to take this ride on a bright sunny day.

We arrived and a young man came around to park our car, a valet, Jimmy Lee called him. Jimmy Lee helped me from the car and held my hand as we walked up a covered walkway. The Flame and Glo Club was a sight to see. When the door opened, and we entered the marble foyer, it seemed to me at first glance that this was the essence of an opulent dining establishment. The floor was laid out in a black and white checkerboard pattern with soft lighting from sconces which looked like glowing torches. There was an elegant young lady waiting to take us back to a table. She wore a sleek sophisticated black gown that swept to her ankles. The tight bodice accentuated the curves of her figure but showed her bare arms. They looked like the arms on a piece of Greek sculpture I saw in an art book at school.

I'm sure I stared at her mouth agape. She might have thought I was staring at her, but I was simply wondering where she got this beautiful dress and how it was made. Mrs. Parker tried to keep me up to date on all the latest styles, but I wondered if she wasn't missing a few of the finer details. Maybe if I came to Newport more often, or if I could have Jimmy Lee bring me back here again, I could discover more about the refinements of the fashion life.

Jimmy Lee looked at me and gave me a gentle shake trying to get a greater share of my attention, "Let's follow her to our table, shall we? I think we need to try and get supper started since I have a young Cinderella who needs to get back to her hearth before midnight."

I looked up at him thinking that he was teasing me, but somehow, I don't think he truly was. Did I sense a bitter undertone to his words? We moved to a table that was a bit remote from the center. Jimmy Lee pulled out my chair with a smile and a bow, and with a sweep of ceremony had me sit. All I could focus on was that the linens and cutlery were the finest. The tablecloth skimmed the table like silken skin as it simply brushed the top of the table. Our waiter brought small plates of things I had never seen before in my life and presented them with a flourish.

"What are these?" I asked Jimmy Lee hoping he wasn't ashamed of this country bumpkin come to town. He told me that the strange looking celery was stuffed with crabmeat, the toast was covered with a mushroom blend, and the other things he pointed out with his tiny fork were chicken livers wrapped in bacon blankets. I had never in my life seen or heard of such.

I didn't trust this kind of information to my journal, but several men came up to Jimmy Lee and me. Most of them smiled, but their smiles didn't leave their lips. Their eyes didn't crinkle at all. A couple of them looked hard and even mean. They all tended to be a bit on the short side and broad. All wore long dark jackets, and oh my Lord, I thought I saw a gun peeking out of one man's jacket. I wondered what I had gotten myself into. For a moment I thought I should have been safe at home, under my covers. When dinner was served, I was so nervous, I could barely eat. We had filet mignon (saw that word on the menu) with some vegetables fixed differently than anyway I had had them before. I wondered what had happened to the fried chicken and fried pies that Jimmy Lee mentioned. Oh well, I wasn't going to ask any more dumb country girl questions.

After dinner though, they had a floor show with lovely ladies dancing to a wonderful small band. I was thoroughly blown away by their gorgeous costumes, lovely skirts covering layers of fancy slips, camisole tops which seemed a bit more revealing than I was used to, and shoes that glittered as they turned. The way they moved together was like a fan unfolding. What a razzle dazzle that was to me.

Once, when I moved my chair around, I thought I saw men moving to a room in the back. "Jimmy Lee," I said to him. "Where are those men going in that other room?" He didn't answer me directly. He only turned to ask me if I wanted more water, or another roll. Thinking he hadn't heard me, I asked again. He only answered by telling me about the choice of desserts. After this, I merely shut my mouth and watched the rest of the show. When the polite applause completed their routine, I looked at Jimmy thinking it was about time we might need to leave. "Jimmy Lee," I said, probably a little timidly, "maybe it's about time we started home."

He laughed, but without much humor. A man was heading toward us. He was a slim little man with thick hair on each side of his scalp, but with a shiny bald spot in the center. He looked full of purpose with a scowl pasted on his slender face. All of a sudden, Jimmy Lee seemed in a hurry to get me up and home. We had almost made it to the door when the man reached us. He reached out with one hand. His long spider fingers knotted with thick purple veins wrapped around one of Jimmy Lee's arms. His nose seemed much too large and bulbous in his pasty drawn face. There was a wave of cigar smoke drifting off his suit jacket. The man seemed to notice me for the first time. "Well, hello, young missy," he said to me. "I hope you don't mind if I take a minute of your fellow's time, do you?"

I didn't think he would have given me the opportunity to object, no matter what I said. He gave me a smile drawing back his lips over large, yellowed teeth. He turned his back to me and edged Jimmy Lee away leaving me standing in the doorway feeling like an embarrassed lump. I heard some threatening hisses about money and Cleveland somebodies. The only thing I knew about Cleveland was that it was a city in Ohio. Somehow, I don't think that the city was what they were discussing. The man gave Jimmy Lee an angry look, and then with a dismissive wave of his hand, turned and walked away.

Taking me by the arm, Jimmy Lee turned and said, "we need to go." He guided me outside. As soon as we stepped out the door, a sheet of rain pouring off the entryway overhang drenched us. My wrap started to unwind and soon my dress was soaked. As I made my way to the car, I looked down to notice a length of my petticoat hanging down. Oh, my goodness, what was happening? In a moment of total humiliation, I noticed that my beautiful seafoam dress was beginning to shrink. I hoped that it wouldn't be too noticeable until the valet brought Jimmy's car around. Thanking goodness it was dark, I pulled my wrap tighter around so it would cover as much of me as possible. Jimmy Lee didn't seem to notice, and I hoped we would make it back to the house without anything else happening.

Jimmy Lee seemed preoccupied with his own thoughts. Probably something to do with his conversation with the man who didn't even have the manners to introduce himself. I couldn't decide whether I wanted this night to be over as soon as possible, or to remember the memorable parts and hope for another better opportunity. We drove most of the way in silence, neither of us seemingly wanting to intrude on the thoughts of the other. When we got to the house, I wasn't certain as to whether Jimmy Lee wanted to take me out again or was this the end of us.

"I had a very special time," I said, thinking to jumpstart the conversation. Jimmy didn't act as if he had heard me. So, I tried again. "This was a wonderful evening. I loved the food and watching the dancing." I pulled my wrap closer around me, partly because I was cold and partly because I was afraid it might be obvious that my dress was gradually creeping further toward my waist.

"Umm, yes," Jimmy said. "Maybe we can try this again soon." He didn't act as though he was seriously interested, although it could be that his mind was still in the lobby of Flame and Glo.

"Who was the gentleman at the door when we left?" I wasn't certain if I should have asked or not.

Jimmy looked at me as if he wanted to tell me it was none of my business, but he answered in a flat monotone expression. "Oh, that was one of the Lowenston brothers," he said. "He and his brothers own this Flame and Glo Club and also the Hey Ho where I work." Pulling a cigarette out of his case and lighting it up, he pulled in a long inhale and puffed out in exasperation. Then he turned to look at me, smiled, took another long inhale and blew out a series of playful smoke rings.

"Let's get you into the house. Maybe on another night when the weather is a bit less blustery, we can try this again." He led me to the door, and with a quick kiss on the cheek, turned back to the car. That was all. There was no more explanation.

October 6

Journal, I guess I don't have much to report to you in the romance department. I have not heard a word back from Jimmy Lee since our dinner, can I call it a date, on that last Saturday night. I guess that is the end of that little romance for me.

I worked, helped Poppa on the farm, and tried to go back to my life the way it was. We had been doing all the fall cleaning, and I had been making curtains for the rooms downstairs as we prepared to move back from the summer kitchen. The summer kitchen was so nice in hot weather. It was a little building set away from the house down a shady dirt path where we cooked, bathed, and did most of our laundry. It kept the house cool when we had to cook and can. We had a big table pushed up against the wall. Most of the time we would put our canning jars on it, but I liked to eat at that table, too. When we ate there, I didn't have to bring food back to the house.

We usually had a breeze at our house from the creek, but the summer kitchen kept the trapped heat from invading the inside spaces when it was sweltering hot outside. In the evening, when I would go take a bath, the breeze kept me cool even wearing a long nightgown as I returned to our back porch. In the fall and winter, though, I realized how much I loved being back in the winter kitchen where the stove and fireplace kept the kitchen warm and dry. The nutty wooden smell of the logs in their rack, and the crackle and spit of the fire gave me a sense of warmth and safety.

I had been spending a lot of my time making new rag rugs because I wanted something cozy to put my feet on at night. Momma had some old dresses and heavy coats that I couldn't bear to throw away or make into cleaning rags, so I thought about putting some of them into new quilts and rugs.

My aunt Flossie helped me some, but most of the time, Jenny Mae and I worked on the rugs on the weekends when she came back home. She tore and cut the material into strips, and I used the old treadle machine to sew the strips end to end. Then Jenny rolled the cloth into balls, and I used carpet needles to sew the yarn into wide circles. This is the part I dearly loved. I loved to weave all the pieces together into a glorious riot of color. I had a loom I could use for this, but the sewing made me feel closer to Momma and the feelings of cozy warmth that I had when we used to make rugs together.

Like Momma, Jenny Mae was there to talk things over with. She helped me sort out my thoughts and frustrations. I wanted her to understand that I loved being a part of her glorious reign as queen of the harvest, but I also couldn't help letting it out that I felt pretty discouraged about my misadventure with Jimmy Lee. "Jenny, do you think he just didn't like me all that much?" I knew I sounded glum and grumpy.

"Well, Josie," she said patting my hand, "I know Winston thought the date had gone well. Jimmy Lee told Winston that he thought you were one swell girl and a whole lot of fun."

I told her all about the disastrous date in Newport. I knew he thought I was a country bumpkin for sure. But even if it was Jenny Mae, I couldn't bear to talk about my dress shrinking. I felt my face turn hot just thinking about it. She seemed a bit more surprised about my meeting up with one of those Lowenston brothers. She looked over at me, "I've heard about those brothers. I know there are lots of rumors and gossip that get spread around. I think they have their fingers in several tills in Newport, but I'm not sure they are the best people to know."

Jenny asked me several questions, with a look of concern clouding her normally happy, smiling eyes. I didn't quite understand why she was concerned, but I told her it was not much of an event. I didn't speak to him, and his conversation with Jimmy Lee was quite short. She still didn't seem confident that was all there was to the conversation. She turned back to me and said, "I think this is probably a busy time of the year for Jimmy Lee, and he knows that fall brings a lot of last minute farm work to do here. I'm sure he will get back with you over the holidays or maybe afterward."

"Do you think for sure he will?" I wanted to believe her, but I wasn't sure I could.

"If he is not around for you during the holidays, you know I will be," she said. "You and I will have all kinds of fun until it's time for me to go back to the University." I felt a bit comforted after this and thought to myself that I wouldn't want to be one of those women who always waited around for others to make things happen for her.

November 3rd

It was a nice day, but a bit windy. I set out some flower bulbs.

November 28th

It's the Wednesday before Thanksgiving. I got home from work, cleaned up around the house. Jenny Mae was home, and she came after eggs. Before she left, she helped me move into the winter kitchen. The new kitchen curtains looked bright and cheerful. They were a nice red and white checked which always made me think of holidays and Christmas. I decided to make some towels and a tablecloth to match.

November 30

Thanksgiving. I canned sausage and rendered some lard. Poppa and I ate dinner with some of our friends, but we didn't stay long.

I had just about given up on seeing Jimmy Lee again. Here we were, close to the holidays, and I had not heard from him. Instead of worrying about Jimmy Lee, I decided to concentrate on practicing for the Christmas entertainment at church and cooking good food for all the friends and family stopping by for the holidays. It snowed nearly all day, and I spent most of the time embroidering on a dresser scarf, but then I decided that Poppa needed a woolly warm muffler to wrap around his neck. Eventually, after looking through all my material in my basket, I decided on a nice rich coffee brown and corn yellow to make his scarf a colorful combination. The day flew by. I looked out the window late in the afternoon and discovered that the snow had drifted up high on the sides of the house. I knew I'd better stop and help Poppa feed or see if he needed help digging out.

The rest of the week, the weather turned off mild. Funny how it can change from one day to the next. I don't know whether it was better to have snow, with all the cold, or have the melt with all the slush. I guess I was lucky to make it down to the bus and get back and forth to work without trouble. We had several wrecks down at the bridge by our house, but so far, the bus had been able to travel just fine. I finished work for the week at noon on Saturday and was told that I wouldn't be coming back until Wednesday. I could hardly believe it. I didn't know if they were giving us Monday and Tuesday off because it was holiday time or if they didn't have enough customers to buy our shirts. One of the women mentioned that there had been complaints about women taking jobs away from the men. Here times were hard, and women were getting the jobs. Her friend answered her by saying that at these low wages, no man would take these sewing jobs.

What a puzzle, but I didn't want to worry about it. I wanted to enjoy this time. I thought it might be fun when I went home to spend the rest of the day decorating the church for Christmas. I had a few trinkets for Helga and Bertha, though, so I guessed maybe I needed to exchange with them before I left for the day. When we took a short break for coffee and chocolate, I thought it was a good time to give them their presents. I had made lovely, crocheted doilies for Bertha, and embroidered hankies for Helga. Helga gave me a pretty, green comb, and Bertha gave me a mirror and brush set. We finished the rest of our chocolate with some gingerbread that Bertha had made. We stood to leave, and Helga turned to me and took something wrapped in smooth brown paper she had laid on the table.

"Oh, I almost forgot this," she said. "This is a small something from Graham." It was a wrapped bag of Chowards Violet Mints. Chowards was a new company that made this confection with a slightly floral flavor. Since I had heard that they were expensive, I was speechless. Why on earth had Graham sent me something? I barely knew him, and even if I did, I had nothing for him.

Babbling my thanks, I could hardly form sensible words to thank Helga and Bertha for their much-appreciated gifts, especially the mints from Graham. We wished one another a Merry Christmas and went home. My gifts were safely tucked in my purse, but on the bus, I pulled out one of those mints to eat. I couldn't believe the taste. Never had I had anything that I thought tasted so good. Even after the chocolate and gingerbread, I still had room for those Chowards mints. That afternoon, instead of going up to church as was my earlier plan, I spent my time baking gingerbread from Bertha's recipe and a date and nut cake. While I baked, I wondered what on earth possessed Graham to give me a gift, especially one that must have been difficult to find and expensive to buy. Maybe, I thought, this date and nut cake would be a nice gift for Graham.

Jimmy Lee, on the other hand, hadn't even given me as much as a card. Since I hadn't heard a word from him, I just needed to accept the fact that he was a cad, and that our relationship was a thing of the past. I knew I needed to accept it, but somehow that didn't change the sad, discouraged feeling that kept bubbling inside me. I decorated the tree on Christmas Eve and put bows around the windows. Poppa found a few boughs of holly and some mistletoe around the farm that I layered across the mantel. There was the sweet smell of the pine tree mingled with woodsmoke from the fireplace. When I stepped back to look around, I thought the room looked nice and festive. It wasn't like the Christmases of the past, but there was a bit of a holiday feeling.

Poppa and I met Jenny Mae and her parents at 6 Mile Church. They gathered in one of the front pews, so Poppa could see me with the rest of the carolers. It was so pretty and special. The singing was wonderful. All the practice we had been doing had been well worth the time. Poppa and I finally made it home just before dark. I thought I saw something bushy and green on the front porch. As we pulled the machine just beside the steps, I saw a big potted plant with bold arrow-shaped leaves marked with silver. The card on it said that it was a Schismatoglottis and not to water it too much in the winter. I was surprised to see it was from Jimmy Lee. He had added in his own hand, that those arrows went straight to his heart, and the silver marked the value I was to him. I knew I had to hide that card from Poppa. Just as I struggled to bring the plant into the house, Poppa came up to the porch.

"Where did that thing come from?" he said shaking his head. It was just about dark, but I thought he looked a little disgusted. "Looks like it will take up more room in the house than your Christmas tree. Who brought that thing?"

I had to confess because I wasn't good at keeping things from Poppa. "It was my Jimmy Lee friend from Lexington," I said struggling to pick up the massive plant.

"Thought he was from closer, like around Newport," Poppa said.

"Well, I met him in Lexington when I went to visit Jenny Mae. You know, he is the friend of Jenny Mae's and Winston's."

"If he is their friend, why didn't he join Jenny and her parents and go with us up to the church entertainment?" Poppa asked. "He sounds a little sneaky to me." Poppa watched as I struggled to get a good grip on the plant.

"Now, Poppa, he probably had to work today. Not everybody gets to start their holiday early like I did this year."

"Well, seems he had time to get a big-assed plant and run all over to dump it down without giving you as much as a 'Hello'," Poppa said. "Don't know what kind of courtin' he's doing, but it ain't like any I know of." Poppa leaned over to grab the side of the plant and help me pull it up the steps to the porch. He huffed and puffed, and I could tell he wanted me to believe that this was a difficult job. I thought he was making it look harder than it actually was.

Poppa didn't say more. He just held the door open and watched me push the plant inside. I tried to remember if I knew anything about this this kind of plant as I guided it into the front room. I moved it away from the fireplace, so the smoke wouldn't bother it. Then I moved it away into the corner, so it wasn't too near the door because of the draft. Poppa simply gazed with a bemused expression as I pushed and pulled trying to find space in my life for this plant.

Chapter Seven

Graham

1935

J*anuary 7*

Not much has happened of interest in this new year so far. Just work in Cincinnati and work here at home. When there is a break in the weather, we go up to the cemetery. Of course, we go to church most Wednesday nights and Sundays.

January 29

Jenny Mae went back to the University.

She seemed glad to be going back. I thought she missed Winston. I asked her to inquire politely as to whether Winston had seen Jimmy Lee. If he had, she was to pass on to Jimmy Lee that the plant was growing and doing well inside the house. It seemed to like the darker side of the house best, although that may have been because it didn't have the cold air from the door or the smoke from the fireplace to contend with. One of Poppa's hounds raised his leg on it once, but that dog didn't need to be in the house anyway, so out he went. That is what we had a doghouse for.

I was a little blue after Jenny Mae left, so I sewed on a dress I had cut out the previous summer that never got made. Maybe, I thought, it could replace the shrunken dress I had worn on my so-called date. Poor dress, it had shrunk so small that I could have easily used it for a blouse. Instead, I put it in the school's poor children's basket. I also crocheted another warm rug for my bedroom. The new dress was made with silk, so I needed to be very careful with it. I washed it out when I got it finished and ironed it very, very carefully. It came out fine. It was sunshine yellow with long sleeves, so I would have to wait until spring or summer to wear it. I thought I needed some place special to wear it, too.

March 11

Poppa seems a little down in the dumps. I don't know if it is the price of hogs, the price of milk, or the fact that his teeth are bothering him.

As the month wore on, Poppa seemed like he was a little better. It must have helped when he got a set of new teeth. He seemed to enjoy his food more and eating wasn't such a chore. Of course, my cooking wasn't always the best. I burned a lot of toast. It seemed strange that I could bake just fine, but putting a meal together, and have everything come out at the same time seemed a skill I hadn't managed.

Poppa told me that a friend of mine from school, Russell, had measles. From the way Poppa talked, it sounded like Russell was really sick. Poppa tried to keep me up with all the local news since I didn't get to speak to the neighbors as much as I had. Spring was in the air. I could go out on the porch and breathe. If I wasn't such a grown-up young lady, I would have turned cartwheels over the front lawn. However, since it was Friday, I needed to step back inside and get dressed for work.

When I got home from work that day, Poppa told me that Russell had died. It made me so sad. We had been in school together since our first grade. It seemed wrong that he was gone without having lived much life. He was his parents' only boy. They set a lot of stock by him. Sitting on the porch swing, I hugged my knees and tried my best not to cry. I did anyway which wasn't pretty. My nose ran and my eyes got all red and puffy. Poppa said the funeral was to be on Monday, so he would go.

March 27

Has been a cold and windy day. It wouldn't surprise me if it didn't start to spit a little snow.

Helga and I thought we would go shopping after work for a bit, and I would catch a later bus. I bought a new pink dress and a black hat. I crossed my fingers that I wouldn't need the money for something more urgent. I wanted a stylish outfit for spring, even though it had been so cold, I didn't think spring was ever going to arrive.

Surprise, surprise. Just as we were getting ready to leave the store and catch the bus, in walked Graham. Somehow, it didn't seem as if Helga was as surprised to see him as I was. It was all I could do to keep my mouth from dropping wide open. It didn't, of course, I just stammered a quick, "hello, there." It took me a minute to remember my manners and thank him for the wonderful mints at Christmas. He didn't say much in reply, just mumbled something about being glad I had enjoyed them. To my surprise, he continued the conversation by saying his co-worker, Carter, said his girlfriend had been coaxing him to get some for her. They were quite the new thing, and she wanted to have some.

I was ready to start for the door, when Helga said we should go up to the second floor and get a Coke float since it wasn't too late. She had heard about the store's delicious Coke floats from a friend and was anxious to try one. According to her friend, you walked up to the marble counter, ordered one, and sat at these cute little iron tables. She thought it sounded like so much fun. The three of us went to the second floor and ordered them. They were delicious, of course, with Coca-Cola, vanilla ice cream, and whipped cream with a cherry on top. We couldn't get these down at our store at home. They were beginning to get in lemon-lime drinks, but that was about all.

Graham paid for all our drinks, which embarrassed me. On the other hand, if he hadn't paid for it, I might not have had the money to get home. Buying the dress and hat left me just enough for bus fare, or the Coke float, but I wasn't sure I could pay for both. I made my own money and partially paid my way at home but didn't have extra for luxuries.

I wasn't sure what to say to Graham, so I asked how his work had been lately. Even though I didn't know exactly what it was he did, I knew most men liked to talk about themselves. How else was I to start the conversation? Since I wasn't certain, I thought work was a safe topic. He told us he had gotten back into town the day before after working in Chicago for a week. He was home for a few days.

Now I knew what I could talk to him about, Chicago. I babbled on about the LaSalle Hotel, and all the places I had been while I was there as a reward for winning the 4-H competition. I talked about the Art Institute and the Alder Planetarium and asked if he had been there too or had stayed at the hotel. "No," he said shaking his head to stop my unending flow of words. "I have never been to those places, but I know where and what they are."

"Where were you then, and what were you doing?" I was shocked at how pushy and rude I sounded.

"I was at work. Meetings and trainings, that sort of thing," he said. He turned back to his Coke float and demolished it with renewed energy. "Helga," he turned to his sister, "I'm so glad you thought of this. Great idea."

I had no idea about meetings and trainings and that sort of thing. I wasn't certain I knew what else to say to continue the conversation. What I did know was I had better get myself back home. Poppa would be worried to death with me getting home so late. "I guess I'd better get my bus back home," I said. "Poppa will worry if I'm too late."

Graham said, "My car is parked a bit away. I could take you home if you like." No, I thought. Poppa would be even more upset if I came home with a strange man after dark when I told him that I would be shopping with Helga. Even if Helga was in the car with us, I don't think that would make Poppa behave better.

"No, I will be fine. Just walk me down to the bus stop. I think I'll be perfectly safe if you walk me there, and then I can catch the bus." When I got on and settled down in my seat, I gazed out the window at a darkening sky as the bus lumbered its way toward home. I was so sleepy after work, shopping, and the Coke float that my chin kept falling to my chest. Finally, I put my shopping bag on the seat beside me and rested my head on it, careful not to crush my hat.

After a few minutes, flickering lights began to nudge me awake. These were the bright lights on York Street in Newport that were flashing and had awakened me. I glanced at the sidewalk and noticed a very sophisticated looking woman sashaying her way down the street. She seemed to have trouble keeping herself upright without hanging on to the arm of the gentlemen she was attached to. They looked at each other nodding with their heads turned toward one another with foreheads almost touching.

At first, I noticed her hat with a feathered band on her head, and the elegant coat swirling around her. Then, I noticed the man with her. There was something familiar about him. As the bus passed them, I turned my head to follow the couple as they walked down the street. Above them, a light from one of the signs flashed, illuminating their faces for a moment. With a gasp, I realized the man was none other than Jimmy Lee.

I was certainly wide awake now. Who was that woman? Why was Jimmy Lee with her and not with me? Of course, he wasn't obligated to me, I thought. There may have been a totally reasonable explanation, but I didn't think so. He must have simply found himself a new woman, I decided. This woman seemed glamorous and self-assured, even if she acted a bit tipsy. I guess Miss Josie didn't have this same charm and appeal.

I was nearly nineteen years old, and I was a mature woman with a job who helped support my family. It was time to make some decisions. When it came to men, I could find a new man, maybe even one or two and pick the one I wanted. I had to decide what they did right to please me, not what I did to displease them. There were plenty of boys on farms around us. Cedric Albert, my good friend and neighbor, for one. He would be more than happy if I agreed to marry him and combine our farm with his. He was the older boy in the family, and his father would be so pleased if he would stay home and work the farm. Their place wasn't big, but if we combined our place and his, it would be enough to support us all.

The more I thought about it, the more it made sense. Poppa had been worried about making ends meet. We didn't have to worry about food because that was plentiful. We hadn't gotten down to coons and collards, but cash was another matter. We had always been able to sell milk, eggs, and of course hams and lard, but now the price of hogs had fallen. Our best cow, Rose, had died, and people could only eat so many eggs. I had always been able to sell my canned goods and produce, but money was just so scarce these days. We needed to replace Rose, but who wanted to trade hams and lard in exchange for a good milk cow when they could get cash.

As for my relationship with Cedric, I did like him. He was good, solid, and honest, but there wasn't any sense of romance with him. No sparks or tingles. If I were to align my future with Cedric, it would be more like a business arrangement. Even if I felt that I could live a good life like that, I wouldn't be happy. I wanted more spice in my life. I thought the best thing for this woman was simply to continue my work in Cincinnati as long as I could, but to set my sights firmly on what I needed and wanted for my future.

April 26

My birthday. They didn't need me at work today or tomorrow, and since it was my birthday, it made me happy not to go in. I still worry about how much longer they are going to need me at the sewing factory.

I baked two cakes, one for my birthday, and the other for my friend, Mavis, who also had a birthday. Lots of people came over to help us celebrate. We had cake, ice cream, and music. Cedric gave me a camera, and I got a dollar from Poppa.

April 28

Cedric came over and went with me to the cemetery to take flowers for Momma. He was excited to start using the camera he gave me. He wanted us to walk down along the river and take pictures of all the wildflowers starting to come alive, trillium, bluebells, blue violets. I loved the wildflowers too, but I didn't want to stand too close to Cedric. I didn't want to encourage a more intimate relationship.

Cedric confessed that he didn't want to be a farmer, but he would if he had to. He wanted to be a teacher, and he wanted to go to teacher's college in the fall if he could manage it. It occurred to me he thought if he married the right kind of wife, she could oversee both places if he were to teach. Whoa, buddy even if I felt that I loved and wanted to marry short little Cedric, I wouldn't be that 'right kind of wife.' No, siree. I thought if he were to go to teacher's college, he wouldn't be around to help on a farm every day. He didn't need a wife. He needed a good, hired hand. It seemed to me it would be best for my future to leave and find another job to help Poppa. My dream was not to spend the rest of my life here as a farmwife.

Of course, I thought, if Cedric were a teacher, that would make him a respectable member of the community. Just as my mind was scrambling through all these thoughts, he leaned over to kiss me on the cheek. I reacted quickly by bringing the big box camera between us. "Saved by the lens," I thought to myself. The thought of those thick wet lips on my face made my stomach take a bit of a flip. I would determine the lips that went there. My idea of romance wasn't one of being face-to-face with a farm boy whose mouth barely reached my chin. "I need to take the picture of that enormous tree with three forks," I said in explanation to Cedric. Waving him around to look at a tree on the creek bank, I asked what kind of a tree it was.

"Um, I guess it looks like a shagbark hickory," he answered somewhat perplexed that I would change the subject so quickly. "I reckon I should see about taking you on home. Dad and I have some work we need to get done before dark."

"Yes, well, it has been fun," I said, patting him on the arm and heading for his truck. "I enjoyed taking these pictures. Thank you for my birthday camera!"

As we pulled up the driveway, a car blocked our way. Not just any car, but Jimmy Lee's beautiful Pontiac. And there, standing on the bottom step of the porch, was the man himself, looking up and talking to Poppa. I wondered if the little trollop he'd been with had left him. Of course, it had been six months or just a bit more. Maybe, I thought, that was a long-term relationship for him.

Cedric looked at the fancy car in the drive, and then pulled his farm truck around it where he could spray a little gravel in that direction. "Well, who is that fancy swell standing on the porch steps talking to your Poppa?" he asked me with a tight look on his face.

"That is Jenny Mae and Winston's friend from the university," I said as nonchalantly as I could.

"He don't look like no college boy to me," Cedric's long bulldog cheeks hung even lower. Adjusting his wire-rimmed glasses as if he couldn't quite determine what he was looking at. He looked at Jimmy Lee and then turned his gaze back to me with an accusing glare.

"I don't suppose he is," I said jumping out of the truck and grabbing at my camera. "Thank you for the lovely day and the pictures. I'll see you later." I shut the door and turned my back to the truck as I headed up toward the house. After a moment, a feeling of shame came over me for the way I'd treated Cedric. Shading my eyes with my hand, I turned and gave him a small wave of farewell. I didn't notice if he even looked at me. As I turned and walked toward the house, the sound of the truck shifting gears and heading down the road roared behind me. A spray of gravel and dirt let me know he was moving faster than he should have.

I didn't want to appear too eager to meet with Jimmy Lee. After all, I should be angry with him. Poppa seemed comfortable rocking on the porch. A pitcher of sun tea sat on the table, and Poppa's dog, Daisy, lay beside him. I supposed I would have to invite Jimmy Lee to come up and sit down since it was a bit awkward to leave him standing there. "Do you want to come up and have a glass of tea?" I asked.

"Don't mind if I do," Jimmy Lee answered. Moving up the steps, I turned to look over my shoulder to make sure he was following behind.

Poppa stood as I reached the top of the steps. "I guess I will leave you folks to talk awhile. It's time to go feed and water. If you need anything from me, just holler." Poppa said, as he took off his house slippers and shoved his feet into his mud boots. Whistling for Daisy, he headed off down the steps. Jimmy reached over to pat Daisy on her neck as she passed him. She looked up and gave a low growl.

"She doesn't really like anybody but Poppa," I tried to explain. "She won't bite or anything. She is just a one-person dog." I thought about telling him my dog, Queenie who loved everybody. She was the pup that Poppa let me keep. It made me a little sad because the others, being good hunting dogs, had to be sold. The mother had to go too. She had one or two litters left in her before she was too old to breed. Poppa had a tough choice about Queenie, but since she was a runt and a bit bow-legged, she probably wouldn't have sold for much anyway. I hated that we had to get rid of the others, but at least I got to keep Queenie. It seemed as if there had been so many things lost and gone recently.

Jimmy Lee looked at me with a bit of a sheepish grin on his face. His eyes crinkled at the corners making him look more handsome than ever, "I guess you wonder why you haven't heard from me?"

Well, I knew I wondered, but I didn't think that did me a darn bit of good. He was probably off with his floozie or another just like her. This was something I wouldn't admit to him. "Oh no," I said. "I have been so busy with work in Cincinnati and work here on the farm, I simply haven't had time to think about other things."

"Does that charming Charley you drove up with have anything to do with it?" he said, his face stiff, cold, and somewhat stern.

"Oh, you must mean Cedric. He is a neighbor and a friend," I said. Jimmy Lee had some nerve asking me all about my business, I thought. Did he believe he could do whatever he wanted, but expect me to explain myself to him? I didn't think so. I squeezed my lips together to keep unwanted words from escaping.

"He doesn't have anything to do with that big box Brownie you have clutched to your chest, does he?" Jimmy Lee asked.

"Well, yes, this was his birthday present to me," I said, clutching the camera a little closer to my chest. "We went out to the river to see how it worked on flowers and ferns."

"Seems like a personal gift for just a neighbor and a friend," he said with a shake of his head. Scratching his mustache with his right finger, he turned to look at me, an unreadable look in his tiger eyes. "However, that isn't what I came about today, but I do want to tell you that I'm sorry I missed your birthday. I hope to make it up to you later." He smoothed his hair back from his forehead. "I have other things I need to talk to you about."

"Oh, that is quite all right. There can be other times and birthdays," I wanted to smack myself for acting as if I assumed he would be around for later, or I wanted him to be. "What else were you wanting to talk about?" I said, nodding to encourage him to get to the point.

"I actually wanted to talk to you about a job at the club where I work. We have these dancers whose outfits are smashing, and they have to stay that way all night. But sometimes, they need to dance twice a night for six days a week. That's a lot of wear and tear. I mentioned to Mrs. Florene, the lady in charge, that I know this wonderful young lady who's a whiz at sewing."

"Oh, I don't know if I'm that," I said feeling a little wheezy in my chest. I gave a short hard cough. Where on earth was this conversation headed?

"Of course, you are," he said with a huff. "I have seen a couple of outfits that you have worn, and all I hear from Jenny Mae is that you sew like a dream. I know all about the sewing competition you won. Jenny Mae spared me no details about that."

"Well, she is my friend, so she would like to believe the best," I said, as I hugged my crossed arms in front of me.

Jimmy Lee continued, "no matter," he said shrugging his shoulders. It sounded as if he were becoming tired of our back-and-forth conversation and wanted to get down to business. "I've heard that the sewing factory is cutting back on its orders and thought you might want something else to fall back on. I mentioned to your Poppa that times are more difficult than they used to be, and I wondered if a little extra cash might come in handy." I was a bit surprised that Poppa would have any kind of discussion with someone he seemed to dislike, but maybe Jimmy Lee was right. The cash would come in handy. "Your Poppa didn't tell me anything directly. He just told me that was a discussion that I would have to have with you." He picked up the glass of tea that I poured for him and drank some of it. Setting it down on the table and rubbing his fingers into the sweaty trickles running down the sides, he continued, "Mrs. Florene asked me if there was a time or place she could meet with you to discuss the matter. It could be after work one day, or on a Saturday afternoon."

"Well, let me see," I said. "Maybe, next Saturday would be okay." I knew full well I didn't have anything else planned for Saturday.

"Done, then," Jimmy Lee stood and brushed off his britches, looking at me with a quirky grin. "Again, I am so sorry I missed your birthday, and I want to assure you that I have missed seeing you." He pulled me to him and gave me a quick kiss on the cheek. I wasn't so sure the missing me part was accurate, but maybe I was closing myself off from a great adventure. It wouldn't do to try to be Miss Nicey Nice all the time.

On Monday, I told Bertha and Helga about the possible job opportunity of acting as a dressmaker and seamstress for dancers. Helga gave a shriek of joy and rushed to give me a hug, "Where is it to be?"

"In Newport," I replied, "at the Hey Ho Club."

"You need to be careful being around those places," Bertha gave me a sharp look.

"Oh, Momma," Helga said with a long sigh. "Don't be so suspicious. It sounds like a wonderful opportunity for our Josie."

"Well, opportunity or not," Bertha added, "she had better keep an eye out is all I can say."

Just as we were heading for a church meeting the following Wednesday, Jimmy Lee rang up. "Mrs. Florene would like to invite you to a high tea on Saturday next at her private apartment at the Hey Ho," he said. "Would you care to go?"

"Oh yes," I said breathlessly.

"Good then," his voice sounded smooth and pleased. "I will come by to pick you up about 3:30 in the afternoon if that is all right with you and your Poppa."

"I think that time will be just fine," I said more to assure myself than him. It was difficult not to sound scared or nervous. Of course, I was both.

When 3:30 came, dressed as business-like as I could, I wore a plain blue checkered dress with puff sleeves and a flared skirt. It was a constant worry as to whether my seams were straight on my stockings or wiggling around like little worms up the backs of my legs. As I stepped my foot on the running board of his shiny Pontiac, I couldn't help but contrast this with the last time I rode in his car. That was the night of the shrinking dress. My face flushed remembering that disastrous turn of events. My hands started to shake a bit as I settled into my seat and adjusted the folds of the skirt around my legs.

"Are you all right?" Jimmy looked over at me. I didn't think I acted scared or nervous, but I guess he realized I wasn't totally comfortable. "You'll be just fine," Jimmy Lee said with a reassuring grin. He reached over and patted me on the knee. "I know Mrs. Florene will be impressed with you and your skills. Simply believe that she will be lucky to have you work for her, and not the other way around." His face crinkled in concentration as he looked at me. His tiger eyes gleamed and with an emphatic slap of his hand on the soft leather seat beside him, "it will be a great experience for the two of you."

As we drove toward Newport, Jimmy Lee changed the subject and chattered away about all the funny things that people were doing and saying at his work. Pretty soon, he had me laughing and giggling until I totally forgot about being scared. It wasn't until I got into the lobby of the building that I started worrying again. I stepped foot into the elegant brass elevator fitted with brass knobs and oak paneling. This was the closest I had come to anything that could compare with the elevator at the LaSalle Hotel.

I realized at that moment I wasn't on the farm or factory anymore. I worried about how I would convince this woman that I could do the job she needed me to do. I was startled to see that there was no one operating the elevator's controls, but Jimmy Lee took complete charge of the situation. He knew what to do with the lever and buttons. As for me, my fingers and toes felt like ice. I realized that I was pretty nervous. I felt underdressed and awkward. "So, will we be having tea?" I asked, hoping my voice wasn't shaking so much he could hear it.

"Absolutely. Don't worry, you'll enjoy it," he said putting his arm around my shoulders giving me a hug of encouragement.

On the third floor, we walked down a long hallway covered with a beautiful Persian carpet ending in a marble offset leading to an apartment. Jimmy raised the knocker shaped like a lion's head on the thick wooden door. Moments later, an elegant diminutive white-haired lady answered the knock. A subtle whiff of scent that I later learned was 'Joy" by Jean Patou enveloped her. "Well, hello there," she said. "I am Florene Ricci, and you must be Josie." She was a full-chested woman dressed in a violet dressing gown that seemed to match her eyes. For all her small stature, she exuded a sense of power and strength. "Jimmy Lee, I am so glad you brought her to see me. Josie, dear, please call me Florene. It doesn't do to be too formal."

Mrs. Florene had a small dog under one arm with a big blue bow containing his topknot of hair. She laid the dog down beside her and reached out her hand to welcome us. Her hand had long thin fingers covered with more rings than I thought our jeweler had in his store. One that I noticed, was a red-purple beryl ring that seemed to glow on her finger. Her rings seemed an essential part of her and looked as elegant as she did. Stretched around her wrist was a ring of keys which she removed and set aside on a nearby table. Around her neck she wore a pear-shaped amethyst necklace anchored to the chain by what looked to be a diamond. I couldn't help but stare at that necklace. She caught me staring. I said to her, "You are wearing the most gorgeous necklace I have ever seen.

She smiled and said, "My late husband had it made for me by a special jeweler. I love it dearly and wear it almost everywhere. It is a special connection and a daily reminder of our wonderful relationship. I had hoped to pass it on to a daughter, but that never happened for us." Taking me by the hand, she led me into the room with the little dog trotting at her side. "Now, Josie, I expect that you are the wonderful master seamstress that I have heard so much about."

"Well, yes, I am Josie, but I don't know that I'm all that about a master seamstress. I just know how to sew." I felt too awed and nervous to say too much. "I make most of my own clothes and alterations and clothes for my friends. May I pat your dog?" I asked, not quite certain if this would be proper etiquette or not. Feeling a bit uncertain as to how to continue the conversation, I thought it best to talk about something comfortable.

"Of course," Mrs. Florene said. "He loves all the attention he can get." The dog nodded his head as if agreeing with his mistress's comments. His blue bow wiggled and wobbled as he did. I leaned over to pat him on his head, careful not to disturb the bow. Oh, merciful heavens, I remembered almost giggling thinking how Queenie would look with a big pink bow on her head.

"His name is Diamond," Mrs. Florene stooped and pulled up the dog's muzzle to show a large, white diamond shape on his chest. "See? He is wearing a diamond, and that's what I like most to wear as jewelry. We have the same sort of taste. That is why I chose him as a puppy." Mrs. Florene stood, straightened, and turned to face me, "did you make the frock you are wearing?" On her lips, it didn't sound like she was calling my dress a frumpy homemade housedress, which in my mind, it now was.

"Yes ma'am, I made this dress," I said, as the heat rose up my neck, through my throat, and all the way to the top of my head.
She looked at one of the sleeves and asked, "May I touch your arm, please?"

"Oh, yes, that is quite all right."

"Hmm, very fine stitches. Did your mother help you with this?"

"Oh, no, my mother has been dead over two years now," I told her.

"Oh, dear heavens, you were little more than a baby," she said as her bright violet eyes shadowed over. "I am so very sorry. That must have been painful for you."

"Yes, ma'am. It happened on my birthday." I thought that made me sound way too pitiful, so I added, "She made me a cake first."

Mrs. Florene took me by the arm and led me to a table. It was right in the middle of the floor in what I would say was a fancy living room. The walls were a shade of green that was the color of new leaves in the woods behind our house. Almost to the ceiling were little drawings of grapevines. I felt like I was lost in a dream. The table itself was in the center of the room with upholstered chairs of green and tan fabric. I wanted to rub on that fabric to see if I could tell what it was, but I didn't dare. In the middle of the table, a circular serving tower held different foods in three layers. Goodness, layers, not food spread out on the table like I was used to. I guess this must have been to save room because there were pots for what looked like tea, sugar, and cream. There were also plates to eat from. I didn't know what to do first.

Mrs. Florene must have sensed my discomfort, and being the gracious lady she was, she led me to a table and asked me to please have a seat. Jimmy Lee did have the presence of mind to pull out my chair for me, and I sat. Mrs. Florene allowed Jimmy Lee to guide her to her place and pull out her chair, and then she said to me very gently, "I suppose your mother didn't get the opportunity to explain a tea to you. Would you allow me to show you how it will be?"

"Oh, please do. I would appreciate it so much," I said

"We are having tea. This is a lovely mint tea that I personally enjoy, and I will go ahead and pour for us," picking up a lovely bone China teapot. "Sometimes, we have wine, but I don't think your father would appreciate that for you so early in the day." She lifted the delicate teapot with her right hand, resting it on her left, with a gentle dance-like movement that was the epitome of grace and sophistication. Deftly, she poured the tea into the three China cups and the aroma of the mint filled my senses. I noticed that the saucer matched my cup. Beside the saucer, there was a dainty napkin and silver spoon with a water glass at one side.

"These three tiers have different foods" she said, pointing to the foods on the tower with her open hand. "The bottom tier holds finger sandwiches. We have benedictine and cucumber, chicken salad, and ham salad. The middle tier has scones, and there are sweets at the top. For the scones we have clotted cream, jam, and lemon curd." I noticed how the little jars of cream, jam, and lemon curd were in lovely matching pots. I was dumbstruck by this wealth of new information. "Now, when you eat your scones, just break them in half and put on your condiments," She said, pointing to the jars again "Just place a spoonful or so on your plate until you are ready for your scones."

I wrapped my hands around the cup of tea. Jimmy Lee looked at me with a slight shake of his head. I took that to mean that it wasn't correct to wrap my hands around my cup. Was I ever going to become a lady? Maybe a farmwife sewing feed sacks was as much as I should hope for, I thought with a sinking sense of despair.

"I love this type of plum jam the best," Mrs. Florene said, as she spread one part of her scone with the lovely dark jam and put it up to her lips. "Go ahead, Josie, and try a bit of it," she said as she gestured with her small knife. Taking a scone and breaking it as she did, I spread a bit of jam on it. It was delicious. Nothing like this had ever come out of our farm kitchen. I knew I would remember the taste forever. "I think Jimmy Lee likes the sandwiches better, don't you? Or is it the cheesecake squares? Gracious, I can never remember," Mrs. Florene said. She sounded as if we were simply a group of friends eating and chatting together. This took some of the awkwardness away from the situation, at least for my part.

"My favorites are the ham sandwiches and the cheesecake squares. The chicken salad is terrific, too," Jimmy Lee answered.

"Isn't that just like a man?" Mrs. Florene looked at me with a wink. "Well, Josie, you might like all of them, so please help yourself." It seemed that although I was being encouraged to try all of those delightful foods, a bite or two of the scone with a little butter and jam was all I could manage. The tea tasted best because it was warm and comforting. My stomach was still knotted with nervous tension. I worried that my manners wouldn't pass muster for for this situation.

At last, Mrs. Florene brought her napkin up to her mouth, and then laid it to the side. Jimmy Lee did likewise, so I did the same assuming the tea was over. I hadn't cleaned my plate, even though I had only taken out the scone and a truffle, but I guessed that was not how it was done around here. Jimmy Lee pulled out Mrs. Florene's chair for her, and she made her way to a brocade loveseat and waved her hand for me to sit beside her. Jimmy Lee pulled up a chair alongside us.

"Now, I want to tell you that my dear, precious girls wear beautiful dresses. There are eighteen young ladies, and they rotate six dancers at a time," she said, staring into my eyes and patting me gently on the knee. "The first six go on at 8:00 and dance until around 9:00 or so. Then, they might entertain young men at their tables, so that they don't become lonely. These men might be from out of town on business or simply visiting and come to the Hey Ho to eat and drink." She pulled herself back to the dress topic. "The second six go on at 10:00, and they dance for an hour and then entertain the gentlemen. Sometimes, the same dresses might be worn by two women on the same night, so that could mean a lot of wear and tear on the clothing, straps, hems, that sort of thing. What I need is someone to keep up with all the fixing and mending of these clothes. Possibly, our seamstress might add a few buttons, bows, little extras that the girls might enjoy."

"I think this sounds like a wonderful sewing project," I said, "but I don't think Poppa would let me stay out that late."

"We wouldn't want you out too late. You could come in early, make the repairs for the upcoming shows, and then leave as the 8:00 show finishes. We would have a Yellow Cab at your disposal to escort you home once you have finished for the evening," she assured me.

"I could ride the bus home," I said, "if it isn't too late."

"Oh no, we will have you back home in your Poppa's care safe and sound. If the weather is cold and dark, we wouldn't want you to stand out waiting for the bus," she said slightly shuddering at the thought.

"How many nights would you want me to work," I asked.

"I suppose Monday through Saturday," Mrs. Florene thought it over carefully rubbing a bejeweled finger alongside her cheek. "We would pay you twice over what the sewing factory is paying. You would be working fewer hours, and you wouldn't have to be sitting at a machine all that time."

This sounded like a prayer come true for me. I was so excited. "I'll have to talk this over with Poppa, but I think it sounds like a wonderful opportunity for me," I said. "Of course, I would have to give them notice at the factory. Two weeks, at least, I think it is."

"Well, let me know sometime tomorrow. You may ring me at this number," she handed me a richly embossed ivory card with her name and number, continuing with a sweet smile lighting her face, "If you choose not to do this, that is perfectly fine. Don't feel as though there is any obligation."

She stood up, and I did the same. As I thanked her for the wonderful tea, I wondered how in the world I would feel like fixing supper for Poppa. I felt stuffed, myself, and even though I hadn't eaten much, that was the least of my worries. My biggest worry was rehearsing ways in which I could present this opportunity to Poppa.

On my way home, I also thought about the fact that I would be paid to sew, my very favorite thing. Poppa would be reasonable. I hoped he would be. Jimmy Lee sat next to me in the car and seemed quiet. Finally, he turned toward me and asked how I felt about Mrs. Florene's offer. "Oh, I am so excited!" I answered him practically bubbling over with enthusiasm. "I think this sounds like a dream job. Mrs. Florene speaks of her girls as if they were her very own daughters. Do you know if the girls are nice? Would they like me?"

"Oh, I think most of them are pretty nice," he said. "I don't know many of them on a personal basis. Some are from around here, and some came from out of town with the people who run the Hey Ho. You might be able to come in before you start to meet some of them and find out what they like in their clothes and such." Jimmy Lee drove me up to the front door and walked me up to the porch. "I hope you decide to take advantage of this situation. Mrs. Florene doesn't make these kinds of offers lightly, and I thought she seemed taken with you."

"Really?" I was plenty surprised.

"You need to call her as soon as you talk it over with your Poppa. That is if your telephone line seems to be working," he said with a grin. He patted me on the arm and turned to go down the steps before adding casually, "Oh, by the way, we'll have to go back to the Flame and Glo or here to the Hey Ho and have drinks or dinner, just the two of us. That is, if that is something that you would like to do."

I thought for certain he could hear the pitty pat of my heart gearing up for top speed. "Oh yes," I said trying to stay calm. "I think I would like that, and I will be certain to call Mrs. Florene as soon as my Poppa agrees."

I realized that Poppa was still at the barn when I got into the house, so I went upstairs to change out of my dress and into my overalls. I didn't want Poppa to think I was just giddying around having tea and such, leaving him with all the work. He was milking, so I started spreading corn and vegetable scraps left from dinner for the hogs. I went back into the barn to see if I could find any eggs. The chickens were firmly on their nests, and several squawked indignantly as I rooted my hands under them. Eventually, I found two eggs we had overlooked this morning.

"Well, how did the fancy tea party go today in the big city," Poppa asked as he picked up the pail of milk and pulled himself to his feet. That is when I told him all about the tea and finished with Mrs. Florene's offer. Poppa didn't look any too happy with what I was telling him, but he didn't tell me 'no' either. He simply headed back toward the house with me trotting at his heels firmly holding the eggs I hoped to put into cornbread.

He laid the milk pail on the table and turned to me. His worn cheeks looked drawn showing a rough, gray stubble. I saw that his hair had gray streaks I hadn't noticed before. For the first time, I thought, he looked like an old man. "I want to say to you that I hope you are making a good decision here," he started. "You do have a decent job with nice and caring co-workers. I understand that maybe this job isn't there for the long term, and the sewing factory may be closing down. But I trust you will make the best decision you can for yourself and not just for the money."

"Oh Poppa," I said. "I think Mrs. Florene is a sweet, caring lady. She seems so concerned about the girls that work and dance for her. You can tell she also cares about the customers at the Hey Ho, and she wants the best for all of them."

"That is exactly what scares me," Poppa said looking at me with wounded eyes. He scraped his thumb along his cheek, "Oh Lordy, I can't really tell you what to do. I want you to be safe and happy. I just don't know." This was the first time that I had ever known Poppa to act perplexed and unsure. I hurt for him since I felt I knew what he must be feeling trying to be mother and father both and to take care of the farm.

"Poppa," I said, hugging him and smelling the good hay and tobacco smells embedded in his shirt. "I will remember all the things that you and Momma have taught me. I won't do anything that would cause you pain or shame.

The next day, I called Mrs. Florene on the phone. The line did work that day. She sounded pleased that I was willing to work for her. I let her know, though, that I must give notice at the sewing factory. It would be at least two weeks. Mrs. Florene thought that after the 4th of July break would be a nice time to get started. The work would be a bit slower in the middle of the summer, and it would be easier to get used to the work when I wouldn't be so rushed.

I purely hated the thought of telling Bertha and Helga that I would be leaving in a short while. They had both been so special and helpful to me. On Monday I explained I would be leaving this job soon. My new position at the Hey Ho in Newport would start the Monday after the 4th of July. I told them what I would be doing. Helga seemed delighted I would be out in a social climate and working with my sewing skills in new and different ways. She seemed almost giddy at the prospect. "Mercy," she said. "I have seen pictures of those dancing girls with feathers in their hair, beautiful flouncy skirts, and lovely satin-looking shoes. Oh, Josie, don't you wish you could be doing that?"

"No, I would rather be sewing," I said. "Can't you just see me? The girls would be dancing and prancing, and I would be falling flat on my face. The first time out, I would probably trip on my hem, tear the whole skirt off, and land with my derriere sticking up to the sky." Well, that started us all laughing. "I think it would be better if I could just sit with my sewing basket, needles, and threads, and repair those things that the others tear. Or sewing together those things that need to be gathered back into place."

"Aha," Helga said. "You are the little Miss Muffet sitting there on your Tuffet except you are also the spider weaving your web, right?" Then we continued our giggling again as Helga mimicked me twirling my carpet needles as she waved her arms around her head trying to be as spider-like as she could imagine.

July 6

Started my new job. It was so exciting for me, and I had primped and worked on my own dress for that first day. This was to show all those beautiful dancers that even though I may have been a farm girl, I knew some stuff. The girls were very nice to me. They were loud and a bit profane, but very kind. What surprised me the most was that they would strip down to their underwear to allow me to mend and pin. They would pull up their hose and show their garters and more so that I could see where they wanted alterations.

Some of the girls who came in for the later show seemed a bit tipsy. They used what they called sen sen, or breath perfume, to conceal the odor from the floor manager and, maybe, each other. I knew the ones who sat with the men after the show had drinks with them at their tables, but I thought these drinks were mostly watered down wine or soda. I didn't think it was the strong stuff that the men drank. However, it didn't concern me much, so it didn't feel as if it was any of my business.

What I was interested in was Jimmy Lee. He had his own office on the 2nd floor. It wasn't a big office, but it was on the floor where the businesspeople were. I peeked in one day while the door was open. His office was paneled in luxurious walnut with a matching desk. There was a globe of the world on a stand, lovely prints on the wall, and a bookcase full of books and ledgers. Wow, he must be an important somebody here. The office next to his seemed a bit grander, quite a bit larger, with an important looking oriental rug in the center of the room. I needed to ask whose office that belonged to, but I managed to sneak a peek in that room, while no one was looking.

The girls asked how I knew Mrs. Florene. One girl in particular, Lila, a tall, elegant brunette who was the lead dancer in the first show and sometimes the second, wanted to know all about me and how I had landed in their midst. Most of the women seemed to have the greatest sort of respect and affection for Mrs. Florene. When I told Lila I met her through Jimmy Lee Reilly, she moved back with a startled look. Her large gray-green eyes widened, but she didn't say much. She asked me how I knew him, but it seemed like a lot to go into, so I merely told her it was through a childhood friend.

After that revelation, the girls seemed to keep their distance a bit. I had hoped Lila would let me know more, but she didn't seem as eager and outgoing as she was at first. Was there something about Jimmy Lee they didn't like? Gradually, as the girls seemed to know and trust me a bit better, they came a little closer. However, they didn't reveal why they seemed to distance themselves from Jimmy Lee.
Lila even offered me a dash of brandy that she carried in a little hip flask for my tea. I didn't want to insult or rebuff her in any way, so I told her that any sort of strong drink might make my stitches all

crooked. I assured her I certainly didn't want to mess up the girls' outfits.

September 18

It is Friday. I have been invited to one of the showgirl's weddings tomorrow. She met her intended groom as one of her customers, we were supposed to call them clients, at the club. He was from off somewhere near Chicago. He wasn't a regular client, but he was a salesman of some kind, paper goods, maybe. He met the girl, Marianne, when he came to town last winter. Then he came in several more times, and they fell in love. So romantic.

I bought a new dress, shoes, and an adorable hat. Cute shoes, too. I think I would have liked a dress I made better, but I didn't have the time. Marianne even let me invite Jenny Mae who was now engaged to Winston. My thought was that maybe the two of us could pick up some ideas for her wedding if I planned this right.

We loved Marianne's dress. It was yellow silk chiffon with sheer puffy sleeves. Even though it was a hand-me-down from her sister, with a few frayed edges, I was able to add a bit of edging which made it perfection. Jenny Mae helped with the restoration of the dress, so it gave her good ideas about stitching and such.

The wedding was very nice. There were only a few girls from Marianne's regular dance shift, Mrs. Florene, me, Jenny Mae, and Marianne's mother. I was surprised, I guess, that the only men there were Marianne's groom, John, and his brother, Gunther.

Marianne carried a lovely bouquet of dahlias. She wanted peonies, but they weren't in season. Mrs. Florene assured her that dahlias were the peonies of the fall. Marianne listened attentively to all that Mrs. Florene had to say, especially since she was paying for all the wedding except for the dress. I made the alterations to the dress simply for the experience of learning what I could. Once the wedding was over, Jenny Mae and I rode back home discussing the details upcoming in her wedding which we hoped to take place in the new year.

In my reading, I had come upon the fact that if some of us chose to have a bridal shower for her, we might include putting her gifts inside a parasol, so it would truly be like a shower. We would, of course, not have any breakables, but I thought it would be fun to shower her with gifts that way. I couldn't wait to discuss this with one of her cousins. Somehow, this seemed to be something of elegance that Jenny Mae would enjoy. Would I ever have a wedding like this? I wasn't so certain. Suppose I would need to have a groom first. Would Jimmy Lee fit that bill? Would he stay with any woman for the long term? But then I remembered this was not about me. It was Jenny Mae's special event.

Chapter Eight

What Myrna Loy Would Do

1936

January 4

Jenny Mae is getting married. This is different from Marianne's wedding in many ways. Jenny's dress is brand new. I had lots of influence in the design and making of this dress. It is made of gorgeous natural silk and French lace. Her parents, Flossie and Oliver, had to send to New York for the material with guidance from Mrs. Parker. I am so grateful that they trusted me to do most of the work. Her rings are white gold, and the engagement ring is 1.66 carats. They are special and lovely.

The wedding was at 2:00 in the afternoon on a cold but clear, lovely day. The church was warm and fragrant, and almost everyone in the community and county attended. Since Jenny Mae and I were both only children, I was her maid of honor. She was always beautiful, but today, she was spectacular. One of the best parts of this event was that Jimmy Lee was my escort and one of Winston's groomsmen. The whole affair was somewhat of a blur to me because my entire focus, other than performing what I needed to do as maid of honor, was having Jimmy Lee right there for me the whole entire time. So exciting. Just being around him made my skin sizzle.

They didn't have a wedding trip since Winston had to head right back down to Lexington to work at the University on Monday.

He was in training to be a county extension agent. Or at least, that is what I was told. They planned to go on a trip sometime in the summer. Jenny Mae told me that she always wanted to go to Niagara Falls as her special honeymoon dream, but I didn't know if that was still on their horizon.

After the ceremony, there was the reception in the church meeting room. Jenny's parents hosted a wonderful meal. All the neighbors contributed to the celebration. Cedric's mother brought chicken salad and mushrooms stuffed with a bacon mixture. My cousin Rose made a lamb loaf with a border of mashed potatoes. I made sure I knew who brought everything, so I could get recipes. We also had a gelatin mold called tomato aspic. I had never had tomato aspic before, but Jenny Mae said her friends at college had it at their parties. It was a tasty concoction of tomato juice, Worcestershire sauce, gelatin, and lemon juice. There was a gorgeous traditional wedding cake, but Poppa and I brought pies of different kinds in case another type of dessert was needed. Everyone must have been extremely hungry or only had a taste of wedding cake because there was not even a scrap of pie left to take back home.

To my surprise, Jimmy Lee came home with Poppa and me. Poppa suggested we play dominoes. I had only played the two-player style before, because it was usually Poppa and me. Poppa knew the rules for playing with additional players, so I learned something that night I never knew before. I was quite surprised that Jimmy Lee was attentive when Poppa was explaining the rules. I thought he might like Jimmy Lee a little better after being such an apt pupil. Daisy didn't seem to like him one bit more. She got in between the two men and cautioned Jimmy Lee with her low growls.

I asked Jimmy Lee to stay for supper, but he said he had to get back. He had some work to attend to. When I walked with him to the car, it started to drizzle rain. This seemed to chill me to the very bone. Since I still had my nice clothes on, I didn't want to get too wet and cold. Jimmy Lee gave me a little peck on the cheek, told me he would call soon and maybe we could see a movie, possibly a matinee. I had heard about the movie, Libeled Lady with Jean Harlow and William Powell, and wanted to see it. At Christmas time, I had hoped to see this with Jenny Mae or Helga, but there had been too much wedding to plan. Now, the thought of seeing this exciting film with Jimmy Lee seemed a lot more fun.

February 1

I feel a bit glum and out of sorts. I haven't heard back from Jimmy Lee or seen him at work yet. He seemed so eager to be with me at the wedding and wanted to take me to the matinee—now nothing. Why is he this way? Worse than that, I heard in town that the movie I wanted to see would end in a few days. Well, I'll fix him, I'll call Helga to go with me.

I cranked up the phone, but the line seemed to be down again. Just my luck. I went out to gather eggs, thinking I would try again when I came back in. When I got back, wonder of wonders, the line was working. I set the basket of eggs on the kitchen table and started my call. Helga was the one who answered, so I tried to get the information out to her as quickly as I could before the line started acting up again, "Helga, would you like to go with me to see a matinee in Cincinnati this week? I see that the movie, "Libeled Lady," is still playing, but I think not for long."

"Oh yes," she said, her voice rose in excitement. I could see her in my mind standing on her tippy toes, trying to make herself heard. "Since this is Saturday, can we go on Monday?" she asked without pausing for breath.

"Yes, I think so," I answered. "I could meet you in front of the theater about twenty minutes before the movie starts. Do you think your mother would like to go with us?"

"Oh, I don't think so," she said. "Graham has been in town this weekend, and she is washing and ironing some of his things before he goes back to work next week. I'm not sure when he will need to leave, but one day next week. Thank you for thinking of me. I've been wanting to go."

Monday was a bit windy, but the extreme cold we had earlier was gone, at least for now. It seemed nice to get out in the air and breathe when it felt like all the hairs in your nose weren't frozen up and your throat burned with every breath. I had barely gotten there and looked at all the coming attractions on the marquee, when Helga came bouncing and jumping like a little kid going to the circus. Alongside her, holding on to his hat, was Graham. What? I thought. Why was he here? Who invited him? Well, I supposed that Helga had. Why she didn't tell me was beyond my best understanding.

We bought bags of popcorn from the street vendor before we went in. Graham insisted on buying us each a large bag. I protested, but since it wasn't too expensive, I let him get me a bag. The smell of the corn and the hot oil was simply too wonderful to resist. I simply hoped that if he talked to me during or after the movie, I wouldn't be left with pieces of popcorn hanging in my teeth.

The movie was as delightful as I thought it might be. Even though this theater was quite the 'picture palace,' I still couldn't sit as far from Graham as I thought I needed to. He started to sit with Helga between us. As we left the aisle for our seats, she managed to skitter behind him forcing him to plunk himself down between me and Helga. I carefully crossed my legs away from him, so I wouldn't bump into him. Somehow, with his shoulders being so broad, my arm touched his several times. Other than having to watch how I sat, I enjoyed the movie a lot. It was so exciting and fun. That Myrna Loy knew how to make those men pay for trying to make her out as a homewrecker. What a smart gal! I wish I had her moxie.

After the movie ended, I wanted to stay and discuss all the fun parts with Helga, but I knew I couldn't stay around and talk too long since I might be late for work. I gave Helga a hug and turned to Graham to thank him for the popcorn. To my surprise, I glanced to my left and saw a familiar car driving down the street. It was none other than Jimmy Lee. I wasn't sure he saw me, but then I saw his gaze fall first on me, and then on Graham.

After that, Jimmy Lee paid more attention to me when I came in to work. Of course, he left for the day not long after I arrived, but occasionally he managed to take a few minutes to stop in to chat. I had a separate area, basically an enlarged closet just off the girls' changing room. It was a handy area for the girls to hand me their garments that needed mending. Jimmy Lee normally came in as they were performing, so as not to get in their way as they moved back and forth trying on clothes and shoes. He did, sometimes, see them in various stages of dress and undress as they rushed in to bring me a piece of work that was urgent, but he didn't turn to stare, well maybe a little. He didn't stay long, just a few minutes to speak briefly and then leave.

I thought surely, he would ask me out, but time went on and he didn't. There were days when I could scarcely breathe when he came close. I could smell the scent of his hair tonic with its hint of sandalwood. I couldn't tell if he was interested in me or just playing. Some days, I thought I just had to know. I wondered if I couldn't come right out and ask him? Maybe I could. That's what Myrna Loy would do. We could go get hot cocoa before work one day. He looked a bit grim the last time or two I saw him. Maybe a cup of cocoa and a muffin would help him relax.

"Jimmy Lee," I said the next time he came by my sewing room, "would you like to have a cup of cocoa or a coke with me one day before work? I know it has certainly been cold, and I would love to have something warm to drink before I start sewing. It is so much easier to sew and mend when my fingers have been around something warm."

He raised one eyebrow, and then laughed at my wide-eyed expression. "Yes, we can do that," he said with an amused look on his face. "The bar downstairs opens early. Harvey, the barkeep, might be able to whip up some cocoa. We could try it tomorrow."

I didn't know whether to be proud that I had asked or embarrassed thinking that he might think I was a total fool. The next day I came in early and met him downstairs. We sat at the bar. I was glad that my Poppa wouldn't have the chance to come by and see me. I wasn't certain I wanted to see me there either, but I felt so grown up and sophisticated. If I had been one of those smoking women, I could have waved my arm in the air with a cigarette in one hand and held my drink in the other. However, this would have been a hard scene to pull off with a hot cup of cocoa.

Jimmy Lee ordered a dirty martini, whatever the heck that was. It didn't look all that bad, and it had a cute little olive on the top. I asked Jimmy Lee if I would like drinking what he was drinking, but he said, "No way in h…eck." I didn't say more but simply drank my cocoa and waved my foot as I tried to strike a bit of a pose on the bar stool like I had seen the dancers do. When my foot got hung in one of the rungs and I almost slid off, I settled down to being regular me and not a fancy show girl.

This meeting led to more meetings which made me proud until I got to thinking, though, there seemed to be nothing personal in our encounters. We were always in a public sort of place, and no place that I thought might be romantic. No displays of affection, public or otherwise. That Lowenston man we had seen at the Flame and Glo came in one afternoon as we were ready to leave. He smiled at me with a tight little smile and asked if he and Jimmy Lee could be excused for a moment. He was slapping a rolled-up newspaper in his hand against one of the barstools. I agreed. What else could I do? They moved away from the bar toward the center of the room and began to talk.

I could see them as they gestured and moved closer and then away from each other. Their voices seemed to grow louder and become more heated. I couldn't make out actual words no matter how hard I tried. At last, the Lowenston man turned and moved away. His shoulders were rigid, and his entire body looked tight. He marched off looking every bit a tense toy soldier. I was puzzled about what was going on. There was surely something happening here that I wasn't aware of. Why would he be angry and upset with Jimmy Lee?

"Jimmy Lee," I said, turning my most concerned gaze toward him. "He seemed a little put out. Is there anything that I can do to help?" I knew full well I probably couldn't, but I wanted to make Jimmy Lee aware that I would support him.

"Oh, I think he's upset because some of our competitors are angry," Jimmy Lee replied. "They think we're trying to take away part of their casino business. They're lobbying the folks in Frankfort to take action against us. It is simply one of those political things that go on all the time. There is absolutely nothing you can do. Don't worry your little head about that at all." He may have told me not to worry, but I could feel the simmer of frustration and concern that seemed to leak out of his very pores. "You need to go on to work now. It will all be fine," he assured me with a wave of his hand to send me on my way.

I felt a bit scattered as I wanted to be concerned over his worry, but I was also frustrated that I had been dismissed with the "Don't worry your little head..." comment. I felt I was being put in a place I didn't choose to be. As I turned to start back to my work area, I noticed that the newspaper was still lying on the bar. Hmm, I thought. Was there something in this that caused this whole conversation between Jimmy Lee and the Lowenston fellow to become heated? I picked up the paper and strolled back to my workspace.

There on the front page was news of the February 3, 1936, Beverly Hills Supper Club fire which was quite a mysterious event. This news article acknowledged that the casino had been destroyed, and a young woman had died. The cause of the fire seemed to be unclear except that a local man with an affiliation to organized crime had bought canisters of gasoline the night of the fire. He seemed connected to another local man who harbored an individual suffering from burns on his legs and hands. The man suffering from burns had connections with a New York gang. These men all appeared connected to an individual, Moe Dalitz, who had tried futilely to buy the successful supper club and casino. I certainly didn't know how Jimmy Lee and Mr. Lowenston were associated with this, but it seemed that there was more to this story than I knew about.

Today, if I happen to mention the Beverly Hills Supper Club fire of 1936, my daughters try to remind me that it happened in 1977. There were 3,000 people crowded into the club at that time and 165 persons died as the result of an electrical fire. It was a well-known tragedy. They scoff when I tell them that the Beverly Hills Supper Club fire that I speak of was one that happened in 1936. It was a result of the club owner refusing to sell out to the mob as others had done. They think my memory is serving me wrong, but of course, I know better.

The rest of the year passed uneventfully, however, I still felt undercurrents of unrest bubbling under the surface. I did my work, kept my mouth shut, mostly, and became better acquainted with the girls. Most of my chatting was done with Mrs. Florene and Lila.

Lila with her beautiful black hair and voluptuous body was a star in the dance line, and a sweet, loyal person to all the girls in the group. She was always free to offer praise and compliments for any work I did for her. The only person that drew her ire was Jimmy Lee. I couldn't quite understand why, but then again, I noticed that he didn't treat her with a lot of respect.

Chapter Nine

The Flood

1937

*J*ournal, *this is a new year, and I always have such high hopes for a new year.*

January 26

The Ohio River has flooded terribly. Record amounts of rain have fallen from the 13th-24th. I think people are saying the river has crested now. One of the neighbors heard amounts from 6-9 feet higher than ever known before. There are hundreds of people homeless around Cincinnati. Lots don't have fresh water, food, or heat.

Even here at home, water has been over the road causing lots of travel difficulties. I feel terrible for all those poor people. I wanted to invite Bertha, Helga, and even Graham to stay with us, but they weren't that much affected. They told me that there was a bridge they could use to get to us if they needed to. I was able to call them one time, but then our phone line went down. Of course, I wasn't able to go to work either.

Journal, this is such a sad year with all the struggles the neighbors have had. I get so blue when I make myself dwell on all the sadness. We haven't been able to get in touch with Momma's cousins down river in Indiana. Can't phone or drive down there. So afraid for them. The Hey Ho has shut down temporarily. I don't know when I will be able to get back to work. I tried to contact Jimmy Lee, but he didn't seem to be available. I wonder if he'll try to get in touch with me.

March 17

We finally got touch with Emeline, Momma's cousin. They lost the power in their house, and the barn washed away. They had good neighbors who took them in. No one was injured and no stock lost. Thank the Lord. They are safe and well. I got a call from Jimmy Lee. He said he would come to see me when he could.

April 26

Today is my birthday. Some of our friends, the Warrens, came to help us paper upstairs. In payment, I fixed a big supper for them. We were just finishing, and I was getting ready to cut the angel food cake I made when I heard the crunch of gravel in front of the house. I went to look out the screen door, and what do you know, there was Jimmy Lee.

I couldn't believe he was there after all this time of not seeing him or not knowing where he was. He beamed and smiled as he bounced up the steps holding a large bouquet of flowers in his hand. "I couldn't let my favorite girl's birthday go by unnoticed could I," he said, opening the door and walking in. He sounded as if we were simply getting together after a day or two, rather than months. He handed me the flowers and gave me a hug that almost crushed me. I pulled my arm out to the side to keep the flowers from being smashed between us.

"Come on in and have cake and ice cream with us," I said. I didn't know whether to be happy he was here or annoyed he had waited so long. "Have you had dinner?" I asked, as an afterthought. "There is still some food left on the stove." I went over to grab a milk jar to put the flowers into.

"Oh, I'm fine," he said with a little boy grin. "I had a late lunch, but I could use birthday cake for sure, especially if it is one you made."

We went into the kitchen, and I introduced him to the Warrens and set about slicing the cake and scooping up ice cream. Jimmy Lee acted as if he had known the Warrens forever, and they and Poppa had quite a conversation. After we all talked and visited for quite a while, Jimmy Lee stood and said he needed to get back to Newport. Even though the Hey Ho still wasn't open, there was a lot to be done on the business end to make it ready for a reopening. I walked him down to the car, and he told me that he thought I would be able to come back to work in the late summer or early fall. It all depended on how the damage could be repaired and what extras needed to be done. I felt almost weak with relief because without my paycheck, we were pretty low on cash money.

As the spring and summer progressed, Jimmy Lee made a habit of dropping by on many Sunday afternoons. He and Poppa talked about politics and the news. We drank tea and ate cookies. Several times, we walked down to the creek and wandered along the bank looking at wildflowers and taking a few photographs. I felt peaceful and relaxed, but I had the feeling that something was missing. At times, he held my hand as we walked. One day, he sat in the grass and made me a daisy chain. We discussed home remedies. He told me the way to cure Poppa's arthritis was to make him a drink of honey, vinegar, and moonshine, but we never had any conversations about feelings or personal things. Where was the romance, the excitement? Did he not like me that way?

July 31

I will have to confide to you, Journal, today I got my very first driver's license. I was so scared. Jenny Mae came home for a vacation, and she went with me. She drove us to the license bureau, and I drove us home. Now I will be legal to drive. Of course, I have been driving since I was 13, but it seems different now that I am legal.

August 7

Another thing that is important to me is that after dinner this afternoon, Poppa and I went to town, and I voted for the very first time in the primary election.

August 23

Yippee! Today is Monday, and I am going back to work at the Hey Ho.

When I went to work, the whole place felt nice, but different. Everything looked clean and fresh. The smell of wet paint still permeated the whole building. Even though it was August, the large ceiling fans pushed the air, so that there was a feeling like a cool breath blowing over your body. Whether it was because I had been away for so long, or because of all the new and bright additions to the design, it felt like the building had awakened after a long sleep.

December 1

When I got home from work, I learned that Poppa had been kicked by one of the colts, and he is suffering terribly. I called the doctor, and even though it was late, the doctor agreed to come over.

"Where did he kick you, Poppa?" I asked. He rubbed his belly and moaned.

Our neighbor Ed came to the door just then. Ed told me that he was with Poppa when the colt kicked him. "Your Poppa must have scared him, coming around behind him like he did," he said shaking his head. "The colt didn't mean anything by it, I don't guess. He just kicked out, hit your Poppa in the belly, and knocked him to the ground. I pulled your Poppa out of the way, and then got him into the house."

"I guess you got the work done, then, didn't you? Didn't you call the doctor?" I asked, not wanting to sound as if I was accusing Ed of being neglectful but needing assurance as much as anything.

"I did get the work done after I got your poppa in the house," Ed said. He didn't think he was all that hurt. He figured he would lie down for a while. I called over to Flossie and Oliver's to let them know what happened. Flossie made him a poultice to put on his belly. She thought he was resting easy the last time she looked. I think Flossie went ahead and called the doctor, anyway, but you'd better check."

"The doctor didn't mention Flossie calling him," I said. "Let me call again to make sure I understood him right." I cranked up the phone and called to make certain the doctor would check on Poppa. He assured me he was on his way. "The doctor is coming out now to check on him," I told Ed. I was certainly relieved since Poppa was still holding his belly and moaning.

"I'll be back in the morning to get the morning work done," Ed said. "Oliver said he would come over and help me. Don't you worry about anything," Maybe he thought I ought not to worry, but he looked worried his own self.

When the doctor came, he poked and prodded a bit. Then, after he shuffled through his bag and picked up one vial and then another, he found what he needed. I held Poppa's hand and gave it a squeeze while the doctor gave him a shot to ease his pain. After waiting a bit, the doctor assured me that now Poppa looked like he wasn't hurting too bad. He had given him a shot of morphine, and he seemed to be resting comfortably. He would come back in the morning and give him another shot if he was still in pain.

Poppa woke suddenly after the doctor left. He screamed and cried in obvious agony. Not being certain as what I should do, I tried to put packs of cold peas from the icebox on his stomach. They weren't too cold, but as cold as I could get them. Since it was colder outside than it was in our icebox, I put a remaining pack of peas on the porch to chill. I finally called the doctor again about 5:00 in the morning. He came down and told me that Poppa would have to go the hospital. He needed to have x-rays made. I went along in the ambulance. They operated on Poppa about 3:30 in the afternoon.

December 3

Poppa passed away at 1:15 a.m. today. The minister came, and he brought me home. Some of the neighbors came over and stayed until 4:00 a.m.

Lots of people came to the house. In the evening, my cousin and I went to town to order flowers.

December 5

I went to town to pick up the flowers, went over the river, and bought a plain sturdy black dress. Had the car washed in Newport.

December 6

Poppa's funeral was today at 2:00 p.m. Sure was a big crowd. He looked so nice and had so many pretty flowers. 25 bunches. All the cousins, aunts, and uncles came back for dinner.

I was completely devastated when Poppa died. I knew I would never recover from the anguish that overwhelmed me. People kept telling me that time would make it easier, but I knew that was a lie. He was my rock and solid ground. What was I to do? All I thought about was how I was supposed to manage a failing farm, with nobody to help run the place. My thoughts ran to selling it. Poppa's dog, Daisy, ran around looking for him. I knew she felt as lost as me. She was the only one I was certain that felt as broken as I did.

I felt like not one trickle of moisture could seep down my scorched throat. My ears rang as if cymbals clanged in my ears, while the shapes of neighbors and relatives rustled and hustled around me piling up dishes and pushing against one another. When each fried chicken or pork smell rose into the air, with the passing of platters, I felt a wave of nausea rise in my burned throat. My breath crushed against my ribs. Despite the crowd around me, I felt isolated in my personal bubble of despair.

As we finished dinner, I heard the familiar crunch of gravel outside on the driveway, I looked out the door expecting to see Jimmy Lee's car. Instead, I saw the Raisch's old Ford sedan rumbling up the drive. Once the car came to a stop and pulled over onto the grass, out popped Bertha, Helga, and Graham. I couldn't imagine how word got to them about Poppa. While it wasn't clear to me how the news had spread, I didn't care. I was so glad to see them and grateful to have them around me.

Bertha gathered me in her arms in a big hug. Enveloped me in her arms, she rocked me like I was her own child, singing to me in a soft low-voiced lullaby. The German words landed like guttural whispers in my ear. I didn't know what she sang, but the words were comforting, nevertheless. "Graham is taking a few days to help you get your work caught up here at the farm," Bertha said in a voice that didn't allow for much contradiction or discussion. "And since it wouldn't be proper for him to be here with you alone, Helga and I will stay as well. We know your family will be around here with you for a few days, but we will plan to come back over the weekend to help with whatever needs to be done," she continued. "I think Graham can stay and help for a while if you have someone to come chaperone after we leave."

I wondered to myself exactly what it would be like if Graham and I were to be alone together at the farm, just the two of us. The feel of electrical twinges pulsing through me, made me wonder where on earth all these emotions were headed. I felt like an emotional tuning fork with waves of all kinds floating through my body.

"Never mind all that now," Bertha said breaking into my reverie. "We will see what needs to be done as it happens. We can't worry about everything all at the same time." Somehow, her brisk comfortable way of speaking made me calmer than anything that had been said before. I supposed it was because she was on the outside looking in that made her seem more realistic and knowledgeable. I felt as comforted as if my own Momma had told me what to do and how to do it. Giving her a squeeze, I turned to introduce the Raisch family to those around us.

My family and other kinfolks seemed glad to meet the Raischs. They appeared to fit right in. Of course, none was in an especially festive mood, but kinfolk seemed to accept this family as equally invested in the gathering. Daisy, for the first time in days, quit her pacing and wandering. She tucked herself under Graham's feet and followed every step he took. I felt a pang of jealousy rocket through me. This was Poppa's dog. She never paid any mind to me. She even ignored my Queenie pup. It had always been Poppa, Poppa, Poppa. Now, without any hesitation, she seemed to transfer her love and affection to Graham. Was this a good sign or bad?

As people mingled and talked, I thought I would hardly make it through all the tears, the blowing of noses, and the same words of pity over and over. I overheard one of the uncles saying to a cousin that I would surely have to sell the farm now that I would have no man to help me run it.

I overheard Uncle Calvin talking to his friend, Walter, about me. "Josie is 21 years old. She should be married by now and raising her own children. Surely, she should have prospects in that direction." He almost sounded disgusted.

"Well, if she sells the farm now, she may have to give it away," Walter replied. "You know times have been hard around here and even worse since the flood."

It occurred to me that the farm and the flood was what Poppa had been most worried about lately. Since January, many people in the Cincinnati area had been without food, water, and shelter. Times had been hard and now, were even tougher. Graham caught sight of my stricken face, and he knew I had overheard the conversation. He simply took me by the arm and guided me away. Then, he looked at me and spoke very gently. "Miss Josie, since we might not have the time to discuss all this before we come back on the weekend, and since it will soon be getting dark, why don't you take a few minutes to show me around the place," he said showing traces of his German accent. "I need to know what to do when I come back this weekend, what stock needs to be fed, eggs to be gathered, and cows to be milked." This felt like an enormous relief to have someone to share my burden. "I know that things aren't as busy as they will be come spring, but work on a farm is never ending," Graham continued with a gentle voice. "You are a sturdy young lady and able to do a lot, I know, but I think sometimes jobs like breaking ice on the pond are a bit too much for one person, no matter how steady or strong."

Somehow, the soothing slide of his voice brought a bit of balm to my suffering heart. He seemed to really know, and care, rather than simply make pronouncements and decisions. I pulled my cape around me and told him that we would slip out and look around. I turned around and gave a nod to Bertha. She nodded back, as if she knew where we were headed. We took a tour of the barn, the barn lot, and the pasture where we kept the horses. I found it difficult to pass the colt that kicked Poppa who was resting his head over the stall door. I paused for a moment knowing the colt was an innocent party, pushing down the urge to cast blame. Graham gave my arm a gentle squeeze.

I showed Graham the chicken house, and where the nests were. They were good layers, and we always managed to have plenty of eggs for ourselves and to sell. Even though it was close to time for them to roost for the night, they clucked with contentment as we passed their nests. We heard the soft snuffling of the pigs, so we turned, and I took him to see the pig lot. My big baby pig, Pea Doodle, who believed he was a dog, rushed over to greet us. He pushed in between me and Graham to remind me that he needed attention. That man was simply in the way unless he had something good to eat in his hands.

The sky darkened, and the clouds hovered over the moon. We walked around the perimeter of the farm, and I felt for the first time since Poppa died, the sense of how he had put his heart's work in this place. There was no noise now in the coming dark, just the crunch of our feet on the icy grass. Poppa had made a difference here even though times were hard. As I showed Graham the side barn, Poppa's pride and care showed with the meticulous upkeep that was obvious in every corner. All his tools were well oiled and hung with precision. The hay was stacked with care and protected from blowing rain or snow.

I turned toward Graham and without thinking put my head on his shoulder and cried all the tears that I hadn't let loose before. I could feel how wet his shoulder was becoming, but he never moved or drew away. He simply rubbed my back and let me cry. Finally, he took a handkerchief out of his pocket. "Here, let's get you a little mopped up before we go back inside," he said as he wiped the tears gently off my face.

I was so embarrassed that I had completely soaked his handkerchief and his shoulder. I tried, as I snuffled holding on and wringing the wet piece of cloth, to apologize. Here, I hardly knew this man, and now I was making a complete and utter fool of myself. "Let me take this in and launder it for you," I finally managed to say.

He tried to take the handkerchief back, but I held on to it. I thought that washing the handkerchief was the least I could do. I needed to do something to try and repay some of the kindness he had shown. I wondered how Jimmy Lee would have behaved under these same circumstances. Why hadn't I seen or heard from him since Poppa died? After I had gone back to work in August, he disappeared from view once again. Surely, if the Raisch family knew about Poppa, Jimmy Lee would have heard.

On the weekend, when things had slowed a bit, I was able to catch my breath and tried to tidy up for when the Raisch family returned. I thought I would give Helga and Bertha my room upstairs, I would sleep in the front room and would give Graham the place in the barn where we let farm workers stay when we had them. It gave me something to do to help fill the empty sore spot in my heart. Putting out a little greenery and holly made me hope it would feel somewhat like Christmas, but of course, it didn't. I didn't know if Christmas would ever feel the same.

When the Raischs arrived, they were gentle and kind. Bertha brought lots of honey cookies, German shortbread, pfeffernusse made from sugar, eggs, and honey, as well as cute spingerle cookies, or little jumpers, which Momma made for us when I was little. Helga giggled as she handed me the spingerle cookies. "I love to make these," she said. "They are so cute when they try to jump out of the pan." The funny thing is that I had forgotten that they did this. Yes, they were cute, but I didn't think there was a lot of cute in the world right then. I wanted to at least act happy and pleasant so as not to make the Raisch's Christmas seem dark and despairing.

All I felt was a glum sense of foreboding and misery. People would tell me, "Oh, it will get better with time." My thoughts were that, if I were lucky, maybe a scab would form. I could only hope that would happen without something coming along and ripping off the scab leaving me raw and wounded once more.

Graham went out and cut down a cedar tree. He said that even though it was a sad time, we needed to brighten up for Christmas. I tried to appear happy because I knew Poppa would have wanted me to be. Graham mentioned putting up an advent wreath. We could put one on the fireplace, and we could spend time around it maybe drinking mulled wine and singing songs. He asked me to go outside with him to pick up pinecones and berries for the wreath. I went with him selecting pinecones and holly berries trying for a gaiety and sense of lightness that I couldn't feel.

Helga and Bertha polished boots to put in front of the bedroom doors where we were sleeping so they could be filled by St. Nikolaus. Maybe with gifts, maybe coals. They also arranged the four Advent candles to be dimmed as we sang and drank in front of the wreath on Christmas Eve. Helga and Bertha made plans to stay here with me, especially since Graham told me he planned to stay here and work the farm a bit longer. I was a bit surprised, and I think was somewhat elated when he said he would stay. Helga and Bertha told me they would wait and leave at the new year. I believed their jobs at the shirt factory had slowed quite a bit, but they didn't seem to miss the work. Bertha was back at baking bread and pretzels since that was what she had always wanted to do. Helga helped with orders and deliveries when they were home. I think their intention was to open a bakery and leave the shirt factory. It was hard to pretend the shirt factory was going to remain in business for the long term, anyway.

We spent the weekend trying for a festivity that we didn't especially feel. Bertha baked some of her good German specialties for Christmas dinner on Saturday, and then we looked over my pattern books. They enjoyed learning how to work on my loom, and we even attempted making some crazy quilt covers for the backs of the chairs.

It rained almost all day on Sunday, we entertained ourselves with board games like Monopoly and Scrabble. We all pretended to have a sense of lightheartedness we didn't especially feel. It was a relief when we decided to go up to Carthage and attend church there. Monday, we got back to a sense of business as usual. I took Graham down to the feed store to check on types of feed we would need. Since the weather had turned off really cold, most of the local men sat around the potbellied stove, eating cracklins, or as my Cincinnati friends called them, pork rinds, out of a burlap bag. I introduced Graham to Mr. Baxter, and Mr. Jones, local farmers he hadn't met before, as well as Mr. Harding who ran the feed store. He spoke politely to the ones he hadn't met before, and he greeted the ones by name who had come to Poppa's funeral. Then we went about the business of buying feed.

We got cracked corn for the chickens, some additional alfalfa and orchard grass for the horses and cows, with a little additional corn for the hogs. It was a good thing we had come in Poppa's truck. We had it pretty well loaded down. I thought it was a good thing that I would have Graham's help unloading all that feed, but I wasn't sure how I was going to pay for it. I decided I would put it on Poppa's tab and figure out how to pay the bill later. I turned my head to watch a small tow-headed girl pulling up to look at the pickles in the pickle barrel and thought I would try to sneak her a few peppermints I had in my pocket. When I turned back, Graham was pulling dollar bills out of his wallet. "Oh no, Graham," I said, pushing toward him. I shoved the peppermints into the child's hand, not wanting to make a scene, but not wanting him to pay my bill either.

"Don't worry," he said. "We'll square up when the fall crops come in."

"I do worry, that is a long time off, and I don't know what will happen between now and then," I said.

"We'll settle this in time," he shook his head at me, but with a smile. "As for now, we need to tend to what is important."

 didn't want to say too much more because the men in the room had stopped discussing their Rook card game and turned to look at us. Even Mr. Baxter, who spent most of his time leaned back on two legs of his chair with his hands folded under his pumpkin-sized belly, brought his chair smack dab down on the floor and began to stare.

We turned and left. I should have felt grateful, but instead, I felt a bit irritated at feeling more obligated than I wanted to be. After all, I was twenty-one years old, a grown woman. I needed to be able to take care of myself. "Graham, I think it is important for me to take care of myself. I certainly appreciate everything you have done and are doing, but I need to be able to make my personal arrangements and decisions."

I felt all these raw emotions running through my brain and my heart. Even though it felt wrong, I couldn't help but feel angry that Poppa had left me with all sorts of problems and decisions that I felt unable to deal with. I felt anger, sadness, guilt, resentment, and I just don't know what all. Christmas was supposed to be a time of peace and happiness. Rubbing my hands together in frustration, I wanted to feel more of that.

"Sometimes, Josie, we can't do everything alone," Graham took my hand and lightly squeezed my fingers. "Those who rise to the top and move forward get there by standing on the shoulders of those who give us a lift. You will be able to manage, but it doesn't have to be right now, right this minute, all by yourself," Graham said as he walked me to the truck and opened the door to have me step up. "I am confident that you will be able to get through this. You needn't feel obligated or helpless when you need a helping hand."

Poppa had always told me that what worries you is usually something you can't do anything about. That it is something in the future which hasn't come around, or things in the past that you can't change. He told me that all you can do is try and make the best choices you can make at the time and move on. I guess that is what I tried to do. To be fair, Graham and his family helped me move forward in the best way possible. Reminding myself that I needed to feel grateful for all their help and care, I decided it was time to make good choices and look to the future.

Chapter Ten

Numbers and Prices

1938

January was the start of a New Year. Not such a happy New Year this time. Graham sat down with me at the table and told me there were important things we needed to discuss before he left. The important things were that it looked as if I needed to sell the farm. Times were tough, and the aftermath of the flood made times that much tougher. I think Graham had talked to some of the neighbors about prices of corn, livestock, and milk. It seemed as if he had received no good news, merely bad. He sat at the table with a pencil and a piece of paper writing and scribbling. I watched him write down what looked to be numbers, mark them out, and put down other numbers.

"Josie," he said, beckoning to me as he looked up. "Come over and sit down with me for a bit. I've been going through some numbers and prices after I talked to your neighbor farmers. You have a job in Newport, but you can't work there and tend to all that needs to be done here. Steve Baxter and Daniel Jones, and even Oliver said they believed that holding an auction might be the best thing for you at this time."

I dropped into the seat across from him, my legs too unsteady to hold me upright. Although I understood his words, I had difficulty believing them. His smile was gentle, but his gaze was steady and firm. "But this is my home," I said, tears threatening. I wouldn't let him see me fall apart as I did the night of Poppa's funeral. A sinking sensation spread throughout my body. I knew, bitter as it was, an auction was probably the wise choice. It just wasn't my choice. I drummed my fingers on the table in front of me trying to come up with a sensible answer and to cover my anguish.

"Why don't you discuss this with your friends and see if they might have another solution for you," he curled his fingers around my left hand that was next to his. "I can't think of anything else to do right now, can you? My thinking is that it would probably be best to hold an auction in March before the spring planting needs to be done," Graham said quietly, tilting his head toward me. "I'll need to get back to my own job after the first of the year, but I will keep in touch and check on you," he continued as he released my fidgeting hand. "There will be work on the farm to attend to between now and March, if selling is what you decide to do. I think maybe Ed, who has always helped your dad, and of course, Oliver, should help keep things going for the winter." Graham squeezed his lips together, trying to be practical but comforting.

I thought for a bit before I answered him, "Jenny Mae and her folks have always been close to me. Now that Jenny is married and living in Lexington, her parents seem to be lonely for her. I will speak to them and see what we can do." I sounded reasonable and calm unlike how I felt. I didn't know how I could manage to get through these next days and months.

"Do you think you would trust me to take Daisy home with me when I leave?" Graham asked. "It seems she is grieving as well as the rest of your friends and family."

At first, I thought that losing Daisy was just one more unbearable loss. Then, I realized that might be one decision I could make that would help make something right. She would be with someone who really cared, and that was probably the best I could do for her. I took a deep breath, knowing that I felt something I hadn't felt in a while. Trust. Graham seemed to be a person who was trustworthy.

When I spoke to Flossie and Oliver, they seemed happy that I could come live with them if I had to sell the farm. I didn't want to take Jenny Mae's room, she needed to have her own place when she and Winston came home. Flossie and Oliver agreed they would give me the space in the connector passage attaching the house to their summer kitchen. They were excited that Queenie would be coming with me since their old dog, Duke, had died in the fall. They were also glad to see Pee Doodle since they needed another boar hog. Of course, Pee Doodle wanted to spend his time following me around anytime I was outside, but he would stay in the pen when I was gone. They would have taken Daisy also, but I told them that she had so attached herself to Graham and he to her, he planned to take her with him to Cincinnati when he left.

When I started back to work, glum was the only way I could describe how I felt. Sore and defeated might fit too. I knew there was a lot needed to do to get ready for the auction. I was at the farm part of the day and at the Hey Ho in the evening. Some neighbor men helped for the short term. Cedric and his father seemed eager to help as well. It seemed as if they would be the ones who would buy the farm. That felt reasonable since they had the adjoining farm and could blend the two farms in a seamless way. We had a small timber property at the back of the farm. I was comfortable with the idea they might clear off a little bit of timber for farming or pasture without allowing loggers to strip the land.

When the Raisch family went back home, I started cleaning out the house in earnest. I planned to take my dog, my pig, and my mother's icebox to Flossie and Oliver's. In addition, I knew I'd need my sewing supplies, patterns, Momma's loom, and the sewing machine, so I planned on those things as well. The area Flossie and Oliver let me use had plenty of room for my sewing things with space to spare, so I didn't feel as if I would be imposing on them for bringing those extras.

Mrs. Florene was more than supportive as well. She had me come to her penthouse apartment more and more to visit and check on me. Even though Mrs. Florene was good and thoughtful with all the girls, she seemed especially kind to me. She talked about her husband who'd been dead for several years. She reminisced about the days of their early marriage and told me how he had given her the best life he could. He encouraged her lively mind and economic acuity. The most supportive thing he had done for her was set her up in the business she was in. He was the only family she had ever had except for a sister in New York whom she rarely saw. She mentioned several times how some day she planned to join her sister, and that the two of them might move to Florida, maybe Miami.

"What would you do in Florida?" I asked. Somehow, I couldn't see her fishing or any of the things I had seen people do in pictures and postcards of Florida.

"Well, we thought maybe we would try our hands at visiting some of the casinos in Cuba. That is where my husband loved to go," she answered. "He enjoyed all the games, but his favorites were craps and the roulette table. I never seemed to make the time from my business to go with him, and I think it saddened him. If my sister, Nancy and I went together, we might make up for lost time. I could feel I was with my Dominic again."

It was hard for me to imagine Mrs. Florene playing cards and gambling, but again, I'd heard that is what they did here at the Hey Ho in the back room. I knew there was the restaurant and the entertainment in the front room, cards, a roulette wheel and such in the back. More went on in the upstairs rooms where the girls lived, but I didn't want to think about all that. That certainly didn't concern me. I was hired to sew.

March 18

We are having the sale tomorrow. I hate it. I have been baking apple and cherry pies to serve to the people who are coming to the auction. The Raischs are coming. Bertha is bringing bread and pretzels to sell. I feel blue, but I know I would feel worse if my friends weren't here. Jenny Mae is making the trip back home to be with me. Guess I should feel happy that at least I have the love and support of good friends. So, I need to stop my sniffling and be as tough as Myrna Loy or one of the heroines in my movie fantasies.

The sale happened on Saturday. The farm sold. Cedric and his father bought it. I presumed that Cedric would be a farmer after all. Guess he needed to give up his dream of being a teacher. I suppose we all must give up our dreams at some point. At least, I didn't have to marry Cedric. He was a great friend, but I was relieved that I didn't have to be his wife to save the farm. He'd started courting another girl further down the road, I'd heard, so I didn't have to feel any guilt about him either.

I had reconciled myself to the sale of the farm, but what I didn't plan on was watching all the household goods being pulled, shoved, and wrenched out the door. The bed I had slept on my entire life was going. The walnut headboard had been carved by Poppa's father. What would I have to pass on to my own children as memories of my childhood? When the rocking chairs on the front porch were sold, all I could think of was Poppa sipping tea and rocking on hot summer days. Our battered kitchen table where Poppa and I had our deepest conversations, and Momma and I had pieced quilts, was dragged off by a nameless buyer.

Jenny Mae grabbed my baby doll in her cradle out of the auctioneer's hands. She handed it to me and said that no other child would have the right to that piece of my childhood. All I could think of was that being a grown-up was not an easy thing to be. I felt as if someone had picked me up and crushed me into an aching, angry ball. Tears leaked from the corners of my eyes as I watched pieces of my life and childhood slip away.

With the farm sold, I could keep my job, stay with Flossie and Oliver, and keep the parts of my homeplace that I could—my loom and sewing material, Pee Doodle, and Queenie. Graham would handle the business part of the sale with Oliver's approval. Oliver assured me that Graham seemed to have my interests in mind. "Don't worry about this too much, Josie. Your Poppa's attorney in town, Mr. Milton, is overseeing everything, so it isn't like Graham would be taking advantage of you in any way. Between me and Lester Milton, we will see that he does the right thing for you," Oliver gazed at me with a soft expression in his sweet kind eyes.

All I could remember about Mr. Milton was he reminded me of a toad. A nice toad, but still a toad. He was short and round and wore thick glasses. He wore a hat most of the time. I supposed it was to cover the shiny bald spot in the middle of his head. He wore a suit and tie to court but whenever I saw him, he wore a ratty cardigan pulled around his shoulders even on pleasant days. I was okay with him, though, and hoped he would help me. I'd heard he was savvy, but he didn't look like it. I hoped Graham was smart enough for both of them.

Mrs. Florene helped me too, like she did all her girls, but I felt as if she treated me more as a motherless child than a woman grown. She offered me a place in her own suite of rooms to stay in after work. She said it was an extra room she didn't need, and it would come in handy when the weather was bad. I could stay with her, she told me, when it was a danger for me to go home to stay with Flossie and Oliver. The extra room was out of my Hollywood dream world. Nice hardly described it. In the center of the room was a carved oak bed with a bold floral print bedspread. The huge cabbage roses seemed ready to jump off the bed ready to go into a vase. The walls were covered with a lovely pale green and cream paper. Crown molding in a cream shade circled the edges of the wall.

There was indoor plumbing, too. I was happy not to need an outhouse. It was hard to imagine that I had my own bathroom here. It sat off to the back of the bedroom with a steam radiator that blew warm air throughout the room. There was an enormous claw footed bathtub. hot and cold water both, perched on a tile floor. I would have stayed overnight with Mrs. Florene for the whole winter, and not only for bad weather nights, if for nothing else, just this elegant bedroom and bath.

After the auction, life went along without too many bumps. Despite feeling the wrenching loss over Poppa's death and the sale of the farm, life settled into a steady rhythm of sorts. Then, one glorious May evening, one that allowed me to come out of my numb shell and begin to feel alive again, I felt an edge of gratitude that at least I lived in the country with good night smells and noises. Oliver came out to where Flossie and I sat on the steps. I bent over Queenie scratching her ears and rubbing under her chin. Her eyelids, with their incredibly long lashes, flickered in delight. "Josie, this Graham boy from Cincinnati is on the phone, and he says he needs to talk to you," Oliver said.

I bolted upright, almost knocking Queenie over since I didn't know why Graham needed to talk to me. I knew he was helping with the financial end of things, but I thought everything had been settled. I ran back into the house, slamming the screen door with a bang behind me. I felt a hard flutter in my chest wondering what else could go wrong. "Graham, this is Josie. Is there a problem?" My breath burst out in gasps, whether from fear or running, I wasn't sure.

"I think everything will be all right, but I need to talk with you. Would you rather I come down there or would you rather come to Cincinnati?" he said, not answering my question. Why did he want this meeting in person? It must be something worse than he let on. "I'll tell you what," he said. "Maybe it would be best if I set up a time with Mr. Melton. We can discuss the situation, and everyone will know everything at the same time."

Now I was beginning to be more than a little worried. I started to twist my fingers together, which was a habit I wanted to break. My fingers needed to stay supple for sewing. If my gut was twisting, that was one thing, but I needed to watch my fingers. What on earth could it be?

"I'll contact him tomorrow during his office hours, and then get back with you to set up a time for us all to meet," Graham said. "Graham, you are scaring me. What's wrong?"

"It will be okay, I promise. We simply need to work out a few financial details concerning the amount that you received for the farm. Don't worry about the details. It can all be worked out."

I really began to fret. When I went to bed, I hardly slept a wink. I reached over the bed, to open the sliding glass windows just above the headrail. The window stuck as if it had been painted shut, but with a firm push it finally opened. The breeze was warm and soft, and a gentle rain tapped down on the metal roof. Even hearing that gentle rhythm, I could hardly bring myself to relax. The next morning, before I even had time to get out of bed and let Queenie out, the phone rang. Aunt Flossie answered it. I knew it was for me when I heard her tiny feet pattering down the hallway. She opened the curtain that partitioned off the connector hall that ensured my privacy.

"Josie," she said softly. It was almost a whisper, as if she was trying to be careful not to wake me if I happened to still be asleep. When she saw me wrap a shawl around my shoulders, she said, "Mr. Graham is on the phone, and he wants to speak with you a minute."

"I'll be right there," I said, as I put on slippers and followed her down the hallway.

"Hello," I said, trying to shake the sleep from my voice. I had no idea what time it was, but the sun was coming in bright through the windows.

Graham sounded wide awake as if he had been up and going for hours. "Josie, I have already called Mr. Melton, and he has agreed to see us on Monday next, if that would be a good time for you."

"How did you happen to get ahold of him so early?" I asked. "Well, Josie, it is 10:00 in the morning. Most of the world is up and working by this time of day, Were you still in bed?" He sounded like he was accusing me of some unforgivable sin. Little did he realize that I had hardly slept a wink until I drifted off near daybreak. I rocked back and forth from my heels to my toes. Why was he being such an ass? I ignored him.

"What time is this appointment to be?" I finally asked, wanting to act as if this meeting was something hard to work into my schedule, and not betray how nervous I was.

"At 10:00, that is a.m. That should give you time to get settled, and ready to go into town," he replied. "Do you want to meet me there, or do you want me to come there and pick you up?"

"Oh, that's okay," I said. "Oliver drives his produce truck to town about that same time, and I will ride with him. Thanks, anyway." I didn't want Graham to think that I was ungrateful for the aid and assistance he offered me.

"All right, then," he replied. His tone was even and smooth. Since I couldn't sense any emotion tied to his response, I supposed it was okay with him.

On Monday, I was scared, but ready to meet whatever awaited me. I looked forward to seeing Graham again, but I wasn't sure I wanted to know what he was going to say. When Oliver dropped me off at the office, I felt a sense of relief that the wait was over. Seeing Graham standing there with his square shoulders, and his easy assured manner, I knew I would be supported and cared for. I realized how Helga and Bertha must feel with a big brother and son who was there to take care of things. Did I think of him as a big brother? I wasn't sure since I had never had one. Maybe.

We met on the porch of Mr. Melton's office and Graham guided me to the door, his hand resting lightly on my back. He reached around me, coming a little nearer than I was comfortable with, but only to tap on the door. When Mr. Melton greeted us with a cheerful hello, the smile on his face seemed forced and barely reached his eyes. Holding his hand out to Graham and giving me a slight nod of his head, he guided us into the office. He pulled the old cardigan closely around him and walked behind his desk as he ushered us to a seat. His office furniture seemed worn and old, a serviceable looking roll top desk with a swivel chair, and a worn rug on the chipped linoleum floor. I stopped short of offering to make him another rug. This was neither the time nor place. The seats he directed us to were stiff ladderback chairs badly in need of painting.

"I think we can get down to business here," Mr. Melton said, placing a worn green ledger in front of him. His fingernails were chewed down to the quicks. This didn't inspire me with a great deal of confidence in the man.

Graham spoke with a quiet, clear assurance as he leaned toward Mr. Melton, steepling his fingers. "I think we need to discuss the proceeds of the farm sale, and the funds that seem to be lacking, is that correct?" I could tell he wasn't bluffing from the easy tone of his speech. "Do you think there might have been something out of order in the sale or the proceeds?"

What? Had I heard that correctly. I looked over at Graham, but he avoided my gaze.

"Yes, well," Mr. Melton toyed with his pen, rolling it in his hands. "I think that although Miss Josie got a fair and equitable price for the land and the house, there doesn't seem to be enough funds to cover all the outstanding loans. You know, since the flood, people haven't had the resources they once had," he said, scratching the side of his nose with his finger." Your Poppa, Miss Josie, had to take out loans to cover some of his expenses. When he took them out, he was sure he'd be able to pay them back, and they probably would have been, Fred being such a hard worker and all, if it hadn't been for his unfortunate and untimely death. Now though, we must come up with another plan to cover the remaining debts."

All I could see in my mind was me going to debtor's prison. I had nothing left to sell. All I had left that would bring in any kind of money were my pig and my loom. Those would bring in so little, it was like spit in a bucket. I did have the money from my job, but I was keeping it in a sock under the mattress at Oliver and Flossie's. Surely that wasn't enough money to amount to much when it came to paying off debts. I simply needed enough money to pay my daily expenses. I realized that I was holding my breath, and I needed to breathe. Hoping my body would relax, I focused on releasing the tension in my forehead, traveling through my body, and leaking down to my clenched toes.

"So, how much money are we looking at?" Graham asked.

"Well, you have to remember," Mr. Melton said. "Cream prices, egg prices, hog prices have been way down the past few years. The flood made things worse, just when it looked like times might be improving."

"Fred was doing better with his horses according to some of the neighbors," Graham said.

"Yes, he was, but not by much," replied Mr. Melton tapping his pen on the desk in front of him.

It was all I could do ignore the hooves that caused his death, were also the hand up he needed to manage his debt.

"Bottom line is what?" Graham asked. He sounded a bit abrupt, I thought. He seemed ready to quit this dilly dallying and get to the point.

"Well, even though he got a good price for the farm, his debts are somewhere around $900. That depends on what the bank will be willing to accept," Mr. Melton replied.

Oh mercy, heavens, I thought to myself. How could I have lost everything, have nothing, and still have more to lose? How do you subtract $900 from nothing? Graham looked at Mr. Melton with his brow furrowed in thought. "I suppose my main question is that with Mr. Kassemier's death, those to whom the debt was owed got nothing. This debt wasn't to be passed on to his heirs," Graham said.

"Well, normally that would be the case. However, as Fred's attorney, I advised him to make Josie co-owner of the farm when her mother died. It would have been a nice dowry if she outlived him, and all debts had been paid."

"So should we be talking to the bankers then, instead of you?" Graham asked.

"No, no. We work together. We don't want to take advantage of the little lady here, do we?" Mr. Melton smiled at me with his beady eyes.

The little lady was seething. Not only did Mr. Melton speak of me like I wasn't even there but acted as if Graham had all the brains and was in control of my life. Not Fair!

"I think Fred probably had some money put by for you, stuck under a floorboard, or in a bowl someplace, didn't he now, Miss Josie? A little money that no one knew about, just the two of you?" He gave me a sly wink.

What was this man insinuating? I looked at his smarmy, oily face with the scattered whiskers over his toad chin. He had a little spittle at the corner of his mouth. If I had been a man, I would have put my fist in his face. Except I wouldn't have wanted my fist stuck in that soft mass of flesh. "No, sir," I said, trying to keep my outrage under control. "He used all our money to pay toward our debts and to keep food on the table. He didn't do anything that he wouldn't have been proud to tell in church each week. He was an honest man if you can understand what that might be."

Graham looked over at me his face trying not to break into a smile.

Mr. Melton looked at me once more. "Miss Josie, are you sure there isn't money in a bag in the henhouse? He gave me a sleezy grin. If there was, for a fee, I could perhaps bargain down your debt a bit." He looked over at Graham and said, "I'm sure you know how business operates."

"I can cover the loan at the bank for the time being," Graham said. "Miss Josie and I will work on the terms of our loan without you, or the bank being involved. Shall I go on down to the bank now, and who should I ask for?"

I believed in my heart that Mr. Melton was trying to take advantage of me. He seemed too overly confident. I wondered if he didn't have a finger in other tills somewhere. I thought about asking him about the rumor I'd heard at church about him having unsavory business partners, but I thought no, I couldn't do that, could I? I kept that thought in the back of my mind.

Mr. Melton answered Graham, "Oh, I think Mr. Taylor might be the man in charge of the loans, but he probably has clerks who take care of details."

Since there was no new business to be had, he rose from his seat, and we did the same. He ushered us out the door rather abruptly. Poppa had certainly done a good deal of business with him over the years, so I felt snubbed and somewhat humiliated. I was also embarrassed that Graham assumed he would pay my loan. It was certain to me that I didn't want Graham to be responsible for my debts. I was determined that I would have to find a way to make more money to repay him as soon as possible.

For the rest of the day, I worked and puzzled over what I should do or should have done. We went down to the bank to meet Mr. Taylor, and Graham explained that he would be paying off my father's outstanding loan. Thankfully, it was only $750. I was relieved that it was lower than Mr. Melton's estimate. Still, I was ashamed to have an almost stranger paying my debts. Mortifying. Mr. Taylor was very pleasant. Assuring me that although I wouldn't be able to have an individual account, I would still have access to my father's account to make payments and deposits. Graham or Oliver would need to sign if I wanted to obtain credit. I wasn't certain I understood all that, I was so befuddled by everything then, it was hard to keep my thoughts from spiraling in all directions.

We left the bank, Graham guiding me across the lobby and out the heavy wooden door. Pausing on the sidewalk, I put my hand up to shade my eyes from the bright sunshine. Still, even with the brightness of the day, the spring breeze had turned off a little cool. I gave a slight shiver, whether from the chill or nerves, I couldn't tell. "Graham, I am grateful that you are helping me out with this payment." I closed my eyes to block out the sunlight and curled my wrap more tightly across my shoulders. "I hate to need others to pay my debts," I said with a slight quiver in my speech.

"How about we go to that little lunchroom down the street. If you have any questions, we can discuss them," Graham said, seeming to sense how uncomfortable I was.

"That would be fine," I agreed. I felt that I must sit down somewhere because I wasn't sure how much longer my legs could hold me upright.

It was early yet, so the lunchroom wasn't crowded. I felt as if everyone was looking at me. Did they know what had happened? Could they read my forlorn face? Our waitress was a girl I had gone to school with. I knew her, but not well. Her smile turned into a Cheshire cat's when she turned her gaze toward Graham. Even as she asked me what I wanted and wrote my order on her notepad, it was clear her attention was on him. She must have thought he was a date or something. I got the feeling she wished he was hers. I ordered grilled cheese and vegetable soup, and Graham ordered the same. The waitress turned and made her way back to the kitchen swishing her hips in our direction as she walked.

Graham and I sat in silence until our food came. I didn't want anyone to overhear the conversation we were about to have. "Since this is a loan or mortgage or some such, I know that I will need to pay you back. I have a job, and I will turn over as much to you as I can until my debt is paid." I picked up my napkin and wiped my dry lips. "I don't want to be beholden to you any longer than I have to, you know."

"Miss Josie," Graham said. "You know, I consider you a family friend, and I have extra cash right now from my job." His gaze softened as he clasped my hand busy rearranging the soup spoons and leaned toward me. It didn't seem like he pitied me, which helped. "I don't get around much of anywhere to spend it. Mama and Helga don't need my financial help, just a bit of assistance with carrying groceries, changing light bulbs, those sorts of things, sure." I looked at him, my face full of unspoken questions. I needed the help, I wanted the help, but I wanted to be strong. I lifted the edges of my mouth in a slight smile which was loaded with uncertainty and doubt. "But no, nothing financial," he said, sitting back. "Since I have the money, and you need money right now, I thought this would work out for both of us. This is a personal loan between friends. There is no property involved, so it isn't a mortgage. How about we simply shake hands on it?"

He reached across the table with a strong square hand and took mine. I felt such a sense of warmth and peace from the sureness and strength of that handshake that I felt an instant sense of calm. Dadgum it. I was so ready to be mad. How could I be mad? I needed to feel grateful that he would support me in this way. Would Jimmy Lee have done the same? Somehow, I doubted it.

The next time I met Jimmy Lee for cocoa it was on Wednesday of that week. I was still mulling over how I would earn money to repay my debt to Graham.

"You are looking somewhat perplexed this evening, Miss Josie," Jimmy Lee said as he pulled out the stool beside me, smiling with a cocky grin.

"Oh, I was trying to think of a way to earn a bit of extra income to pay off some of the farm expenses," I answered.

"Well, now," he said as he twirled his drink around in his glass and took a few random sips. "I possibly might have the answer to your dilemma." I looked up at him, not sure if he was being honest with me or joking. "Yes," Jimmy Lee continued. "You know the time I brought you to the Flame and Glo for dinner and you so admired the hostess?" He gazed into the depth of his drink, probably considering a reorder.

"Oh, yes," I couldn't help but give a big sigh. "I loved her elegant clothes and manner."

"Well," Jimmy Lee said, wiping the moisture from his drink onto the tiny cocktail napkin. "We need someone to do that job here on Fridays and Saturdays for a while, not sure how long, but we might need her right away."

"Do you think I could do that?" I asked, a bit awed to think that Jimmy Lee believed I could be that elegant, sophisticated person. "What would my duties be? How late would I have to be here?" I felt tingly all over as I envisioned a picture of me, sweeping across the floor with my dress floating down from my hips and across the backs of my legs. Maybe a little bolero jacket covering my arms.

"Now, I'm just guessing here," Jimmy Lee answered, "but I think you could probably stay in your room with Mrs. Florene on the nights that you would be working. You stay with her on bad weather nights anyway. I believe she would allow you to stay on a regular basis. She has mentioned repeatedly how much she enjoys your company."

"What is it that I would be doing? Taking people to their tables?"

"Well, what we do is that people make reservations for certain nights they will be coming in to eat, playing cards, or any other sort of entertainment they enjoy. You want to be sure they're treated as special customers, so you ask them their names, where they're from, and maybe what kind of work they do, so that they feel that we here at Hey Ho are interested in them personally. Let me refresh my drink before we continue." I watched him saunter up to the bar, a bit put out that he didn't ask me if I wanted more cocoa, but I was too excited to drink more. He came back, settled himself in his seat and continued, "sometimes, our hostess, after she knows them better, recognizes their preferences, and what they like to eat and drink. We want our customers to feel special. I think with this job and your regular sewing duties, you would make more than enough to pay off any debts."

"I only saw the hostess when we came in taking people to their tables," I said. "I really didn't know it was more than that."

"That happens also. At times, people come in off the street. We take them if we can or have someone not show up. However, with our special customers, we treat them as if they were family, important members of society. We make a few notes in our hostess book, so that we can remember who they are and what makes them special."

I felt a bit awed over this prospect, but I also felt strange about asking people about their personal information. At home, I knew almost everyone's personal information, their names, their children's names, their dog's names. Maybe, this was the city version of the same.

Looking back at this magical solution to my financial worries, how could I have been so naïve as to believe that there were no strings attached? But at the time, it seemed like the perfect answer.

"When would I have to start this job? This Friday, next week?" I asked.

"Let me speak with Mr. Barbee, the manager first," Jimmy Lee said finishing his drink. "You remember him, don't you? I'm certain that my recommendation will be enough because he doesn't make actual hiring decisions for the Hey Ho unless it is for a senior job. On other matters, he mostly leaves that up to me or Mrs. Florene."

I remembered briefly seeing Mr. Barbee, but I don't think I could rightly say I knew him. He had that big office next to Jimmy Lee's. He had a pleasant look, but I hadn't met him. The only one I had sort of met was Mr. Lowenston, the man of the long bony fingers. I remembered him from our meeting at the Flame and Glo when Jimmy Lee told me he and his partners owned both businesses. No one seemed to want to know him. They even acted a little fearful when his name came up in conversation.

"I will leave word with Mrs. Florene or the girls upstairs when I know the answer," Jimmy Lee said. "It shouldn't take more than a day or two to find out."

Possibly, I would need the time. I had enough nice frocks for a week or two, but then I knew I had better get to sewing. Most of the clothes I had since my move were basic house wear. I knew I needed more dresses that would be elegant and work for warmer weather.

May 2

Journal, it is time for me to get more of my own spring and summer clothes on the way. I need to work this extra job, I know, because I don't like not being able to pay my bills. Sometimes, it weighs on my heart so much, I can hardly sleep. I will see it through!

Several weeks later, I hadn't heard back from Jimmy Lee. I knew as little as I did at our last conversation. He hadn't come to the house, either. Thinking I would have a chance to sit down with him and have a drink in the afternoon, I showed up early several times and had a glass or two of cream soda. I felt silly sitting at the bar by myself, even though there were only a few customers there in the afternoon. Harvey, the barkeep, kept up conversation with me as he wiped down the bar and washed what looked to be already clean glasses. At last, I asked him if he had seen Jimmy Lee. "No," he said. "Not lately, but this is his busy time of the year. Probably in his office most of the time now." That's it, I thought with a flash of surprise. What I should do is drop by his office one day if I come in early and surprise him, or at least simply let him know I am here.

I waited a day or two because I had a big rush of business. With the warmer weather, the Hey Ho became busier with more people who wanted to be out in the lovely spring evenings and to dine places other than their homes. It seemed that more of our dancers were breaking the straps on their gowns, more buttons were coming loose, and more tears were showing in the dresses. When the opportunity came, I went up to the second floor and walked down the long carpeted hallway to find Jimmy Lee's office. The transom at the top of his door was open, even though his office door was closed. As I grew nearer, I heard loud voices and shouting. I only recognized one voice, JimmyLee's.

The door opened. Out stalked Mr. Lowenston, his face a mask of deadly menace. His starched white collar and trim bow tie gave him a decided air of icy authority. To get out of his path, I ducked into an alcove. Just looking at him gave me cold chills. Jimmy Lee came to the door of his office and looked in my direction. I knew he didn't see me. His focus was on Mr. Lowenston's back. When I stepped out of the alcove, his face was a picture of shock. It seemed to take him a moment to register that I was there, and to finally recognize me.

"Oh Josie, what on earth are you doing here?" He barked.

This was not exactly the welcome I had expected. I answered him in a huff, "I merely came by to ask about the hostess job. I am so sorry that I have come by at a time which seems inconvenient for you." I really wasn't sorry. I hated being abrupt, but I needed answers.

"Oh, and I am sorry to be so gruff with you," Jimmy Lee glanced away from me for a moment, seeming a bit embarrassed. "We have had a lot going on in the past few weeks, and I have neglected you. Please forgive me. I meant to leave word with Mrs. Florene, but that hasn't happened. Now, we are sorely in need of a hostess, so I will have to ask you to start this weekend if you can manage it."

"Well, I suppose I can do that, but did you mention to Mrs. Florene that I will want to spend Friday and Saturday nights with her?"

"No, I haven't done that either," he replied. He rubbed the side of his neck and looked at me with a sideways grin.

"Well, let's go up and take care of that now," I replied. I didn't want to be rude, but I felt I was owed the respect of some answers. The weight of my debt to Graham compelled me to act in ways that I otherwise wouldn't.

When we reached her apartment, Mrs. Florene didn't look surprised to see us. She was busy retying the ribbon on the top knot of her little dog's head. She pulled the keys from her wrist and set them down on a small table. "Well, hello, to you both," she said. She beamed at me as if I were an unexpected visitor and not an employee.

"Josie, would you mind seeing if you can make a pretty little bow on Diamond's head?" she asked. "My fingers are a bit sore with arthritis these days, and I can't seem to get the hang of making this turn out right. The lace seems all wrong. Diamond keeps panting and wiggling, and I don't know if I am hurting him or simply taking too long. I think those keys might not have helped either." She cocked her head and looked at Diamond one way and then the other. Mrs. Florene always carried the keys with her. The lockers holding the girls' street clothes and the doors to the building were constantly needing to be locked and unlocked. The keys jangled as she leaned down to pat Diamond on the head.

"Certainly, I will," I said.

"Seems like you are a little early for work this evening, aren't you?" Mrs. Florene said.

"Yes, Jimmy Lee and I came to discuss something with you," I said as I fussed with Diamond's bow. "He can explain while I make Diamond into the lovely young man he needs to be."

Diamond seemed to know we were talking about him as he preened and strutted like Mr. Wren's pet rooster at home. Then, when he was certain he had had his full share of attention, he quieted right down and stood still as I worked.

Jimmy Lee hadn't opened his mouth, so I turned to him and tried unsuccessfully to raise one eyebrow. Naturally, it didn't have quite the effect I wanted, so I nudged him in the side with my elbow. He seemed to wake up then and went on to explain his plan and asked if I could stay with her two extra nights during the week. He explained that this probably wouldn't be on a permanent basis, but there was a need now that business had picked up. Jimmy Lee was careful to clarify that these new duties wouldn't interfere with my regular job.

It occurred to me that men seemed to explain me and my needs to other people with me standing right there. I had the ability to think and speak for myself, or I thought I did, and yet, there was always a man doing that for me. I looked up and caught a strange expression on Mrs. Florene's face. She had a stern expression as she looked at Jimmy Lee, "I can see why you might want Miss Josie to act as a hostess because no one could be any prettier or better dressed when she wears the clothes she designs. However, I must say it concerns me that you want her to become too personal with our customers."

"Oh, Mrs. Florene," I broke in. "Jimmy Lee wants me to find the information we know about people we like, so we can treat them like treasured guests while they are away from their friends and family. We here at Hey Ho want them to feel special." I wanted to put my new duties in a more favorable light than I thought Jimmy Lee presented.

"Oh yes we do," her voice was stern and forbidding. Not the Mrs. Florene I had grown to know and respect. Jimmy Lee looked down and shuffled his feet like a schoolboy. Even his ears blushed. This seemed odd to me. I wasn't sure what was going on, but I knew everything wasn't as it appeared on the surface. I looked from one to the other, but I couldn't tell if it was something real or my imagination.

Suddenly her demeanor changed. Mrs. Florene turned and looked at me with her normal sweet and loving expression, "I'm certain you will make them feel welcomed and appreciated, no doubt, Josie." She fussed a bit with the shawl around her shoulders and continued, "of course, I would love to have you here for two extra nights. You can stay for as many as you like. Sometimes, the girls pop in and out, but other than that you should have all the privacy you want. You can feel right at home." She then looked over at Jimmy Lee and panned her gaze over to include me as well, "I guess you probably know, Jimmy Lee, that we are adding a new tap dance routine for our dancers. They will be wearing lovely plumes on their heads which will take some talented needle work to keep them attached during the performance. I needed to ask Josie for a bit more of her time, anyway."

"Thank you so much, Mrs. Florene, I appreciate your kindness. I won't be able to stay too many nights since I do have Queenie and Pee Doodle at Flossie and Oliver's. I don't want to impose on them."

"Didn't your Poppa have a dog as well?" Mrs. Florene asked, wrinkling her forehead in concentration.

"Oh yes," I answered. "But that unfaithful mutt has gone home with my former co-worker's brother. I also have some financial affairs to complete back home as well."

"We would like for her to start here this Friday if that is agreeable with you, Mrs. Florene." Jimmy Lee said.

"Of course, it will be. I think the armoire in your room has enough space for your frocks and essentials, doesn't it?" Mrs. Florene asked.

"Oh yes, ma'am, it does." I thought of the large piece of furniture with its shelves and hanging racks. It had more room than I would ever need to hold everything I owned. I felt truly valued and loved here. This wasn't my true home, but I was beginning to fit into this new place with a warm feeling of belonging. I still missed my Momma and Poppa so much that at times I cried myself to sleep but, in this place, I didn't miss seeing them and didn't think of them every time I turned a corner or opened a door. Now that the farm was sold, and Cedric and his family were in my old homeplace, it was easier not to have to see different people in my house. I did miss Pee Doodle and Queenie terribly, since I felt they were the only parts of my close family I had left. Oh, I knew that all my aunts, uncles, and cousins loved and cared for me, still it wasn't the same. I felt all betwixt and between. Where did I truly belong?

Since I had a couple of days before the weekend, I would head home to pick up clothes and tell Flossie and Oliver I would be gone for most of the weekend. I also needed to talk to Graham about repaying my loan and setting up a schedule of payments. As Jimmy Lee and I walked down the hallway, I thought about the arrangements I needed.

"You mentioned the reason you wanted to add to your job was to make additional money to pay off farm debts, isn't that right?" he asked, pulling me closer and coiling his arm around my shoulders. "I think I have a proposition that might help."

I felt a twinge of concern since I wasn't sure what to expect. On one hand, this answered my vision of us becoming more involved, but with Jimmy Lee's arm pulling me closer, I had the image of a snake curled around me. I took a deep breath to settle my thoughts. Why was the image of a snake inserting itself into my brain? This was a man who was the object of my romantic fantasies. Where had that picture of perfection gone?

"You know, we are just coming out of a bad time with the banks," he continued. "I know times are better, but I don't know how much trust I have in the banking industry, right now." I listened intently to all of this since I wasn't sure what this had to do with me. "I've made money over the years in this job, but I don't trust putting all my money in our local banks. There may be a bit of corruption going on in some of our banks and other corporations. I don't like to put all my cash in the same place."

I wondered how and what he knew about corruption going on. I felt fluttery on the inside while restrained by Jimmy's arm on the outside. My first thought was to push and flail him away from me, but I willed myself to remain still. He made it worse by drawing me tighter and allowing his voice to drop to almost a whisper against my ear.

"I was wondering if you would allow me to put a thousand dollars in your account at your bank," he said. "In exchange, I could pay you a cash percentage to apply toward your debt in exchange for using your account as my safety net," Jimmy Lee said. "You can be my little layoff bank," he said with a snicker.

I thought about this for a moment. This whole conversation seemed to move into an even darker place. I tried to remain calm and envision how Mrs. Florene would handle this kind of situation. "How long would this be for and what would be my percentage?" Would this be legal, I thought? "Do I need to talk this over with my attorney?"

"Oh no, this is just between us," he said quickly. If you talked it over with your attorney, then he would have to be paid out of your percentage. How does one percent sound?"

"I think ten percent seems nicer, but I can be satisfied with three percent."

Jimmy Lee looked a bit startled at my response, "all right. I'll go with three percent. You seem to have more of a business head than I thought."

I felt a bit proud of myself that I could put myself out there a bit. After all, if I ever had my own sewing business, I would have to be in charge like Mrs. Florene. "Don't forget my Poppa was a farmer and a good businessman. You know it wasn't his lack of ability, but the times that caused his financial problems. Poppa was a smart, honest man." Looking Jimmy Lee square in the eye, I laid out my terms, "I'll agree to three percent. I do believe that is the going rate in banks now." That was one piece of information I was able to find out when I had gone with Graham to my bank.

"Done, I guess," he said. "We can discuss more details and make arrangements when you come back on Friday. It is important to know how I will have you withdraw cash for me when I need it and so forth."

"Let me ask you one more question," I said. "What the devil is a 'layoff bank'?"

"Oh, it's a term that some of my associates have come up with. If you are my 'layoff bank,' that means you keep me from taking as big a risk as I would with some of the local banks. Not all of these banking folks can be totally trusted."

I had the feeling Jimmy Lee might just fall into that same category, but I would wait and see. "Very good," I said. I put out my hand to shake his and I didn't get a good feeling from his touch. I still wasn't totally clear as to the true meaning of a layoff bank.

Going home that evening, I was perplexed as to what I needed to do about my current financial situation. Should I tell Graham about my arrangement with Jimmy Lee? Something about it didn't smell quite right. I thought Helga and Bertha mentioned that Graham had some sort of police connection, maybe with the government. They weren't clear about that. I didn't want to get anyone in trouble, but I was concerned. And I wasn't sure if the person who'd get in trouble was me or Jimmy Lee. My regular cab driver, Morris, looked at me through his rearview mirror, "Miss Josie, you seem all quiet back there tonight. Most nights, you are talking a mile a minute about dance routines or clothes."

"Morris, so many things have happened in the last months that I don't know exactly which end is up sometime."

"I'm sure you will work this out, doll," he said. "You are quite the smart girl. You aren't going to take sh… stuff from anyone." I knew Morris would be in a bit of a hurry to pick up regular fares going from Newport to Cincinnati, so he didn't normally take the time for too much conversation. I had heard cab drivers who took passengers from Cincinnati to specific restaurants and casinos in Newport were paid an extra fee by the clubs. I didn't know how accurate this was. Probably more of those dirty rumors.

Maybe, I thought as I mused over my situation, I could call Graham and see what he might want to do about when, where, and how much I would pay him. Arriving at Flossie and Oliver's, I was tired, hot, and feeling a little blue. I simply said "Good Night" to Morris and walked up the hill to the house. When I looked up at the stars and felt the soft air, it reminded me that there was peace and goodness in the world. Smelling the rich earth of Oliver's produce garden and listening to the soft lowing of his milk cows comforted me like no other sounds and smells could. Even with all the sadness of the last years, I knew I had a lot to be grateful for. Breaking into my thoughts,

I heard Queenie barking out behind the house, and her baying as she caught wind of my scent and came scrambling toward me.

Flossie was glad to see me when I came in the door. She must have been waiting as she completed a little mending and darning. This was Oliver's busy season with his produce patch. What he didn't sell in town, she had to can. Evening was her time to rest as she listened to the radio while darning holes in the heels of Oliver's socks and patching the knees of his overalls. "Well, hello, Josie," she said. "I am so glad to see you home. Such a pretty night. I thought about setting on the porch awhile, but then I got to doing all this for Oliver."

"Flossie, put your work down and let's step out on the porch a bit," I said.

"Is something troubling you, Josie or did you simply want to sit outside?" Flossie asked.

"A little of both, I guess," I said. "I sit inside at the Hey Ho in the evenings, and I don't get to enjoy the stars, the sky, the smells. Of course, I guess the smells outside in Newport wouldn't match the clean, soft country smell that we have here." In my mind, I could smell the thick heavy exhausts from cars, the oily smell of gasoline residue, and the smoke from chimneys where houses nudged close to one another. Flossie set her basket and her work aside. She was a stout woman and held tightly onto the arms of her chair to pull herself to her feet. I wanted to help but didn't as not to insult her.

They had two large, caned rocking chairs on the porch, and I sank down gratefully into the one farthest from the door. It was covered by a crocheted pad I recognized as one Momma had made for Flossie. It made me a little teary-eyed. Some days I felt like I was moving past their deaths, and then something would jab me with a pain so intense it was hard to ignore. Everyone told me time would heal this pain, but I didn't truly believe it. At least not yet.

"So, tell me what's on your mind, Josie," Flossie said.

I paused, listening to the sound of the cicadas, such a welcoming summer sound. Some thought their sounds were raspy and intrusive. For me, they were the perfect harmony for summer. "Oh Flossie," I finally answered. "I'm confused about some decisions I need to make. I thought our sale was going to pay all Poppa's debts until I found out they didn't. I thought Poppa's debts were not to be mine, and then I found they were."

"How did you find out about that? Oliver wasn't told about it," Flossie shifted weaving side to side in her seat.

"Graham called me," I answered her. "He said the bank people who phoned him believed he was the one handling my affairs. Because I became joint owner of the farm, I now had joint responsibility for the debt. That's as it is, but I can't see why they didn't call me."

"I don't see why they didn't get in touch with Oliver, but I think Graham assured him he would handle everything," Flossie said. "But why not me, Flossie?" I stammered, my voice rising in frustration. "You know better, Josie," Flossie said gently. "If a woman doesn't have a father or a husband to handle business affairs, a male relative or family friend is responsible. Especially when it comes to money."

"You mean, I can't take out a loan myself? I must have some man do that for me?"

"Yes, I guess that's what I mean. Loans and such need to come from the man. You knew that didn't you?"

"Well, I guess I do now, but I'm going to see how I can do it differently." I knew Mrs. Florene seemed to do business and make money. Maybe staying with her was a good thing. I could probably learn a thing or two from her. There might be a good reason that I was taken in this direction. "What I wanted to tell you, though, Flossie, is that I will be staying with Mrs. Florene on Friday and Saturday nights for a while."

"Why is that honey?" Flossie started to blink her eyes. I realized it was late, and she needed to get up early. She was on the verge of falling asleep right there. I didn't know if I could get her up out of her chair if she did.

"I'm going to add a bit to my job duties on those nights." I didn't think that I needed to go into more detail. Somehow, I wasn't certain that she would feel entirely comfortable with my additional duties. I'm not sure I was either after seeing the expression on Mrs. Florene's face when we told her.

"Well, let's go in and make ourselves ready for bed. I'm certain that things will look different in the morning. I know you have to be up early, Flossie, and I have clothes to get ready to take to Newport. We can talk more about these things tomorrow when our minds are clearer, and we're bright eyed," I said. "I'll need to call Graham about my repaying the debt."

I wasn't about to tell her that Graham had already paid the loan. I knew she and Oliver would be offended if I told her that Graham paid it. They would insist on paying themselves, and I knew they probably had debts of their own from Jenny Mae's college. I wasn't sure how that would work, since she was now a married woman. Oh well, some things a woman must keep to herself.

The next morning, I called the Raisch home. When Bertha answered, she said Graham was out of town for a few days on his job, probably in Kentucky. If she heard from him, she would let him know to get in touch with me. She was glad to hear from me, wanted to know all about my job, how I liked living with Flossie and Oliver, and to please come see them. "I want to tell you all about my job and all that has been happening, Bertha," I answered, confused about so many things. "When I get the chance to talk to Graham and have more details, let's have a visit and get caught up."

I set about washing, ironing, and packing up the dresses and blouses I thought would work for my new job duties. Many of them seemed a bit worn and faded for hostess duties, but I didn't have time to make new dresses and definitely no money to buy them. I was focused on mending a collar on a blouse when Queenie jumped up from the rug and ran to the front of the house. Only then was I aware of the crunch of gravel and thud of a car door closing.

"Josie," I heard Flossie calling from the front of the house, "I think you have someone here to see you."

When I came out to the porch, there was Graham looking as though he had materialized from my thoughts, "Graham, what are you doing here?"

He looked up at me in surprise, "I thought you were the one who asked to see me." He scratched his head as if he didn't know where this conversation was supposed to head.

Flossie stepped into the awkwardness of the situation, "I need to go out to the garden while it's still cool," she said. "But why don't you all sit out here on the porch while it's still nice. I have some strawberry pie I baked this morning. Why don't I give you all a slice of that. Josie, get the milk out of the icebox and pour you each a glass, and I will go in and bring the pie slices. You can carry on your business here as well as you can in the kitchen."

I felt awkward with Graham standing in front of me with hardly any room between us and the porch post. Then, he turned and sat on the porch swing. I went inside to get the milk. When Flossie brought out the pie, there was simply no place convenient to sit except beside him on the swing. Balancing milk, pie, and my skirt with Graham wedged in beside me was a bit uncomfortable. He didn't seem at all uncomfortable. I guess it was because he was with his mother and sister all the time, so these situations probably seemed normal.

"Tell me, "He began. "What was it that you wanted to talk to me about?" It was hard to start a conversation with pie in my mouth, so I washed it down with a big gulp of milk and set my plate on the floor.

"All right," I said, dusting my hands to knock away any clinging crumbs. "I know that you paid the bank loan, and I wanted to discuss that. I have added extra duties to my job at the Hey Ho, and I will be able to repay you faster than I thought I might be able to originally."

"May I ask what these extra job duties involve?" he asked.

This sounded a bit offensive, who was he to oversee my actions and career? "Yes, I will be the hostess on Friday and Saturday nights," I said. "It will involve a bit more time, and I'm able to stay with Mrs. Florene on these nights, so I won't be late coming back."

"What will these hostess duties involve?" Graham asked.

"Oh, I will take clients to their tables. For the ones who have reservations, I might ask their names, where they're from, and the kind of work they do. You know, things you would ask friends to make them feel comfortable." I heard a gasping, choking sound. I looked up and thought Graham was choking on his pie. I grabbed his plate and his milk glass out of his hands and placed them down on the porch. "What is it?" I asked in alarm. "Are you all right?

He didn't speak kindly to me for having saved him from choking. He looked furious when he barked, "What are you thinking? Who asked you to do this? Why would you agree to that?" For an up and coming business woman, I thought I was going to burst into tears. In fact, that is exactly what I did. He looked back at me a little more gently, "do you know why you were asked to do this? The real purpose behind these questions?" He handed me his handkerchief to mop up my tears.

On, no, I thought. I am not doing this again. Straightening up, I handed him his unused hanky. I would not have him thinking of me as a child. I answered him, "the reason is to make these out-of-town businessmen feel comfortable and at home."

"Well, let me tell you what I think," Graham said. "Do these men come to eat and drink only? Do some of them go in the back room and play cards and other games? Do some of them go upstairs with the women?"

I remembered Marianne and her client turned husband, and I stuttered, "I guess they sometimes do."

"What do you think would be the purpose of knowing the

names, the hometowns, and the occupation of these men? Let's say they were married and engaged in gambling, card playing, and consorting with exotic women and showgirls?"

I was totally stumped. I could hardly breathe. "I wouldn't think knowing these simple things about a person would have the slightest connection with wrongdoing if they were married men or not," I said. "I truly don't see any sort of connection here."

"Here is what I think," Graham said. "I think these men are being set up for extortion. The men will be threatened with exposure if they don't play by certain rules. If you know where a man lives, his name, and his occupation, it wouldn't be any too difficult to track him down if someone in these places wants to do it."

"Graham, hogwash," I protested. "That is the most ridiculous thing I have ever heard."

"I'm simply warning you, Josie," he said softly but seriously. "You have to be careful unless you know exactly what and with whom you are dealing."

"I suppose I could say the same thing about you, Graham," I said firmly. "But so far, you seem to be reputable. I've only known you for a few months, and you have inserted yourself into my business and financial affairs. I trusted you because I trust Bertha and Helga, and I trust Jimmy Lee because of Mrs. Florene." He looked at me and shook his head. "Anyway, what I wanted to discuss with you is when and how much should I pay you."

Graham paused for a moment and rubbed his chin, "what would you say to $18 each month at the first of the month?"

"Hmm," I considered. "That will take me about three and a half years if I see that correctly. What would you say to $25?"

His eyes widened, and he drew back his head in surprise, "how on earth can you afford that? Surely you can't be making that much money at your job. Are you sure that sewing and seeing people to their tables is all they are having you do?" His eyes narrowed, and he gave me a hard stare. "They aren't asking you to suggest other activities like going into the casino areas or over to a roulette wheel, are they?"

Who did he think I was? An idiot? An unnamed fury swirled inside me. How could he believe I was stupid enough not to realize what was happening. I wasn't raised in a padded cotton box. I was aware of what people did at the Hey Ho. I wasn't involved with all of it, but I was aware. "Well, I certainly don't know all the details yet," I answered Graham, sounding sharp, if not a little mean. "If you remember, I haven't even started my new duties. I won't start until Friday."

"I'm only saying you need to take care of yourself and watch what you are doing. You don't want them to take advantage of your generous nature." I think he knew he was getting on my last nerve and was trying to pacify me. He sounded like he could have been my older brother and possibly the most opinionated person I'd ever met. Even my Poppa had given me more credit for being able to care for myself and I thought he was overprotective.

Friday rolled around quicker than I thought possible. I got up early and packed my trunk and hope chest with the essentials I needed to spend weekends at the Hey Ho. Oliver loaded the produce truck, empty of produce, and smelling reputable, thank goodness, and took me to Newport.

When I unloaded my clothes and other necessities into the wardrobe at Mrs. Florene's, they were dwarfed in this huge space. Mrs. Florene looked over my outfits, checking carefully, assessing for my new duties. She lifted her head in a study of memory, then shook it as if to bring herself back to present. "I do have a few outfits that I have saved from an earlier time," she said, "when I was much younger and slimmer. With your skill with the needle, it wouldn't take a great deal of effort for you to have them ready to wear once again."

For the first time, I became aware of the vulnerability behind Mrs. Florene's façade of unflappable composure. "Don't know why I saved them," Mrs. Florene ran her fingers along my dresses. "I think I always had the idea in the back of my mind that I would have a daughter to wear them. Even though that time has passed, I can't bear to throw them away. They represent the glamorous edition of who I was. It wouldn't take much for you to make them modern and glorious again." She paused, drawing herself to a different time and place. Going to her cedar chest, she pulled out a dress which was a glorious jade green. "See this flapper dress? It shows a lot of leg, but you have the legs to wear it," she held it up to me. "I have a beaded headband that goes with it and some Art Deco jewelry. You don't think it is too old fashioned, do you?"

"Oh, no, ma'am, I certainly don't," I was delighted to be able to wear a dress so elegant and charming, like something a star would wear. I needed to keep these kinds of designs in mind if I ever wanted to approach this level of allure in my own work. "I could make a few adjustments if needed."

"And oh look," she exclaimed, her face alight as she pulled another from the chest. "This one is much longer, and you could make more alterations. I have several strands of pearls that would go well with either. They may not be real, but they look smashing with the outfits." Mrs. Florene pointed out others that lay in the chest, "feel free to take any others that appeal to you. I'll bring the pearls and other jewelry to your room before you start tomorrow." I was totally overwhelmed with her kindness and generosity. I wished Graham could understand what kind of people Mrs. Florene and others here at the Hey Ho were. Maybe, though, I thought with a twinge of unease, only some of them.

The next night, starting my new duties, it felt a bit strange but after a few minutes everything seemed to fall into place. The first thing I did was simply greet people who came to the door and ask their names. There were mostly men but some couples. Then, I consulted the sheet at my podium and led them to their tables. A couple of times I almost forgot to include any extra details, if I found them out, in my hostess book. Graham had such a distorted view of what took place here. Goodness. Couldn't elegant, sophisticated people come out to dine with their friends and be honest and respectable? When Helga and Bertha said he was involved in some sort of police work, it made me think he saw criminals around every corner.

On Saturday night, things settled in the same easy routine. There were a few more people there, but not the crowd I would have expected on a pleasant summer evening. I caught a glimpse of Jimmy Lee, but only for a second. He was placing the hostess book beneath the podium for me. I guess this was one of the things he checked on from time to time.

Later that evening, two men in dark suits came in the door. I thought one looked familiar. It was Graham with someone I didn't know. He was barely recognizable in a fashionable outfit, a suit with pleated pants, a double-breasted jacket, and what looked to be a beautiful silk tie with matching handkerchief. All I could say was he looked like all my movie star idols rolled up into one. The man with him was handsome, too. If he weren't standing next to Graham, he would have been a looker. As it was, he looked like a faded image of his companion. I went up to them, but was struck dumb, hardly knowing what to say or how to begin. The copies of the beautifully embossed menus were clutched tightly in my hand. My tongue lodged in the roof of my mouth. I couldn't seem to find my voice right away, and I must have had nothing on my face but a blank stare.

"I believe you need to ask my friend, Carter, and me if we have reservations," Graham looked down at me with a smirky kind of grin. Obnoxious. "And no, we don't. Since we don't have reservations, either you tell us to wait until you check to see if you can find us a table, or 'Right this way, sirs, a table for two.'"

I didn't even look back at Graham. I simply turned on my heel toward his companion, and giving him my sweetest, most simpering smile, said, "Oh Carter. It is so nice to meet you. We love having you here with us tonight. Will you come right this way, so that I can seat you and the person you are with." I led them to a table off the proper edge of the main seating area explaining we had a larger party with reservations coming in a bit later. "Is this satisfactory for you? You should still have an excellent view of the floor show beginning shortly." My focus was on Carter. His eyes were a bright little boy blue that gave him a helpful, hopeful look. Other than that, he was sturdy and muscular with mud brown hair. He wasn't as handsome as Graham was, at least tonight, but as Lila, our head dancer, would say, I wouldn't kick him out of bed for eating crackers.

As they took their seats, I handed them their menus, saying their waiter would be with them shortly. When I say I handed, I sort of pitched Graham's to him, but I leaned nicely toward Carter and politely handed him his. Making my way back to the hostess station, I stopped at several tables to answer questions. Most were questions about the types of flowers in table arrangements from some of the women, or brands of alcohol available from men. Nothing too personal or intrusive. I did look over and notice Graham looking at me. He probably thought I wouldn't be able to handle myself, but I thought I was doing just fine.

When I went back to check on setting up an extra table for the large group, Jimmy Lee met me in the back hallway. I knew I couldn't be back here too long because I had to get back up front. Still, Jimmy Lee grabbed me by one arm and almost hissed at me, "who were those G-men types you were talking to out there?"

"G-what?" I asked. "I don't exactly know what you are talking about. The one tall man was my friend, Helga's, brother. The other one was probably a friend or co-worker. I don't know. All I was told was that his name was Carter."

"I can tell you that I don't like the looks of those two. Do you know what they might be up to?" Jimmy hissed so hard that spittle flew out his lips.

"I think they might be up to checking on what I'm doing," I said. "I'm sure Helga and her mother want the big brother to see where

I'm working and what I'm doing." Of course, I didn't have any such thoughts, but I couldn't think of anything else to say right then. Also, I was in a bit of a hurry, and I didn't want to spend it trying to mollify Jimmy Lee. As it happened, though, Mr. Barbee helped me out.

"Jimmy Lee," Mr. Barbee said to him coming down the back hall. "I've been looking everywhere for you. Can you come to my office for a few moments?" Mr. Barbee smiled at me, but it was a tight, closed smile with no humor.

"Sorry, Miss Kasenmeir, is it?" Mr. Barbee looked at me with a questioning look on his face.

"No, Kassemier, Mr. Barbee, but most people don't get that close, anyway." I gave him a smile back, but this whole thing seemed awkward. "I need to get word about setting up another table for our large party group, and I must get back. So glad to see you again." What I really meant was I was so glad to get out of there.

The rest of the evening went smoothly for the most part. As I walked between tables and spoke with the diners, I kept thinking to myself, though, what the heck was a G-man? Who would I have to ask to find that out? Normally, I would think of asking Graham, but I couldn't ask him. I thought his job was police work, and I didn't think a G-man was that. Was that what Helga meant when she mentioned that he did police work for the government? I wondered if I could ask Mrs. Florene? Would Lila know? Being a sophisticated grown-up was not easy.

The rest of the summer and on into the fall, things settled into a steady rhythm. I came in about 5:00 p.m. every day, adjusted the girls' clothing during the first of the week and prepared for hostess duties on Fridays and Saturdays. On weekends after the 8:00 show, I made any clothing repairs since I was spending the night. This routine seemed to work well for everyone. I got to know many of the customers, and nothing seemed out of line. Yes, I knew that many, mostly men, but sometimes women, stayed on to play cards and games in the next room. Some of the men followed girls to the third floor, but everyone seemed to have a good time. Graham didn't come back, so I was spared the indignity of having to put up with his ungracious comments.

I mailed Graham's money once each month since I knew his home address. One night, as I was addressing the envelope for my loan payment, it occurred to me that I didn't know Jimmy Lee's address. Really, I knew nothing about his personal life. Did he have siblings? Living parents? Where he was from? The next time I saw Jenny Mae and Winston, I would be certain to ask if they knew about his personal life. Surely, if Winston had asked him to be the best man at the wedding, he would know. I decided right that very evening I would ask Mrs. Florene if she knew anything about him.

When I got back to the apartment, I took off my jacket and kicked off my shoes. "Mrs. Florene," I said, as I walked barefoot into the main room where she was sitting at her desk sorting through various stacks of papers.

"Josie, dear, please call me Florene," she said, removing her reading glasses, setting them on the desk beside her, and turning to look at me. "Mrs. Florene makes me sound like an old maiden aunt. Now maybe that might be the way you see me, but I don't want to think of myself that way."

"Florene, I will remember to do that," I said thinking to myself how much she meant to me. I was so glad she had come into my life and was guiding me through this maze. When I remembered my trip to Chicago a lifetime ago, I thought I wanted a life of adventure. Little did I realize, then, that you needed others to make this a successful journey.

"I came here at the urging of Jimmy Lee," I began, "but I realize that I don't even know where he lives, or that much about him." I hoped Florene would give me some of the missing details without my having to fish for them too hard.

"I'm not sure I know that exactly either, Josie," she said looking up at me and pursing her lips. "He spends much of his time here, and, perhaps, going to places with his friends," She paused for a moment, scratching her chin in thought. "His office is well equipped to make it more homelike. I don't know if you have spent any or much time in his office, but he has an alcove off the back. There is a built-in chifforobe and a Murphy bed, you know one of those beds that pull out of the wall at night and close up during the day. I think he lives in that office for a good bit of time. Otherwise, I truly can't say." She shook her head, "I do believe he might be one that you could give your time, but I would never, ever, suggest you trust him with your heart."

My mouth flew open to ask more questions, but we were interrupted by a knock on the door. Mrs. Florene rose to answer the knock. It was Lila bringing in the cash proceeds from the evening in a leather bag. "Thank you so much dear," I heard her say. "I will turn it in later tonight. Thank you for being so prompt and diligent."

When Mrs. Florene returned to put the bag on her desk, she seemed distracted from our previous conversation. I didn't ask more questions about Jimmy Lee since she appeared ready to close off our discussion. Maybe when I went back home at Christmas, I would be able to find out more from Jenny Mae and Winston. I forgot to ask what a G-man was.

December 22

Journal, Christmas will be on Sunday this year, and I am so pleased because I am off work on Friday and Saturday. Winston and Jenny Mae are coming in for Christmas, and I can't wait to see them. It will be easier to be with them on the anniversary of Poppa's death.

I was excited to have time with Winston and Jenny Mae at Oliver and Flossie's. We made boughs of greenery to put around the house. We found pinecones in the yard and sprigs of holly to decorate the windows. Of course, we always waited until Christmas Eve to decorate the tree and popped popcorn to string with thread. I certainly had plenty of that. I even made Pee Doodle and Queenie little collars of greenery which stayed on for about 5 minutes. Winston got their picture before Queenie pawed hers off and Pee Doodle got rid of his on a fence post.

Saturday was Christmas Eve, and we baked most all day. I made a jam cake, coconut cake, two types of fruit cakes, and lots of cookies. Always lots of cookies. I hoped Jenny Mae and Winston would take some back with them. I certainly didn't want to eat too many, but Flossie and Oliver had all that fresh cream, eggs, and canned fruit from the orchard, begging you to bake with them.

On Christmas, Winston got a brand-new camera, and he had the grandest time taking pictures of all of us. Sometimes, I look back at those pictures and wonder who those people were in that moment and feel a great sadness that they are all now gone. Did their lives turn out the way they wanted and imagined? Oh well, that is part of life, I suppose. As I now know, all relationships end, and you must make the best of the time you have. Funny, I didn't realize this then. I guess sometimes it is best when one doesn't know.

I thought I would ask Winston more about how he knew and met Jimmy Lee. It was hard to find a time when we could be alone to talk about these things. With all the hustle and bustle of Christmas, a quiet time was hard to find. Late on Christmas Eve when the household had quieted and Flossie and Oliver had gone to bed, Jenny Mae, Winston, and I were sitting on the sofa drinking a glass of eggnog. I had made it using the recipe my Momma had given me, and it tasted better and sweeter because of that. Holidays were hard. I had people who had somewhat adopted me, but I felt like a peripheral member at times, not completely embedded into the fabric of their lives. I missed my Momma and Poppa so much. The people at the Hey Ho and Bertha and Helga had become an extended family, as well as Jenny Mae's family, but it wasn't quite the same. I didn't have the intimate relationships to help guide me through this maturing process. I had so many questions about what to do and whom to trust. I casually brought up Jimmy Lee in my conversation, "Winston, have you seen

Jimmy Lee Reilly since your wedding?"

"No," he said. "Come to think of it, I don't believe I have. Odd. I would have sworn I would have, but no, I don't think so."

"So, have you been friends for a long time?" I pressed.

"Actually, no, we haven't. He and I got to be friends over cars. At the time, he was getting a Cadillac V16 All-Weather Phaeton, and he wanted my opinion."

"Why would he ask you?" I asked. "Were you friends?"

"No, we weren't," Winston said. "We were at a car dealership in Lexington, and I was looking at all the cars I couldn't afford as a student and struggling academic." He looked a bit puzzled, as if uncertain as to what he needed to say. "He seemed to have all the money to buy any fancy car he wanted, and he wanted to know my thoughts on all of them."

At the time, I thought this was rather strange. Why would Jimmy Lee have approached a stranger to ask his opinion? Maybe, I thought, since Winston appeared to be local, he might have useful connections Jimmy Lee could use to his advantage.

"It seems he comes down to Lexington every few weeks to look at cars for the partners who own his club," Winston continued. "Sometimes, they want super fancy ones, and at other times, they need nondescript unnoticeable ones. When we met at the car dealership, we went out for barbeque and beer after. Jimmy Lee told me he thought I had a good eye for the types of cars he was looking for. He said I could be paid a commission for cars he purchased when he came down," he looked over at Jenny Mae. "That sounded like an easy and good way to make some money, since money was always tough for me to come by as a struggling student."

"Oh, I didn't know that," Jenny Mae said with a puzzled look on her face. "I thought he kind of hooked onto you, Winston. Your life became his for a while, then he disappeared."

"But not until after your wedding, though, right?" I asked. I could easily understand how Jimmy Lee could take over one's life. He had a way of acting as if you were the most important person he knew until he no longer benefited from it. I couldn't help but wonder what the attraction to Winston was. Probably, because he was knowledgeable and responsible. Jimmy Lee seemed attracted to those who put him in a favorable light. It seemed strange that no one appeared to have a clear picture of the 'real' Jimmy Lee.

I couldn't dwell on things I couldn't change or understand right at Christmas. Instead, I needed to focus on what was happening now. Earlier, I had started working on some rag rugs for Mrs. Florene. Not the rag rugs for everyday use, but ones a bit more fancy using beautiful colors and soft fabrics that would fit into her lovely living quarters. I wanted to have one that was somewhat oversized, so that she would have something warm and lovely to put by her bedside and have under her feet. I had thought I would have them completed in time to take back with me before Christmas but realized that between Christmas and the new year would be a better choice. I also worked on needlepoint designs for Bertha and Helga which again, wouldn't be ready until after Christmas.

Other than my uncompleted projects, I had everything finished and bought for those I spent Christmas with. We had a warm happy time. We got to visit with neighborhood friends and relatives, went caroling with church friends, and made baskets for the needy and orphans. One of the neighbors coming from Florida brought home a basket of oranges which we shared at the church Christmas celebration. I put away questions about Jimmy Lee, money, and all the turmoil surrounding the Hey Ho to focus on my hometown friends and family whom I had known and loved forever. I would save those until after the holidays.

I went back to the Hey Ho on the Tuesday after Christmas. I had expected lots of holiday celebrations at the restaurant, however, things seemed subdued. Three dark suited men came to visit at odd times, and I wondered if that had something to do with it. They were there on Tuesday. Then on Wednesday evening, as I was going downstairs, they were coming up to the 2nd floor. No one was talking about who they were or why they were there. Even Mrs. Florene sweetly skirted my questions about them. Since things were slow, I must have been noticing things out of the ordinary. But, as it didn't concern me, I put it out of my mind.

With New Year's Eve approaching, I thought it best to set aside some time to visit Bertha and Helga. We made plans for me to come visit on Thursday, where we'd have lunch, and exchange gifts. I didn't have a gift for Graham, but I hoped that the loan payment which was due on the first was gift enough.

That day, even though it was gray and overcast, I walked to the Raisch's apartment from the bus stop with a lift in my spirits and a sense of excitement. It must have been because I hadn't seen or heard from them in a while. Even from the hallway, outside the apartment, the smell of freshly baked pastries and yeasty rolls filled the air. Helga opened the door almost before I could finish knocking. Her bright sparkling face lit the gloom of the hall. Her squeals of excitement leapt over me with an almost physical force. She grabbed me in a hug and pushed her head under my chin like a loving sister.

"Welcome, come in. We are so excited you are here," Bertha took her spoon from the pot she was stirring and placed it on the spoon rest on the stove. She untied her apron, placed it on a chair, and bustled toward me, her arms outstretched and welcoming. Even though a bit of garlic essence pervaded her hair, she still smelled warm and motherly. I looked beyond her, but no one else seemed to be there.

"Tell us all about your Christmas," Helga said, still bouncing with excitement. She wanted to know who was there, what we did, what food we had. Even though she didn't know many of the people involved, just the ones that she had met while they were at the farm, she seemed to take joy in all the activities and events of a country type Christmas.

"Was Graham here with you on Christmas?" I asked.
Bertha raised her eyes in question, "Oh, he's still around. He took

Daisy for a walk and to buy a newspaper at the store down the street. That boy won't miss a meal. He should be back in a few minutes."

"Do I have time to give you my gifts before lunch?" I asked.

"Of course, let me get yours," Helga said, stepping into the hall leading to the back of the apartment. She came back moments later with several packages in her hands.

I took the paper wrapped parcels from my bag. For Bertha, I had needlepointed a chair cushion with a pink rose on a dark background and lovely green foliage. I made three matching crocheted doilies of different sizes.as well. For Helga, I had a lovely dresser scarf with needle-worked pink and yellow butterflies on soft green material with an edging matching the butterflies' colors. I was very proud of my needlework gifts, but I had nothing except the money folded into a piece of stationery for Graham. Even though I was starting to feel a bit ashamed that it wasn't more, I could do nothing about it.

The women were delighted with their gifts. Bertha turned hers over and over in her hands as she examined every stitch. Helga laid her dresser scarf on different pieces of furniture throughout the room and said she was going to put it in her hope chest.

They gave me a very nice cloth clutch purse that was small and dainty, just large enough to carry my essentials if I went out for the evening. I thought it was so nice to have something elegant to use on special occasions. I loved its shades of purple shimmering fabric. Every other bag I owned seemed large, lumpish, and plain compared to this. It was a bag I would use and cherish for years. I gave each of them a hug of appreciation. What a marvel it was that we continued to be close.

"I had a date, last night," Helga confided with a sheepish grin. "Such a sweet fellow. I don't know if it will go anywhere, but he is to come here for dinner on Saturday night. Momma will be here, of course, but I hope Graham has gone by then."

"You don't think Graham will approve?" I asked.

"I don't know, but he seems to scare off every boy I see. I

think Momma likes him, don't you Momma?"

"He is a delightful young man," Bertha said. "I understand that he sells men's clothing in one of our nice local stores. His dress is impeccable. I believe he is very much taken with our Helga." Helga looked over at me beaming with pride but seemed a little exasperated at Bertha's assessment of her new beau. "Let me finish getting this dinner together," Bertha said. "Graham will be here soon, and we do need to eat, so we can have time to visit before you go in to work, Josie."

Not a moment after she finished speaking, the front door opened, and in walked Graham. With him came the scent of the outdoors and fresh winter cold. Daisy took one look and came at top speed to greet me. Graham seemed to fill the space in the doorway with his size, and the controlled energy of his movements. I was glad we had finished the gift giving. I believed he would think this was trivial and too banal for his approval. Not that he would say anything. He had a way of assessing a situation wordlessly, yet letting you understand how he felt without speaking. I felt stiff with my greeting of Graham, so I leaned forward to ruffle Daisy's ears and tell her how much I missed her.

"Did you miss both of us or just Daisy?" Graham said with a grin spread across his face. That grin caught me by surprise. I wasn't used to seeing a smiling, happy Graham.

"Of course, I have missed Daisy," I said, intentionally ignoring what I thought was his intent.

"Do you have any Christmas for me?" he asked in a way I knew wasn't serious.

"Well, I do have something for you," I said, as I dug into my purse and drew out the cash, I had saved back for him. I wish I had thought to ask the women if there was a small gift I could have brought. Maybe it wouldn't have been appropriate. Darned if I knew. "Here is my payment for this month. I know it's a few days early, but

I thought it best to give it to you while I was here."

"You knew I would be here?" he said.

"No," I answered a bit spitefully, maybe more than I should have. "I could have left it with your mother." I don't know why I couldn't be my nicer self.

"Oh, I suppose I would have gotten it sooner or later. How about let's have our dinner," he said sniffing the air in the room. "All that fresh air has made me hungry. After, I'll sit and read the paper while you ladies have your chat. Then, I can walk you to the bus when it's time for you to go."

"You needn't worry. I can manage by myself," I said.

"Daisy and I need the exercise," he answered. "We'll be glad to walk down to the corner." That seemed to end the discussion for him, as he turned and headed into the dining area.

The lunch Bertha and Helga had prepared was delicious. I thought Flossie was the best cook in the world, but this meal was darn close. After all the good food at Christmas, I didn't think I could eat another bite, but I was wrong. We had duck, which I hadn't had in the longest time, sweet potatoes, green beans, and Bertha's delicious yeast rolls. I ate three. I was so full I could hardly push myself away from the table when we finished. Then, Bertha brought in a wonderful apple torte, so I didn't move, simply ate more.

I decided then that I would make Helga a nice tablecloth and embroidered napkins for her hope chest. She seemed so taken with fancy needlework, I thought a design of green, gold, and red for Christmas with holly berries and pinecones would be great for future holidays. The rest of the afternoon was filled with cheer and laughter as we discussed all the fun events that had happened since we had been together last. Helga told us more about her chance meeting with Albert, her date. She had gone into the store where he worked to buy a belt for Graham. When he asked if he could help her, she questioned him about which of three belts she held looked best with dress slacks.

In turn, Albert asked whether this belt was for a boyfriend or father. When he found it was for neither, he asked to call on her. She kept her conversation somewhat muted, I suppose, so Graham couldn't hear all of it.

I hated it when it was time to leave since I had so enjoyed the time and conversation. Graham insisted on walking me to the bus. As we walked to the bus stop, he casually asked about my job at the Hey Ho. I told him that it was slower than I thought it would be at holiday time. I did mention that there were three men in dark suits who seemed to be hanging around at odd times. I didn't think it was of much importance, but I had to have something to talk about. He seemed more startled and interested than I anticipated. "Three men in dark suits?" Graham asked in an abrupt tone. "What did they look like? Who did they talk to? Where did they go?

"I just thought that they came in for dinner or cards or the usual activities most people come in for," I said. "They went on up to the 2nd floor. I thought maybe they were there to speak to Mr. Barbee, or maybe Jimmy Lee."

"Wonder if they were there on behalf of the top management?" Graham said talking more to himself than to me. "Do you know anything about the owners of the Hey Ho?"

"Not really," I said. "I did see Mr. Lowenston there once or twice. From what I have picked up from conversation, I think he might be one of the partners or owners or something, but I don't know that for sure."

"Oh, he is definitely one of the owners," Graham said. "I wonder why these men were there?" We couldn't finish more of this conversation since it was time for my bus to come. Daisy suddenly noticed a squirrel dashing up the tree in front of us. She wrapped her leash around the two of us pulling us closer together. I almost tripped, but Graham wrapped his right arm around me and pulled Daisy to a stop with his left. We were so close I could almost taste the fresh spice of his cologne. It filtered into my nose, down the back of my throat, and cascaded into my lungs. I stood there allowing myself to feel cleansed and somewhat overwhelmed by the aroma. So wonderful. I had to make myself aware of his voice when he spoke. "Well, maybe another day or time," Graham said, trying to finish our conversation and hold on to Daisy. "Let me know if you discover any more about those people, will you?" He released me slowly, with a lingering squeeze. I willed myself to step away and move to the bus.

"I will let you know if I learn more," I said as I gave him a small reluctant wave and climbed on the bus. "Oh, and Happy New Year. I hope this year brings bigger and brighter things to you and the rest of the family."

"You never know," was his cryptic answer. I turned away and climbed the steps.

Chapter Eleven

The Gala

1939

January 2

Journal, as this new year begins, I wonder what it will bring. I always hope for the unexpected and the magical. Don't know how this will work out. The beginning of the new year was on Sunday. Jenny Mae and Winston had stayed on to celebrate New Year's Eve and Day with their family and relatives. We all visited with friends and went to church, so there weren't any wild and raucous celebrations. I probably wouldn't have gone to any anyway. It was pleasant to rest and to be at home with everyone.

When I went to work on Monday, everything started back on an even keel. It was a bit slow, which we anticipated after the holidays, expecting things to start humming again soon. The humming that I didn't expect was from Mr. Lowenston and the men with him. He came in on Friday with the three dark, brooding men following at his heels. The men struck me as menacing. The one in the lead looked briefly over in my direction. He was square and boxy with a heavy black wool coat draped around his hefty girth. His plaid newsboy cap held long greasy hair sliding out the back and turning up in a slick curl. The other men wore black suits with white ties and fedora hats. I thought they looked like an ominous set of matched monster penguins, and I shivered as I looked at them. They marched toward Mr. Barbee's office. I pretended not to see them but acted as if I was focused on going to Mrs. Florene's apartment to dress for my hostess duties.

When I came back down, I saw Mr. Barbee. He staggered down the hall supporting himself with the walls. Through the dim light, he looked as though his right eye was swollen and his bottom lip split. As he drew nearer, I could see his blackened eye and bleeding lip more clearly with light of the slag lamp in the hallway. I nodded and said, "Hello," and scurried with all the grace I could muster down the steps. I felt a strange chill that had nothing to do with the faint breeze in the open room.

When I finished for the evening and returned to the apartment, I saw Mrs. Florene seated in her parlor. As she turned pages through what looked like letters, she seemed lost in a remembered conversation or memory. "Have you noticed anything strange going on?" I said to her. "I thought I saw Mr. Lowenston earlier with three rough looking men when I came to dress for work. They were headed to Mr. Barbee's office. That was odd enough, but when I came back down, I saw Mr. Barbee in the hall, and he looked like he had been in a fight. His right eye seemed puffy, and his lip was bloody. Scared me a bit."

"Oh, dear girl, I guess you saw him before the show when I was going through a dance routine with one of the girls," she said, laying her letters beside her. "Goodness. Josie, please forget what you saw. I'm sure it was nothing, but it doesn't pay to ask too many questions. Sometimes it's best to keep a blind eye." Now that she put it that way, I wasn't sure I could forget. So strange, maybe it was a simple misunderstanding, but I was more than a little scared.

I had almost forced all this out of my mind until I ran into Jimmy Lee on Saturday. "Can you come up to my room for a minute for a soda or perhaps a cup of tea?" He asked. "I want to go over the business arrangement we talked about earlier." I meant to mention it to Graham that Jimmy Lee wanted to deposit money into my banking account, but he had been so flabbergasted by my new duties, I didn't ask. All I remembered was that Jimmy Lee wanted to deposit $1,000 in my banking account for which he would pay me three percent. Whenever he asked for it, I would withdraw what he needed from his portion. I was to be a 'layoff bank' was the way he put it.

"I think I can come for a bit if you like," I said. Still, in my mind, I was a little uncomfortable being this close to Mr. Barbee's office in case more strange men came along. I would have invited him to my room but didn't want him to get any improper ideas. Hoping Jimmy Lee didn't sense my nervousness, I went to his office. He showed me around his workspace and then guided me to his private quarters in the back. Once I looked over the area with a flickering gaze, I nodded in what I hoped looked like approval, and then shot right back up to his office.

"Well, have a seat," Jimmy said, sensing my discomfort. "I'll get you a Doctor Nut soda I brought back with me from New Orleans." He strolled over to a recessed cabinet and pulled out two elegant crystal glasses. Reaching into an icebox, he pulled out the soda. "Now, are you sure you don't want a martini?" he said with a grin.

"I am perfectly fine with that nut drink since I've never tried it before." I wondered if something with alcohol might keep my hands from shaking but was worried that it would lower my inhibitions. He brought back the glasses and bottle, setting them in front of us on a small clawfoot table. As he poured our drinks, I thought the most interesting thing about it was the label. It showed a picture of a squirrel taking a bite out of a huge nut. After a tentative sip, I found it not displeasing. It tasted like almonds. Not bad, but not great. I slowly sipped it trying my best to be polite.

"Okay," Jimmy Lee said as he leaned forward, his gaze searching my face. "I thought I would like our arrangement to be more like $2,000 rather than $1,000. Would that be all right with you? I'd be happy to give you the cash tonight. You could take it to the bank when you get home. You still have access to your father's account, don't you?"

Since Jimmy Lee had become so insistent on my participation in his banking and money schemes, I realized that I didn't feel nearly the same way about him as I had earlier. It seemed as if he was interested in me only when he needed something. I felt as if he was using me in a manner in which my father would not have approved. I took a big gulp of my drink. Gracious. I had never seen $2,000 in my life. The banker would think I'd robbed somebody if I brought in that kind of cash. I truly didn't know what to think or say. I set my drink down on the table, careful that I didn't spill it. "Yes, I do have access to that account." I truly hoped so. "You know tomorrow is Sunday, and the bank isn't open. Could we wait until one day next week when I could take it straight there?" I felt cold sweat running down my backbone. My fingers and toes were ice cold, and the weather had not one thing to do with it.

"Okay," he said, patting my hand, and then running his fingers down my arm. "Let's talk about this next week. Give it more thought, and we can make whatever arrangements you think would work."
My thought was that I wanted to get my arm out of his reach. What was this all about? A few weeks ago, I would have loved to have him touch me. I realized my feelings had changed. I couldn't allow him to run his fingers over my arms. Now, it felt repulsive. The arrangement I thought would work was talking to Graham. I had to find someone with more answers than I had. Not that I thought Jimmy Lee was a crook or anything. He did seem a little shady, but I wasn't sure who he was. I couldn't find anyone who seemed to know the real Jimmy Lee. Maybe tomorrow being Sunday, I could get hold of Graham and find out what he thought I should do.

I was so glad to get home on Sunday morning. My safety net was still in place, at least here. I wanted to talk to Flossie and Oliver about my dilemma, but I didn't think they would understand. Jenny Mae would, but she seemed far away from me now. Her life in Lexington felt distant, not so much in miles, but in sense of place. She was living in an academic world, and I didn't think she could relate to this sense of sinister intrigue. I worried she might think this was my imagination running wild and would say I'd seen too many movies. Maybe I had.

Oliver and Flossie encouraged me to go with them to church at 6-Mile, but I stayed home pleading weariness and needing to rest. As soon as their truck pulled out, I cranked up the phone. Thank goodness the line wasn't down. Bertha answered immediately. "Josie, is that you? Are you all right?" Her voice was heavy with concern.

"Oh yes, Bertha. I'm fine. I need to speak with Graham if he happens to be around."

"Well, he is just starting out the door, on his way back to Chicago, Detroit, or one of those big cities. Let me see if I can catch him before he gets away." I heard her lay the phone down and run through the hall hollering for him. I suspected he thought I was a royal pain interfering with his family and his job. What was I thinking? After a few minutes, I heard the phone being picked up and a loud breath in my ear.

"Josie, are you alright? Is there something wrong?"

"Oh no, not exactly," I said. "I have some things I need to talk over with you." I felt a bit embarrassed I assumed he would drop everything to take care of things in my life that might be imaginary.

"Well, I'm on my way out of town, but I should be back toward the end of the week. Can I come see you then?" His words sounded clipped with concern.

I noticed my words were a bit shaky, stuttering around in my mouth, "Of course. Could we meet in the tearoom where we had coke floats that day or somewhere else?"

"You don't want me to come by your work?" he said. "I'd hate for you to have to come over to Cincinnati to talk."

"I don't feel like I should be discussing too much at work," I said, hoping he didn't think I was being evasive. "There is a drugstore with a soda fountain on Monmouth Street. Maybe we could meet there."

"Better there than this party line," Graham answered. "But are you scared? Do you feel safe?" His voice rose sharply upward.

"Oh, I'm sure I'm safe. I simply don't want to talk too much about things I might not want others to know about," I said twisting the phone cord between my fingers. It was slick and wet now drenched with worry. "Often, Flossie and Oliver's line is down, and even if it's working, all the neighbors will want to ask them about the man calling on their line."

"Yes, there is always that," he said, giving a huffing sound which I realized was a chuckle. I didn't think I'd ever heard Graham laugh or even come close to it. The last time I went to dinner at the Raisch house, he'd grinned, and now here, a chuckle. He was turning into a person I hardly recognized. "Do keep safe," he said. "Would you rather have me call at Florene's if I get in on a night you are staying there?"

"Mrs. Florene's place would almost be better," I said. "Do you want her number?"

"Oh, I don't have any paper handy to write it on," he said. "I have her number here somewhere."

"Well, have a safe trip, and I look forward to your call," I said.

"You, as well," he answered, "and if you can, write down anything that happens that you might think I would need to know."

"Oh, I will," I said. After our call ended, I wondered why he had Mrs. Florene's number. So many questions these days, and so few answers.

February 6

I returned to work today. For a Monday, things seemed slow, but steady. I wonder if I am making more of the situation here at the Hey Ho than is true. Maybe my imagination is working overtime.

On Wednesday, I brought in Mrs. Florene's rugs. Christmas had long passed, but they were finally done. These rugs weren't intended to be a Valentine's gift. When I was almost at the apartment, I heard Mr. Barbee talking to Mrs. Florene. His voice was sharp and angry. I stood there not knowing whether to stay or run. "You know better than to cross Mr. Lowenston in any way," he said. "Remember, that you are the longest remaining Madame in Newport, so you best mind your P's and Q's."

"I don't suppose you are referring to Pints and Quarts, I dare say?" Mrs. Florene responded, the acid fairly dripping from her tongue. "Young man, you don't know all the things that are going on here. You'd best be aware. Let me tell you another damn thing, you had better not involve my Josie in any of your shady and sordid dealings. I will not have it. Do you understand?" I stopped in my tracks. What was going on? Standing a bit closer to the door, I listened for more. Scrunching my body into a soundless knot, I hoped no one could hear my heart hammering in my chest. Why was Mrs. Florene protecting me and from what?

"Lady," Mr. Barbee replied. "I am simply trying to save you from anguish and possible physical danger. You saw those thugs Mr. Lowenston has running all over the building. You'd best not use your sassy tongue on him or those brutes. Either one of them could take you and smash you like a matchstick."

"Thank you, Frank, I appreciate your concern." Sarcasm stretched each word to its fullest. "Remember my warning about little Josie. I will use any and all connections and allies I have to protect her and my other girls."

"I don't understand why you are so adamant that I am going to involve Josie. I hardly know her, except by sight. Also, I wouldn't call her little," Mr. Barbee said with a huff. "She's easily a head taller than you. I will admit, though, you do notice her in a crowd."

"She is as stately and elegant as a queen," Mrs. Florene said. "Don't you forget that and don't treat her as anything else." My mouth flew right open. I couldn't believe my ears. What was all this I was hearing? I almost burst into tears right then and there, but I didn't have time. I had to get to my sewing station and take Mrs. Florene's rugs with me until I could deliver them to her. I needed to find a pencil and paper to start writing this down. I had so much I needed to tell Graham.

When Graham called on Friday, Mrs. Florene was dressing to go down the street to meet a friend. I had sewn a little jacket for Diamond to wear in the cold, and I had to dress him in it and his little bow. As Florene's heels tapped on the marble floor, I spoke into the phone, "I have so much I need to discuss with you! When can we meet?" I said all this without giving him a chance to speak.

"Well, hello, to you too," he said with a laugh. "Yes, I had a good trip. We ran into a lot of snow and bad weather in Chicago. We were lucky to return safely, which was a blessing. Thanks for asking."

I felt so ashamed and blurted, "Graham, I am so sorry to be so rude, but I really need to talk to you. When would it work out for us to meet?"

"If you come to Newport a bit early tomorrow, perhaps we could get together at the drugstore, have a muffin and cocoa or coffee, and get caught up on our stories," he said.

"I would be so grateful," the warmth that spread through my chest and down to my toes melted me in relief. With a big sigh, I let all the air slide out of my body. Hopefully, I could turn everything over to Graham and let him help me handle this situation, not that I wanted him to solve all my problems for me, but I needed help. After he hung up, I simply sat on the bench by the phone alcove giving my thoughts time to digest.

Graham and I made plans to meet at the drugstore at 3:30. That would give us time to eat, discuss what we needed to discuss, and for me to get over to the Hey Ho by 5:00. It was a cold, blustery day. I had wrapped a full woolen cape around me. An emerald green felt hat and woolen mitts of the same color added color. Feeling warm and toasty on the outside, I was a mushy mess inside. Since he wasn't there yet, I found a table at the side of the soda fountain that was a bit secluded. If we sat here, I thought, we could discuss our business privately. The soda jerk with his white paper hat looked up rubbing his thumb along one acne scarred jaw, but otherwise he ignored me.

When Graham came in, I wondered how he ever did police work. I thought they were supposed to fade into the woodwork and not be noticed. Not Graham. When he swept in, the girl in the five and dime section stared. He strode over to our table. The soda jerk sprang to attention adjusting his cap. Graham casually pulled the scarf from around his neck and put it down in the seat across from me. He asked me what I wanted. I told him even though it was cold and blustery, I craved a hot fudge sundae. He walked to the fountain and ordered for the two of us, bringing back a hot fudge sundae for me and a cup of black coffee for himself. I curled my nose at the coffee. How could he drink that? I truly appreciated the sundae, and I took money from my purse to pay him.

"So," he said, with a flourish of his napkin, waving away the coins I offered, "tell me what is happening that has you so upset?" He leisurely pulled out a packet of Lucky Strikes, took one out, offered me one, like he thought I would take it. Then, with practiced ease lit it with a slim, polished lighter.

I pushed my spoon into my ice cream, swirling the fudge through it aimlessly. Laying my spoon to the side, I told him the long story, no short to it. I told him about Jimmy Lee wanting me to put money into my account from which I would receive a percentage, the fact that Mr. Barbee had called Mrs. Florene a madame, and about the men looking through the building for Mr. Lowenston. Graham listened thoughtfully, as he stirred two lumps of sugar into his coffee.

"All right let's see what we need to do here," he said. "Let me simply say to you that the Hey Ho's owner/partners are under investigation for financial and tax irregularities. We don't know exactly who is responsible, but we're trying to find out. I need you to keep your eyes open, and your mouth shut. If you could see what sort of information you can get without getting into the line of fire, it would be helpful."

"Like a gangster movie?" I asked with a gasp.

He looked at me and shook his head with a smug grin.

"Does that mean that I can take Jimmy Lee's money, and put it into Poppa's bank account? I won't get into any trouble, will I?" I didn't mention the fact that he called me his layoff bank.

"Let me say to you that the bank doesn't have to report that particular sum, and as long as I am informed about it, we could work on that angle. If it seems that you might be liable in any way, we'll get changes made," he said.

"What about Mrs. Florene? Is she going to get hurt? I don't want that to happen."

"Oh, I think she has a few connections who will keep her safe. She has a special friend in New York, Al Segoritti, who was her husband's enfor... good friend," Graham said evasively. "Let me simply say that Al is a man who is feared and loathed by many. When her husband was unexpectedly killed, Mrs. Florene's life and safety became his mission. I can tell you that she and, possibly, others believe that the Lowenstons may have been involved with the death of her husband."

"Did they murder him, maybe?" I was so shocked and maybe a little thrilled. This happened only in the movies. "Is this why you have Mrs. Florene's number? Are you investigating her husband's murder?"

Graham didn't give me a direct answer, "I know you have a million questions, but I believe they will be answered in time. Try to be patient, and I will answer what I can when I can." He knocked the ash off his cigarette into the ashtray at his elbow. He looked up at me raising his eyebrows but offered no further explanation.

"What about Jimmy Lee?" I questioned. "Nobody seems to know much about him, what he's doing, or who he is."

"I would play along with him for the present, but I can tell you this. He is not an entirely trustworthy player in this story," Graham took a long drag from his cigarette gazing into the distance and then back to me. "See if you can get information from and about him, if you like, but do not, and I repeat that, do not, raise his suspicions. I'd say if you need to confide in anyone, either confide in me, or, maybe, Mrs. Florene."

"I'm safe then in speaking to Mrs. Florene?" I was so relieved that I could trust the one person whom I believed in my heart was trustworthy.

"Probably, but don't say too much," Graham said. "Does she talk to you or say much about her dead husband?"

"Constantly. It was a case of true love," I said with a long sigh. I looked down at my watch to see if I was short on time.

"Well, whatever it was, let me remind you of this again. Her husband, Rocco, was a person of considerable influence in New York and here in Newport. I will let you know that while you are under her wing, you should be safe, unless you act foolishly. As I said before, keep your eyes open and your mouth shut."

"I guess I can go along with that," I said.

"Do you have other questions?" he asked. "I think you are a smart, brave girl, but you need to stay calm and keep your wits about you. Now, eat your sundae and quit smushing it into slop." It was none of his business how I ate my sundae, but I tried to eat what I could, the spoon scraping against the bottom of the cup. He continued to drink his coffee and smoke his cigarette. The smooth taste of the vanilla ice cream layered with the warm fudgy chocolate was comforting given all I now needed to do. When we had finished, we stood, he laid two bits on the table as a tip, walked around the table and gave me a gentle hug and a soft smile, "I will try to be available whenever you need me. Of course, I do travel a bit, but if you leave a message with my mother, she will get word to me."

I had the full weekend to mull over what I would have to say and do. I was a bit more confident when speaking with Graham, but after I left him, I felt a disturbing sense of unease as to what to do next. I guessed the best thing was to get with Jimmy Lee to handle the money situation he'd proposed. At least I had the weekend to try out different conversations in my mind to consider how I'd handle myself. By Monday morning, I still didn't feel confident. However, I decided to get in touch with Jimmy Lee and see if there was a morning we could go over this transaction. Again, my thoughts chased all over each other like crazed cats trying to figure out the best way I needed to handle making a deposit in the bank. When I first spoke with Jimmy Lee about this, he assumed I could make a deposit into the account he spoke of as mine. I needed to make sure my father's account was still active, and confirm I was allowed to make deposits. Why didn't I think of asking Graham about this when we talked? It was so hard to think of everything I needed to do. My own earnings, I never put in the bank. They stayed in a sock in my room at Flossie and Oliver's. I took out only the cash I needed when I wanted to use it.

I put on a pair of coveralls and boots to protect against the cold and the icy slush of the frigid January day and told Flossie I was walking down to the bus stop. I told her I needed to go into town to take care of some business, but I shouldn't be gone long. The path seemed longer than normal with slick spots and holes left by melting and refreezing snow. When I finally got to the bank and went in, the heat from the steam radiators was stifling. The coveralls and boots were way too warm inside. The teller at the first window looked at me with a condescending smile, "Well, hello, young lady, and what can I do for you?" His voice and words slid out snake slick as he drummed his fingers on the counter.

"I am checking to see if I can make a deposit into an account," I announced.

"Well, you know that women don't have accounts here," he said. I wish he would choke on his muttonchop sideburns, with the mustache part coming down over his top lip. Didn't he know they were way out of style? Ugly!

"My father was Fred Kassemier, and I believe his account is still active," I said with what I thought was a firm authoritative voice. "Please look up the last activity, since I plan to make a deposit in the next week or two."

"Will you have Graham Raisch or Oliver Aldrich sign for you?" he asked.

"I didn't think with a cash deposit that I would need anyone's signature," I said, trying to be an echo of Mrs. Florene in my mind. How would she have handled this type of situation, I wondered?

"I suppose not." For the first time, he seemed at a loss for words. In my own mind, I sounded tough. What a surprise. "Yes," he said as he shuffled through his papers, "that account is still active, and I do believe that you can make a cash deposit."

"Very well," I said. "It will be a sizable cash payment, and I will come in shortly."

His eyes widened. I gave him a smile and a sideways glance that a queen might bestow on one of her subjects. I sashayed out the door as much as I could wearing coveralls and rubber boots.

"Oh, by the way," he called out as I walked away, "You will need a man's signature to withdraw any money." I turned and acknowledged him with a smile and a slow wave of my fingers.

In the afternoon, I hurried up the steps to Mrs. Florene's to take off my outerwear and prepare for work. I needed to check on the girls and see who needed what to be sown. Stopping off at the 2nd floor, I went to Jimmy Lee's office to leave a message in the drop box beside the door. It requested that he get with me about the business matter we had discussed to sort out details. The lid of the drop box closed with a metallic clang, and I gave a satisfied nod.

Surprisingly, I didn't hear from him that evening or the next. As I worked diligently on a torn piece of lace on a skirt hem, I wondered about his on again off again insistence. He made it seem so urgent earlier, and now no word. At least I was somewhat prepared as to the action I was going to take. I attacked the skirt hem vigorously until I stuck a needle into my finger. To protect the material, I stuck my finger in my mouth to get rid of the blood. I hated the metallic taste, but it made me aware I had best keep my eyes on business.

Jimmy Lee didn't contact me until Thursday. I had just settled into my sewing alcove, next to the dressing room behind the stage, when he tapped on the slightly ajar door. "Jimmy Lee, you shouldn't be in here," I said, nervous he might see the girls in various states of undress.

"Oh, they're used to me," he dismissed. "I'm in and out a lot around here." It didn't seem exactly proper for him to be here, no matter what his job was. I thought I would mention it to Mrs. Florene. Maybe this was a city way that I didn't know much about, but it seemed too familiar. Especially, when he walked out and patted Lila on the rump. He treated her like she was a cow. She turned and smacked him a good one, but I still didn't think it was proper. Jimmy Lee acted as if it was all in fun, but I saw fury as she scalded him with her eyes. She didn't say a word, but I knew she felt disrespected.

"Now," Jimmy Lee said, as though we were simply finishing up a conversation we started minutes ago. "It seems as if we will be able to carry on with our business arrangement?" He adjusted the crease in his slacks as he settled into the other chair in my sewing area. Normally, one of the girls would perch there as she spread out the dress she wanted mended or adjusted.

"Yes, I spoke with the banker earlier this week, and he seemed to think we could make this happen." I didn't mention that I would have to have a man's signature to withdraw the money. I wondered if Jimmy Lee's signature would work. Of course, if Graham and Oliver's names were listed on the account, that might not be able to happen. That was a problem for another time.

"Okay, you sweet thing," he said. I cringed as he said that. Just who did he think he was speaking to?

I looked at him sharply, "I'm Miss Josie to you, Jimmy Lee." He thought I was joking but I wasn't.

"We'll take care of this tomorrow when you come in for your hostess job," he replied, taking a small Cuban cigar out of a gold case and lighting it with flair with his matching lighter. I simply said that was fine and please not smoke in here because it left an odor in the girls' clothes. "Oh, Missy," he said with a tone I didn't like even one little bit. "They are used to more than odors in their clothes."

The next day, Friday, I came in a bit early to try and catch Mrs. Florene before I started working. As I moved through the dining area, I saw Jimmy Lee putting the hostess book back where it belonged. Now that I was more familiar with how work was done here, I wondered why on earth he needed the hostess book. It was not the first time I'd seen him do this. It did have the names of the customers for the evening. Maybe he needed to know how many people were expected, or if there were diners he needed to pay more attention to. I chalked that up to one more question I needed answered. Another note for Graham, I thought.

When I reached Mrs. Florene's apartment, I put away the clothes I brought with me to wear that night and set out my mirror and comb on the dresser with the lovely three-way mirror. I was thinking about the questions I needed to ask and how I needed to ask them. Mrs. Florene tapped on my door and came in with powder and brush and a Limoges perfume atomizer. "Now, young lady, you have an important grown-up job. You will need to look your best and use the best scent. I know you aren't exactly trying to attract a beau here, but you want to project the image of importance that you deserve. Correct?" she said, handing me the powder and brush.

"Yes, I do. I'm not exactly sure how to go about all that, though."

"Well, let me turn you into the elegant young lady that your mother would have, had she had the opportunity." My Momma wanted me to know and do lots of things, but hair and makeup weren't exactly on her list of essentials. Mrs. Florene, being a New York girl, had different city ideas than Momma.

As Mrs. Florene bustled behind me, combing and pinning my hair in different ways, brushing powder on my face and adding lip and cheek color, I watched the transformation in the mirror. Who was this person? I thought I would look like a clown, but I didn't. I wanted to ask questions, but I didn't have a chance to open my mouth while Mrs. Florene was performing her wizardry. I closed my eyes and for one moment of magic imagined that it was my Momma combing my hair. "Florene," I said, mumbling with my eyes half closed. "Most of the hair styles I see in magazines and in store windows are short styles with bangs."

"Josie, no short hair for you," she said to me. "I think that your hair is long and lovely. A real dark-haired beauty you are, and I love the long waves. Maybe a center part would show your face to a better advantage." She continued, knowing how I loved movies and movie stars said, "think of Vivien Leigh. Think of how her lovely hair gives her the very essence of sophistication. I know that you are apt to pull your hair back in a loose ponytail but let's try for an air of elegance."

When she finished, she dusted me off and told me I could put on the dress that I would wear for the evening. I looked in the mirrors and admired Florene's handiwork. The first thing to come to my mind, was this really me? I don't think I had ever looked this way in my life, but I decided I liked it. However, I needed to get my mind back to those questions I wanted answered. "Florene, I don't quite understand who Jimmy Lee is and exactly what he does. I know he keeps the books here, but he seems to be in a lot of different places. I don't know who all these men are who are looking around either. Can you tell me anything about all that?"

"Child," she said, patting my shoulder softly. "Don't ask a lot of questions, at least not now. There may be some business irregularities happening, but they don't involve you. I'm certain all this will be straightened out fairly soon. Most likely, the less you know, the better. If there is anything I think you need to know, I will tell you. My first priority is to keep you safe. Just trust me, and all should be well." I looked at her not knowing exactly what to say or do. "Jimmy Lee has his fingers in a lot of pies at the moment," Mrs. Florene said. "Sooner or later, we'll know if the fruits of those pies are sweet or tainted."

"I will try to do that," I said. Looking back at this conversation, I think she believed tainted, but didn't want to scare me. Mrs. Florene just gave me the sweetest smile and a hug. I felt warm and safe like nothing could endanger me if she was there.

Down at the restaurant, there was already a customer waiting to be seated. It was Phil DeMarco from Detroit. He had been here several times during the fall and winter, not consistently, just now and then. I knew he liked large medium-well done steaks, great roasted potatoes with lots of butter, and expensive liquor. He had dark, dark hair, and lots of it, large fleshy hands with black hairs sprouting all over, and the heartiest chuckle I had ever heard. When he laughed, his large white teeth gleamed in his swarthy face.

Tonight, he wasn't laughing. In fact, he looked rather grim. Had I kept him waiting? I was a bit nervous, and I hoped my voice didn't shake, "Mr. DeMarco, have you been waiting long?"

"Oh no, dear," he said with a tiny smile breaking through. "I simply have to have a conversation with one of your management members."

"Oh," I said. "Let me take you to Mr. Barbee on the second floor in the business section. He may have already left for the evening. I think he and his wife had a dinner to attend, but I can go up and check."

"Fine, you can do that, but I will go with you. I know Frank Barbee, and I need to get my business with him taken care of," he said, chopping his words abruptly. He didn't sound at all happy. Scurrying up the stairs with Mr. DeMarco at my heels, I didn't know what to say, so I said nothing. I did worry that maybe we could have taken the elevator, but since it was so slow, I thought it would be best to go up the stairs. Also, I knew that Mr. Barbee normally came down the steps, and we might very well miss him if he hadn't already gone.

As we started down the hall of the 2nd floor, Mr. Barbee was just coming out the door turning to lock up with his key. He seemed surprised and not altogether happy when he turned to see Mr. DeMarco, but he kept a polite insincere politician's smile on his face. He rubbed his hands together and fiddled with his jade cufflinks. "Well, Phil, it's a nice surprise to see you," Mr. Barbee said as he reached out to shake Mr. DeMarco's hand. "Is there anything I can help you with?"

"What I need Frank is an answer to why someone is calling my office and asking for additional funds to cover an overdraft on my account here," Mr. DeMarco said, waving off the extended hand. "I also happen to know my account here is fully paid, and I do not understand why these questions are being asked."

Mr. Barbee recoiled with a look of total shock on his face, "someone from here? At the Hey Ho?"
I couldn't stay and listen to the rest of the exchange between the two men. I had to get down to my hostess duties. Just as the conversation was getting interesting, I had to leave. So much for keeping my ears open and my mouth shut. It seemed that my ears weren't getting enough information to do me much good. Putting aside my double agent duties, I returned to the hostess desk. Later, I needed to meet with Jimmy Lee, so he could give me money to deposit into my account. How confusing and exhausting.

The evening went smoothly after this. I didn't see Mr. DeMarco, so I guess he didn't come down for dinner after all. I couldn't help but wonder about the outcome of his conversation with Mr. Barbee. By the end of the evening, I was weary. I don't know if it was the work or the worry that made me so, but all I could do was think about meeting Jimmy Lee and collecting his deposit. I wanted to meet with Graham again to discuss my worries and anxieties. What I really wanted was to hand the whole situation over to him and let him solve the problems.

Jimmy Lee suggested he meet me at Mrs. Florene's, but she was still out with friends. It wasn't proper for a single man to come to a woman's apartment or at least I didn't think so. I told him I would drop by his place to pick up the money. When I came in, naturally he was looking as fresh and energetic as a new day. I felt like I had been chewed up and spit out. Of course, he didn't act as if he thought that was how I looked. He put his arm around me and tried to lead me into the back of his office, the home of the Murphy bed. I told him I needed to get back up to Mrs. Florene's because she had left Diamond in the apartment, and I thought he needed to go out. When he persisted, I said I didn't think Diamond could wait until Mrs. Florene returned.

He gave me a sulky look and handed me a bag with cash inside. I took it and asked if he needed a receipt. He said that the bag contained $2,000, and that I could give him the receipt from the bank. I gasped to myself, knowing I had never seen this much money before in my life let alone held it. "I will deposit this tomorrow morning," I told him, backing my way to the door.

Sometimes, I simply stayed all weekend at Mrs. Florene's. Of course, since Mrs. Florene knew so many people and had such an active social life there were times it was downright lonely here. I could catch the early bus and go home the next morning. That would give me time to go to the bank before they closed. I was truly exhausted, but still had to take Diamond out. He had been quite patient waiting by himself in the apartment. When I went back to Mrs. Florene's, I walked up the stairs since it was only one floor up. I wanted to take Diamond back down in the beautiful elevator since it was so elegant, and I had few chances to use it. But I knew the dog was very nervous in the elevator. The clanging of the gears and the opening of the door caused him to shake and shiver the whole time.

I opened the door to the apartment and Diamond was excited to see me. He twirled and bounced in excitement while I put on his collar and leash, even though I knew I would probably be carrying him down the steps. He would most likely be fine when I walked him outside and onto the green grassy area beside the building. As I passed the landing on the 2nd floor, I heard Mr. Barbee and Jimmy Lee's voices. They seemed low, but angry. I held onto Diamond and ducked back into the alcove by the stairwell. That way, I would remain out of sight but still be able to catch some of the conversation. After all, wasn't I supposed to keep my ears open, and mouth shut?

"Phil DeMarco was here a bit ago," I heard Mr. Barbee say in a tight, strained voice. "He is extremely upset that someone from here is calling him at his workplace, asking for funds to cover a shortfall with his casino account. I told him I had no idea how and why this was happening. Do you know anything about these calls?" I couldn't exactly understand Jimmy Lee's answer, but it sounded like a placating denial of some sort. "We'll have to set aside a time one day next week. We need to go over the receipts and revenue. It's important to get to the bottom of this," Mr. Barbee's voice became louder and a bit more strident. "I know Mr. Lowenston thinks our profits are down, he and his men are investigating reasons why. He seems to believe I've been hiding assets. It seems that the receipts are there, but the profits aren't. Some of the cash is not showing up at the end of the night." Jimmy Lee mumbled something in return that sounded as if he agreed and was also befuddled. "He certainly doesn't want us to be late in paying taxes," Mr. Barbee continued his voice raw and insistent. "That would be a red flag to the Treasury department. They keep close eyes on what the restaurants and casinos bring in. If we aren't at the same level as we have been in years gone by, and if we are way out of line with our neighbors, something is going to smell bad."

What was going on, I thought to myself? I realized I was squeezing Diamond more than I should, when he gave a little umph. I didn't want him to bark and give me away. Loosening my grip, I rubbed him under his chin. It was hard to understand much of this, but I didn't imagine it would lead to anything good. I tried to remember what it was that Graham had said, something to the effect that the Hey Ho was under investigation. I wonder how he would have known that, and who was trying to find out what? What do they tell you about eavesdroppers hearing no good? Now, I really had to hurry to get poor little Diamond outside before there was an accident. I didn't want to take responsibility for a dribble of something down the front of my dress I truly didn't want.

Once I stepped out the door, I realized the meaning of March coming in like a lion. It wasn't quite March, but that wind was sure cold. Maybe it could have been my thoughts and feelings. It was a struggle to keep my coat wrapped around me with Diamond trapped in my arms. I knew I needed to clear my thoughts and decide what it was I must get worked out for tomorrow. I would take the bus home early in the morning, help Flossie with a few chores, then go to the bank and deposit the cash. I thought I best count it first.

When I got to Flossie and Oliver's, it seemed like spring. Crazy. Yesterday morning, it was twelve above zero, now this morning, spring-like warmth. I helped Flossie bake a cake and prepare pie filling before I went to the bank. It was hard for me to imagine how heavy a bag of $2000 would feel. I wondered where it came from. I wasn't told, but I didn't feel it was my place to ask. I took out $60, my three percent. I wasn't about to ask some man to take out money that was rightfully mine. At the bank, I spoke with the same teller whom I had spoken with before. Those muttonchop sideburns were marching in order as he counted out the $1940.00 from my bag. Then, he gave me a fawning smile and asked if he could help me further.

"Yes, I said. "I would like to have a receipt."

"Well, you know," he said, "a deposit of this quantity has to be counted by a second person, and you may be here for quite a while until they count it."

"I'm sorry," I said. "I don't have the time to sit and wait." I tried to mimic Mrs. Florene with a bit of an imperious overtone in my voice.

"Well," he said. "I will give you a receipt, but if there is a shortfall, it will come back on you, you know that." His voice took on his former high-handed tone. I thought that the little worm was showing his true colors. "And please remember, Sweetie," he said shoving the receipt at me, "you have to have a man's signature to remove any money." Sure, I thought to myself. That was a problem Jimmy Lee would have to work out.

Later, at the Hey Ho, I took the elevator up to Mrs. Florene's. I didn't want to encounter any more shenanigans in the hallway if I could help it. For a moment I considered making my own receipt on Mrs. Florene's receipt booklet to show the full $2,000, but decided I couldn't do that. To be a better person, I would give Jimmy Lee the bank teller's receipt and tell him I had already withdrawn my share.

After I had put away my things, talked to Mrs. Florence, and given her part of the cake I baked, I went on down to my hostess station. With the receipt tucked into my pocket, I hoped I would see Jimmy Lee somewhere in the restaurant or around the next room where they played cards. Lo and behold, there he was at my station, his back turned toward me, copying something from the hostess book onto a notepad. Now, why was that?

"Jimmy Lee," I spoke rather loudly, making him jump and whirl around to face me.

"Goodness, Josie," he said. "You scared me out of a year's growth, at least."

"Yes," I said, pleased as punch that I had caught him unaware. "I wanted to give you the receipt from the bank," I pulled the receipt from my pocket. "You will notice that I have already taken my three percent from the total, that way you wouldn't have to withdraw that as well."

Jimmy Lee looked at me with a strange speculative look and with a chill in his voice responded, "thank you for letting me know that. I'll assume I have the correct remaining balance."

"Do you find anything of interest in my hostess book?" I said, taking one side of the booklet and pulling it around so I could read its contents more closely. "Is there anything amiss here?"

"Oh, no," he answered, almost ripping the booklet out of my hands. "I simply wanted to get an idea of how many people would be here tonight and who might be coming. I needed to make certain that we had enough money for the Blackjack table and so forth." I wondered if I really believed him. I decided I didn't.

December 1

Journal, I am so excited. When I got to work this evening, I found the Hey Ho was planning a big New Year's Eve event. Now, since New Year's Eve this year is on Sunday, and there should be no liquor sales on Sundays, well ordinarily not, this is to be a super Gala, by invitation only. Mrs. Florene will be in charge of designing the invitations, and Lila and I will help her. We will have feasting, dancing, fireworks, outside, of course, and revelry of all kinds. I guess they don't remember the admonition in Exodus: 'Remember the Sabbath Day to keep it Holy.'

Since things had settled into an uneventful rhythm during the summer and fall, I hoped that this Gala would make things more interesting. I was ready for a little excitement and thought this might be the beginning of an entertaining adventure. I hoped to learn from Mrs. Florene about the materials used in the tablecloths, the outfits the girls would showcase in their Broadway-style extravaganza, the types of foods served, and the liquors selected to go with them. Another learning experience for me, that was for certain. Since it was a Thursday at the beginning of the month, I thought we would have plenty of time, but Mrs. Florene told me we barely had moments to spare so we spent most of the time in her apartment, gathering materials, sending invitations, and making necessary plans for the big night.

One upside was that I could invite Jenny Mae and Winston. They would be home for the holidays, and I would certainly hate to miss them. Of course, I would miss all the other friends and neighbors, but at least I could go back after the Gala and see them. If I didn't see Jenny Mae and Winston during the holidays, it would probably be quite a while.

The days seemed to fly by. I don't think I have ever worked so hard. I didn't know if it was day or night. I stitched, sewed, cut, and basted endlessly. Mrs. Florene was sweet as she could be, but a tough taskmistress. She had lists that seemed to sprout other lists. Never ending. I finally had one weekend off when I planned to meet with Bertha and Helga for a day of shopping in Cincinnati. Mrs. Florene gave me a list of things she needed, but it wasn't long. I would still have time to visit my friends and buy a nice outfit for the Gala which was of major importance to most of us at the Hey Ho. I also didn't want to forget Christmas. It was important for me to buy gifts for my friends. I wanted to see delight and happiness on their faces.

We finally had a Saturday to all go shopping. I had my duties in the evening, so we planned to meet early. We met in front of Shillito's department store and spent time looking at the elves in the windows. Helga and I were enthralled by the adorable Christmas scenes and the mechanical workers in Santa's workshop. Our arms threaded around each other, we grinned and giggled as the elves toiled at their tasks. Bertha laughed and smiled along with us until she put a hand on each of our arms, shaking her head, "Girls, we'll be all day and miss our shopping if you two don't quit lollygagging around these elves. Let's say we split up for our shopping and meet back here in about an hour."

It took me a while to decide what to get, but I finally settled on lovely, gift-wrapped boxes of candies for my two friends. It didn't take me long to find the items on Mrs. Florene's list. I found most in the notion's department just steps away from the candies. Since Graham had taken the time to tend to my financial needs during the year, as well as acting as a sounding board for my questions, I needed to get him something. The men's accessories department offered options like men's key rings. A lovely copper key ring with a soft leather handle caught my eye immediately. Visualizing it held gently in his hand, I picked it up and paid with a wistful grin, imagining how pleased he might be.

In the women's department, a bias-fitted calf-length garnet red dress with puffy long sleeves stood out. It had adorable buttons on the sleeves and the front. It fit me like a second skin, but only in certain places. In a stack of sale items, I found a beautiful silk slip to wear under it. Mrs. Florene had promised to lend me a mink stole in case there was a chill in the air. I felt like I would be a woman of fashion at this event, a star in this show.

When we got to Helga and Bertha's apartment, the women were all ears wanting to know about the Gala, who would be there, what sorts of foods and beverages would be served, and what entertainment would be offered. I spent a few minutes loving on Daisy before we discussed the whole affair from top to bottom. Talking about it excited me all over again. When I left, they gave me a basket full of baked goods covered with a handmade cloth over the top. The smells made me so hungry I could have plunked myself on a park bench and eaten all the sweet rolls and cookies, but I needed to share them with Mrs. Florene. She definitely had a sweet tooth, and I knew how much she would enjoy them.

I had just let myself into the apartment when the phone rang. Mrs. Florene talked to the caller for a bit and then turned to stop me as I was going back to my room. "Dear, don't go. This call is for you," she extended the receiver toward me.

"Who is it? Do you know?" I couldn't think who would be calling me on Mrs. Florene's line.

"It's Mr. Graham Raisch. He says he needs to speak with you if you are available."

"Of course," I said, taking the receiver from her hand. "Graham?" I wondered why he was calling me on Mrs. Florene's line.

"Yes, it is I," he said with a chuckle in his voice. "I need to find time to talk to you, and not on the phone. It must be soon. I need you to do a favor for me."

"Yes, certainly," I said. "When and where would you like to meet?"

"There is a large church down the street from you," he said. "It has a protected courtyard in front, and we could meet there if the weather is nice."

"Now, Graham, you know it is in the middle of December, and it isn't likely that it will be all that warm or inviting outdoors," I said, trying to come up with an alternative plan. "Mrs. Florene has a ring of keys to everything. Since the Hey Ho isn't open on Sundays, and neither is the drugstore, you could come here to the back entrance just off the alley to the restaurant kitchen. No one will know you are there. I can use her keys to unlock the doors and have you come in the back and up to her apartment." I thought this was a reasonable choice.

"Will she be there?" Graham asked. He sounded a bit concerned and confused.

"Probably not," I said. "I think she might be gone to church, since she takes some of the girls to services on Sunday mornings. She usually leaves her key ring here and only takes the one to open the front door. She's afraid the keys will clatter and clang too much in church. I can pick them up after she leaves."

"Aren't you worried about protecting your virtue?" he said with a hint of levity in his voice.

"I don't have a thing in this world to worry about with you," I said with a grin.

"Very good," Graham smiled. "Let's plan on about 10:00, would that suit?"

"I will see you then, keys in hand," I said, shaking imaginary keys.

Sunday morning came earlier than I was ready for. I don't know why. Since I was a farm girl, I was early to wake up and go.

Now, I had a tougher time. On the farm, I never stayed up late. Of course, I never had to take a dog out on a leash late at night, down three flights of stairs and then back up again either. Diamond had to take his time picking the choice spot. To be honest, I also had to take in what I looked like. Did I do this often? Was I always this particular about my appearance in the mornings? Surely Graham coming had nothing to do with it. Still, I thought I would practice with the powder and lip color. It would be good to have the opportunity to practice before I had to look good for the Gala. I was tingling with curiosity about what favor Graham needed from me.

A few minutes later, I felt I looked acceptable with time to spare. I decided to look around to see if I had something to serve. All I had was the basket of baked goods from his mother's house the day before. I could always boil some water for tea. I thought I could manage to put tea into one of those little holders and put it in the pot to steep. Other than that, I knew next to nothing about making tea. I tried to remember some of the details from Mrs. Florene's tea, but none would come to mind. There was a honey pot if he liked it sweet. I was getting all twitchy and worked up. Mrs. Florene would be back with the girls before I could even talk to Graham if I continued to flutter over all these details. I tried to compose myself, seem competent and assured, when promptly at 10:00, I heard a tap on the door. Graham stepped in from the alleyway, removing his gloves and overcoat as he came in the door.

"I can't stay but just a bit," he said. "Let's find a place to sit in the back of the kitchen."

"You don't want to come up to Mrs. Florene's place where we can be comfortable?" I asked, kicking myself silently for all that worry about tea.

"I'm not sure I'll have time today," he leaned against the counter while I found a stool. I felt a flutter in my tummy. Was it hunger? Fear? Maybe something else? "I can't give you a lot of details now, but I need to ask something of you," Graham said. "You know about the Gala?"

"Do I know about the Gala?" My eyes widened. "It's all we've talked about and prepared for over the last two weeks."

"My men and I are planning to raid the Hey Ho at the stroke of midnight," Graham said. "We understand from Florene the plan is that when the clock in the foyer strikes midnight, champagne bottles will pop, the band will play, and fireworks will rocket outside the front door. When the outside doors open, we will launch our raid. Mr. Lowenston and his men will be there, so they won't be hard to catch. The wild card is Jimmy Lee." I put both hands to my chest in alarm or excitement, I didn't know which, but emotions were slamming me on all sides. "What I want you to do is to devise a plan to entice Jimmy Lee into your bedroom. This will put him on the 3rd floor, away from the main action. We'll send someone to overtake him there. Whatever scheme you come up with, it needs to be kept under wraps. This plan cannot afford a single slipup."

Graham couldn't look me in the eye as he said this. I was totally flabbergasted. I couldn't think of what to say or how to answer him. All I could come up with was, "let me think about it. I just don't know."

"Josie, you don't have time to think. Remember, this is going down in about two weeks. I have faith in you. You can do this," he held me by both arms and looked into my eyes with warmth and affection, but also determination. The faint sounds of the girls laughing and talking drifted toward us at the front entrance. I knew I had to get Graham out the door and Mrs. Florene's keys back in their place. "I'll call you later today, Josie," Graham said folding me in his arms for a quick squeeze. "We can do this."

Shutting the door quickly behind him, I raced up the stairs to replace the keys. I was breathing so hard my chest ached. I was beginning to think I wasn't built for a life of intrigue. I knew I needed to talk to Jenny Mae. She was always the one with great ideas. She could tell me what I needed to do about enticing Jimmy Lee without it going too far. Graham seemed to be giving me credit for being able to do more than I could. I needed to see if Jenny Mae could meet the next weekend. We needed a plan. I knew she had been sent an invitation to the Gala. I would use that as an excuse to see what sort of plan we could devise, and then sort it out later with Graham. That man had a way of getting me into all sorts of situations. Was I the perfect spy or the perfect fool who seemed to fall for his schemes?

Near supper time, I managed to call her. I knew she would be at home in the evening helping Winston prepare for his classes. She would be studying for her own final exam as well. Jenny Mae had made the decision to be a news writer. I was so proud of her. She wasn't surprised when I called. She was stirring a pot of tomato soup made from tomatoes she and Flossie had canned, along with making grilled cheese sandwiches. I wish I could have been there to eat with her instead of simply on the phone. I told her I suspected that Jimmy Lee was taking advantage of Mrs. Florene. I wanted to use my feminine wiles to entrap him into revealing his secrets without endangering my virtue, and I needed her help to do this.

"Oh ring-a-ding-ding, how exciting" Jenny Mae burst out. "A real movie heroine spinning your web of intrigue. I'll ask Winston to help too." She agreed to come home on Saturday, so we could come up with a plan. I could feel her sense of mischievousness vibrating through the telephone wires. Thank goodness, I had someone to unburden myself, as well as someone with a good brain to help come up with a solution. Of course, I couldn't tell her everything. I didn't want to burden her or put her in danger, but I wanted her help.

I didn't think that Graham would call that evening, but he did. I was glad to have the chance to tell him I was making a plan with Jenny Mae without giving away important information. He sounded pleased, his voice slow and relaxed, but not particularly surprised. It gave me a jolt of satisfaction that he had faith in my ability to work this out.

When I met with Jenny Mae and Winston, we talked about a way to lure Jimmy Lee to my bedroom in Mrs. Florene's apartment while making sure his romantic plans went nowhere. We decided I would have to flirt with Jimmy Lee over the next two weeks to make him receptive to my wiles. When it got down to the basics as to how to handle the party, things seemed pretty easy. He and I would have cocktails, dinner, and dancing. After this, it seemed more complex. Jenny Mae and I planned that around 10:30, I would lure him upstairs with the promise of a drink. I would use my well-known clumsiness to fake a fall and a broken heel. Promising to go ahead to replace my shoes, I knew that, with a wink and a nod, this would give me time to set up our drinks. I couldn't figure out the details of exactly what I could do after that. How would I hold him in my bedroom without giving in to his amorous advances? Jenny Mae and I thought that I could sew up this situation in a web of my own design, maybe in the coverlet or snare him in another way.

Winston came up with the final blow in my attack. He had a friend in Pharmacy College who had heard of the Mickey Finns that they had served in Chicago. A Mickey Finn had a draft of chloral hydrate in it which would put him fast asleep, at least for a short time. That would give me time to ensure that Jimmy Lee stayed in place until Graham arrived. Thinking that would be perfect, but not entirely certain how the plan would progress, I was determined to relax and let our strategy and timing unfold in its own way. No matter what happened in the next few days, I was determined to be charming and alluring to Jimmy Lee, knowing in my heart I was the spider in this web of intrigue. I hoped to lure him into my trap tangling him irretrievably without endangering me and mine. Made me feel kind of daring and captivating.

During the next few days as the plans for the Gala became more detailed, I had to spend most of my time at the Hey Ho. I hated that I wasn't able to get back home. I knew, however, there were many things that needed attention, and help was in short supply. As I bustled to and fro, I saw Mr. Lowenston and his men again and again. I didn't have time to pay a lot of attention to them other than note they spent more time on the 2nd floor. They were around at the same time Jimmy Lee was, and because he was now my main focus of attention, I noticed them more. I heard angry voices coming down the hall a time or two, but mostly when Mr. Barbee was in his office. To be honest, the raised voices frightened me, so I resorted to leaving messages in Jimmy Lee's mail slot. One unseasonably warm day, I left a note asking Jimmy Lee if he could take me for a ride in his beautiful car. I said I needed to get away from the pressures of the Gala preparations. This was a favor I could never have asked him in person.

Shockingly, later the same day he found me in the dining room cutting out decorations for the red tablecloths we were making. He asked if I still wanted to take that ride. "Of course, I do." My voice was a little shaky, but I didn't want to seem as though I wasn't truly sincere. "I have to finish this work that I have here," I said, lifting one of the decorations hoping it would camouflage the shaking of my fingers.

"Give me about thirty minutes to complete some accounts I'm working on, and then I'll meet you here," he said, giving me a conspiratorial wink.

"Of course," I said with a smile that spread to my lips but didn't make it up to my eyes. I wondered if these were accounts he was truly working on or simply altering. Chastising myself for not being kind, I reminded myself Jimmy Lee needed to believe he was the love of my life. Regardless, all I could picture in my mind's eye was Graham.

Thinking of Graham made me think I needed take a little extra something to Bertha and Helga. I had given them the candies on the day we went shopping but wanted to give them a bit more. Packing two parcels of party favors, and one of the red tablecloths with napkins we were using for the Gala would make fine presents. I doubted if I would give party favors to Graham, but I still had the keychain I bought for him on our shopping trip. The more I thought about it, I decided, no extra gift for him. It would appear I was pursuing him, so the keychain would be enough. Helping with his scheme would be gift enough. My gifting plans in place, my thoughts returned to my ride with Jimmy Lee.

I put away the decorations and my scissors, then went upstairs to put on outdoor boots and a warmer jacket. I also needed a hat with ties to keep my hair from blowing away. Not a romantic vision of me with my hair flopping in my face. Jimmy Lee met me in the front foyer. His lovely Pontiac was waiting at the door. The red was so glorious, it simply gleamed. The black fenders and running board made such a contrast. Honestly, I was now more smitten with the car than the man, and I was not normally a car enthusiast. He was wearing his normal long-sleeved shirt, but he had a sweater thrown over his shoulders and a fedora hat perched on top of his head. I wondered how he could keep the hat from blowing away, but that was his worry and not mine.

He gallantly helped me into the car, and we drove all around town, as he pointed out all the sights of interest. We drove through Cincinnati, and we were able to see several sights along the river. I was surprised that so much flood damage from '37 was still in view. I would have thought after two years that much of it would have been erased, but still the broken stubs of trees and the crushed barns and sheds were very much in view. They bore quiet evidence of the pain and suffering that had been endured by so many.

Pulling my concentration away from this sad scene to the matters at hand, I leaned into Jimmy Lee a bit. I pointed out features of the car and the interior and asked him to explain what the dials and knobs were for. Placing his hand over mine, he showed me how to shift the gears. I knew how to shift gears and use the clutch of our old truck, but still acted dumb and innocent letting his long fingers guide mine. Although I felt a big urge to pull away, I didn't. I looked at him with a coy glance and pulled my hair back over my shoulder flirtatiously as I nodded with what I hoped was encouragement. He leaned toward me with a lewd smile. I kept my feelings of nausea barely contained. At last, the tour was over, and we were back at the Hey Ho.

He came around to open my door. With the excuse that I needed to get more done on decorations, I gave him a quick kiss on the cheek, pulled off my silly hat, and ran inside. I needed to change my shoes and leave my hat and gloves in the apartment. Thankfully, I only had to work with dancers tonight and not hostess duties, so I could be comfortable in the shirtwaist dress I wore. When I reached the 2nd floor landing, I heard more loud talk from Mr. Barbee's office. Although I couldn't identify the voices, I assumed they were Mr. Barbee and some of Mr. Lowenston's men. In my hurry, I thought no more of it as I had work to do but made a mental note to tell Graham later. I didn't think Jimmy Lee was involved in the argument, since he hadn't had enough time to get back from parking his car.

During the evening, as I worked in my sewing cubicle, Jimmy Lee came by several times each time giving me a lascivious grin. He didn't stay around too long, though, and I managed to look even busier than I needed to be. As I worked, I thought since tomorrow was going to be a quieter day, and since I had so much of the Gala work done, I would go see Helga and Bertha to give them their baskets of favors. If Graham happened to be around, I could let him know that Winston, Jenny Mae, and I had a plan in place. I hoped Helga wouldn't feel insulted that she and her fellow hadn't been invited to the Gala. I needed to make it clear to her that I wasn't in charge of the guest list.

I called Bertha between floor shows to make sure it was all right to come in the morning with small party gifts for them. I assured them that it wasn't much. Bertha seemed more than delighted to hear from me. "Oh Josie," she said. "I am so happy to hear from you. We hadn't heard from you in it seems like forever. We have heard that you are having to prepare for a big party, but we didn't know anything more than that." I assumed they had heard about the party from Graham, but I didn't know how or what he had told them. I didn't know if I hoped he would or wouldn't be there. Part of me said yes, and the other, no.

The next morning when I started off for the bus to Cincinnati, I paused at the 2nd floor and looked down the hall at the business office area. There were no lights on in Mr. Barbee's office. He was usually in by this time, but I shrugged it off and went on my way. Walking to the bus stop, I felt the full force of the December day. It was strange that yesterday had been so mild and balmy, and today was pure winter. I was so glad I didn't go for a ride in that convertible today. A wintry mix of frozen rain and snow began to pelt down the back of my hat and dripped on to my coat collar. I was super glad when the bus came.

It was heaven to step into the warmth of the Raisch apartment after the chill of outside. They had already put up a few decorations for Christmas, but the main thing I smelled as I walked in was gingerbread. Oh, the lovely gingerbread. Their gift to me was a basket of gingerbread cookies and jam cake. What a lovely Christmas surprise. I couldn't wait to get back to share this with Mrs. Florene. She would love it with her tea.

The ladies seemed glad to receive their party favors. It seemed like a truly special treat when I gave them the red tablecloth and napkins. I even included a small box of gold glitter to spread onto the table if they wished a more festive look. We were using red and green balloons, but I knew that I couldn't have managed to bring them, and they probably wouldn't have used them anyway. Graham wasn't there, but that didn't spoil my happy time with Helga and Bertha. I left the keychain with Bertha in case I didn't see Graham before Christmas. When I left, I asked them to let Graham know I would like to hear from him in the next few days, if possible. I could see questions in their eyes, but I didn't want to say more.

When I returned to the Hey Ho, I noticed that the business section was still dark. I supposed Mr. Barbee had taken a day off to shop with his wife, or they might be visiting friends. As soon as I saw Mrs. Florene's reaction to the gingerbread and jam cake, Mr. Barbee's absence slipped my mind. She was delighted. The aroma filled her small kitchenette area without me even having to take the cloth off the basket. "Josie, dear girl, this is delightful. I must fix us a cup of tea right this minute." She bustled about putting water on to heat and pulling loose tea out of a cannister. Her small nimble fingers glided through her task, and she hummed to herself as she worked. I watched carefully as she made these preparations wanting to be ready if I decided to try and make tea for Graham at another time. Realizing I would have done it all wrong, I was grateful to have the opportunity to learn how to do it right. That is, if I ever decided to fix him tea at all.

We had such a nice time, eating gingerbread cookies, drinking our tea along with a nice thick piece of jam cake with the caramel frosting thick and brown half soaking into the cake. I was so warm and contented. It was utter heaven having someone wait on me, and simply allowing the taste to fill my all my senses, the spice, the sweet, the tangy aftertaste. This was one moment I hoped to remember forever. It vaguely crossed my mind to wonder if Bertha had taught Graham the secrets of her baking skills, seeing as he was a man who cooked.

Bringing my mind back to reality, I thought of how to reach Graham. He needed to know my plans and what was going on at the Hey Ho which brought my thoughts back to the darkened business section on the 2nd floor. "Mrs. Florene, I noticed this morning and again this afternoon that there were no lights and no activity in the business corridor," I said.

"Why, I'm sure I don't know anything about that. It seemed to me that Mr. Lowenston and his men were in Mr. Barbee's office until rather late yesterday evening, but I was so busy with this and that, I didn't keep my eye on the time. I simply assumed that they were going over receipts and such. You know, I don't believe I have seen any of them today." Mrs. Florene had a puzzled look on her face, "You know, dear, that when these men are taking care of business, their hours are not what yours and mine might be. They can be an odd lot for sure."

I didn't know if she was reassuring me or herself. I felt more and more puzzled about the mysterious circumstances in which I was becoming enmeshed. This was a tangled web. How were all these strings connected? "What about Jimmy Lee? Has he been about?"

"Oh yes, he was working with some of the newer girls on some of their dance moves," she said. "He will probably be in the staging area when you get there. In fact, if you will take Diamond out for his constitutional, I will tidy up here, and then come on down."

When I went down with Diamond, I saw Jimmy Lee talking to one of the men who silently followed Mr. Lowenston here and there. I didn't know his name for certain, but thought I heard someone call him Duncan. Indeed, he was the same one I saw earlier who was built like a barrel. Before he had been wearing a plaid newsboy cap with his long greasy looking hair hanging out, so I wasn't certain. Now, as he spoke and nodded to Jimmy Lee, I noticed he was bareheaded, which was probably why I didn't recognize him right away. His dark thinning hair was slicked back. He wore a black wool vest over a long-sleeved shirt with the sleeves rolled over his massive arms. Most of the men here seemed to have pants with tapered waists, but not this one. The buttons on his trousers and the buttons on his vest were a strained fit. I watched him thinking that any minute everything would explode, and buttons would be popping everywhere. This didn't happen. I couldn't make out much of the conversation except there seemed to be a lot of hand waving, sputtering, and gestures, some of which were not pretty.

I hurried Diamond out the door onto the grassy strip in the back. Diamond always seemed to do better out here with the large shrubs that offered him more privacy. Of course, this was probably my imagination. I did notice something had crushed into the shrubs and had broken off several branches. There was a scraped and muddied patch beside the shrubs. I craned my neck to look up to see if anything had fallen off the awnings or ledges of the building, but all I noticed was the darkened window of Mr. Barbee's office. Looking down to check on Diamond, I saw a faint glitter under one of the broken shrubs. Digging at it with the toe of my shoe, I noticed it looked like one of Mr. Barbee's jade cufflinks. Leaving it on the ground and shaking my head, I wondered what had happened here. Nothing good, I was certain. I was getting no easy answers. Since the wind had picked up and it was a bit chillier, I hustled Diamond back inside when he finished what he had to do.

Later, when Jimmy Lee came back to the dressing area, he seemed calm and collected. Sitting down beside me, he looked over my shoulder at the piece I was working on. He leaned in way too close, and I could feel his warm, peppermint-scented breath on my neck. When I turned and looked at him, I tried to give him a flirtatious smile which was only a grimace with my lips pulled back. I licked my lips. Not in invitation, but mostly because they seemed tight and dry. I laid my needles aside as I stood, telling him I needed to find Lila, so she could try on a head plume I'd adjusted. It had become easier for me to make up wild stories to fit situations. I don't think Poppa would have been proud, but he wouldn't have liked me to be in these situations anyway.

As I started down the hall on the pretext that I was looking for Lila, I ran into Mrs. Barbee. I was surprised to see her here, since she seldom came to see Mr. Barbee at work. She was a small curvy young woman who normally had a bubbling air and a smiling face, but now she was not smiling. A worried frown drew a deep line between her eyebrows. "Have you seen my Frank? He was supposed to meet me here for drinks and dinner. I thought there might have been some work problems, so I came to check on him. I have looked everywhere I can think of in this building, and nobody seems to have seen or spoken to him today."

My mind immediately went to the broken branches and the muddy patch under Mr. Barbee's office window. I wondered again if that was one of his cufflinks I saw. Shaking with nerves at my thoughts of what may have happened, I tried to answer her the best that I could, "No, Mrs. Barbee, I haven't seen him, but I will ask around. If I find out any information, I'll have someone call you."

She didn't look reassured at all, "I may have to call the police to see if they can locate him. I am becoming more and more worried. It isn't like him not to even call."

I was becoming more and more worried as well. I didn't have words to reassure her. She trotted down the hall with quick steps. Her head was bowed, and it looked as if she were pressing a small hanky to her eyes. Slowly, feeling sad about Mrs. Barbee, but knowing I had other things to attend to, I went back to Mrs. Florene's apartment. I needed to put in a call for Graham. It was time to let him know our plan was well under way. I didn't think I would reach him, but surprisingly, he answered the phone. "Hi," I said. "I wanted to fill you in on what Jenny Mae and I have agreed on for the Gala." I went on to let him know what we had discussed and the plan for the chloral hydrate.

He laughed as I gave him this information, "You are going to Mickey Finn him, huh? Will this be before or after you seduce him?" That really hurt my feelings. Did he think I would go that far with Jimmy Lee? Did he think that was necessary? I didn't know whether to keep talking or just hang up. I didn't feel like discussing more of the plan.

"All right," I said. "I just wanted to let you know." I put the receiver down a little less than gently.

Christmas seemed to be not much of an event since Gala preparations took up most of our time, and I didn't have time to go home to celebrate with friends and family. Mrs. Florene had Lester, the doorman, bring a small tree from his home in the country which we decorated with small bits of ribbon and lace. On Christmas Eve, Mrs. Florene had the girls come up to sing carols, drink eggnog, and exchange tiny baubles wrapped in brown paper and sealing wax. My gift from Mrs. Florene was a tiny pair of sparkling clip-on earrings that had what looked like small diamonds in them. I gave the girls and Mrs. Florene handkerchiefs that I had embroidered and hemmed.

December 30

Journal, Mrs. Florene tells me that she will be leaving in the morning on the train to visit her sister in New York. I hate it that she will miss the Gala. I had so hoped that she could have the opportunity to enjoy this grand party that she helped to create. I wanted her to meet Winston and Jenny Mae. They had heard me talk so much about her and how much she means to me. I will have to write her all about it.

Mrs. Florene flabbergasted me by telling me, not that she was simply leaving to visit her sister but leaving tomorrow for good. Not simply a visit. I had no warning that I could think of. I knew she had been pulling out suitcases and rearranging clothing in her armoire, but I didn't think much about it. She was always sorting through and giving away accessory items to the girls, so it seemed as if she was doing a bit more, but not a lot more. She did a bit of cleaning and rearranging, but I didn't think about that either. I thought she was only going for a visit, because she had said earlier that she and her sister in New York were planning to go to Florida and then on down to Havanna to play the cards and the numbers a bit. That surprised me since I hadn't noticed her paying all that much attention to the cards here. I supposed it was her sister who had most of the interest. I had no idea that she would be gone for good. I would miss her dreadfully.

Jenny Mae called to let me know that she and Winston would be there at 7:00 as planned. Winston would have the vial in his pocket. Cocktails were from 7:00-8:00, dinner from 8:00-9:30, and then dancing from 9:30 until midnight. When they arrived, we would coordinate our plans, then meet up with Jimmy Lee who was to be my date, and the evening would move on from there.

December 31

Journal, this is the day of the Gala. I don't know how it is going to come down. I am excited and nervous, but I'm certain that the New Year will happen, and all will be well.

I needed to get up bright and early to help Mrs. Florene make all the final preparations for her last-minute packing. Although I was happy Mrs. Florene would get to see her sister whom she hadn't seen for the last year or more, it left a bitter taste in my mouth. I would miss the person I now considered to be as close to me as the dearest of family members. This seemed to be a pattern, for another year to end, and with it, for me to lose someone near and dear to me. If life meant constantly losing everyone whom I loved, then I believe it would be hard to meet each new year with gratitude and hopefulness.

Mrs. Florene would not allow me to wallow in self-pity. The look in her eye told me to get over myself and move on. "Here," she said, handing me the phone. "Call Lester at the front desk and ask him to come up and help me with my trunks. I want you to gather all the valises that are in my bedroom and carry them into the hall in front of the elevator."

"What about the two valises beside your armoire?" I asked.

"No, not those. The little one has a few accessories and things I have saved back for Lila. I would like you to give it to her before you go down to the Gala," she said, looking up at me with a gentle smile. "You know, I have always had the greatest affection and respect for Lila, but she is nearing the end of her time here. She is already thirty-five years old, and it is uncommon for girls who are getting a bit long in the tooth to continue in this business. She will have to move on soon. The management will not want her here much longer."

When she said management, I thought maybe Mr. Barbee, and again wondered at his absence. "Mr. Barbee doesn't want her?" I asked.

"He wouldn't care one way or another, but I think maybe some of the higher up folks want only young and fresh girls here. However, I don't think we will be seeing Mr. Barbee again around here again." I looked at her with surprise and questions in my eyes, but I didn't say anything more. "The larger valise is somewhat the same. That one is for you. Please don't open it until later tonight or in the morning. This is your New Year's present and the gift for the daughter I never had. Oh, and let me give you my beryl ring." She pulled the large piece of beautiful purple-red jewelry from her finger. "It will go beautifully with your dress for tonight."

Now, I did start to bubble up. But of course, I had to swallow my tears as Lester was at the door for the trunks and baggage. I had to head out with dignity and take the remaining valises to the elevator door. "I can take these down with us to the cab," I said pointing at the door.

"No, we need to say our goodbyes here," Mrs. Florene said. "It will be too painful for me to watch you at the door as I drive off in the cab. I must let you go now." She took my chin in her fingers and gave me a look of gentle warmth and caring. She folded me in her arms and rocked me back and forth as if I were a young child. I cried softly into her shoulder. Then, pulling on her gloves, she wrapped her stole around her shoulders, picked up her travel bag and Diamond's carrier, and walked out.

I gazed at the door with a sense of total loss. The room now seemed empty and raw. All the charm and elegance of the apartment was as so much gilt and floss without substance now that Mrs. Florene was gone. I turned back to arrange the valises, the large and small so that I would remember which went to whom. They were the only bits of Mrs. Florene left to light up the room.

I worked hard to get through the day. I had to carry out the plans Jenny Mae and I had devised. When Winston and Jenny Mae arrived at 7:00 along with my date, Jimmy Lee, they needed to see me as the most fun date at the party. I would make Mrs. Florene proud of me. Since I would have the apartment to myself until then, I could use Mrs. Florene's liquor cabinet to access the champagne I thought I needed. I looked through the cabinet at all the offerings there. When I saw one that I had heard of from a customer, 'Moet Et Chandon,' I decided I would chill a bottle.

Next, I laid out my lovely dress and the beautiful matching shoes. Cleaning my shoes carefully, I filed where the heel attached to the base of the left one and then applied a light layer of glue to hold it together. I needed a nice normal touch to disguise my tripping plan. There, I thought. Ready for the performance of my lifetime which I hoped to survive. I would not dwell on my loss of Mrs. Florene or wonder about the contents of the valise.

After a long leisurely bath in the big claw footed tub complete with scented powders, soaps, and fluffy towels left by Mrs. Florene, I felt like a movie star preparing for a role of high drama, which I suppose I was. I put on my everyday dress to go downstairs and make sure everything was ready for the Gala. Did Lester, the doorman, have someone to help him check the invitations to make certain that those who came in were allowed? Were the women who were to dance the elegant numbers prepared with all their routines? Of course, with Lila in charge of the dancers, they should be. Did the band members have questions? Most had prepared Glenn Miller swing music which meant there would be lots of noise and movement. When I was satisfied that there was nothing left to do downstairs, I went upstairs for a nap. I thought I'd even take a taste or two of Mrs. Florene's champagne to make me a bit less nervous of the night to come.

I couldn't sleep. I paced, I rearranged odds and ends of things sitting on the dresser and cabinets. I took Lila's valise down to her. Lila's eyes brimmed with tears as I placed the valise at her feet. It was a bit heavy, and although she didn't open it, I assured her that Mrs. Florene said it held items she thought Lila would treasure. "Oh, Josie, I can't believe that she has left us. She has meant so much to me over the past years. She took me in when I was down and out and gave me the will and the means to move on. I need to take care of a few things now, but I want to drop by and thank you when I have had the chance to open this," she said mopping her eyes with the backs of her hands and nodding toward the valise.

"You don't have to thank me, Lila. It was all from Florene," I said. "She was a wonderful person and one that I won't forget in my lifetime. I have a few other things to take care of myself, so let me get back upstairs, and we can talk later."

When I went back to the apartment, I dressed Mrs. Florene's beautiful bed for the amorous events of the evening to come. I put on her scented satin sheets and pillowcases and dusted them with additional lavender scent before piling high her gorgeous pillows and folding the pink satin bedspread over the top of the bed. I laid my sewing basket beside the bedside table and placed fresh cut flowers into a cut glass vase on top of the table. It was a special Sunday delivery, but the florists were more than willing to accommodate the Hey Ho's owners every whim. I arranged the oversized rug close to the side of the bed.

At last, it was time to dress and go downstairs. I wish I hadn't chosen to wear nylons, but of course, I had to try to look like Greta Garbo, with her sultry sweeping looks. Her seams would stay straight, no doubt. Mine would become all twisted. Maybe I should try for a Ginger Rogers look. With all her dancing and twirling, no one would notice her seams.

I put on my slip and pulled the dress over my body. The feel and texture of the dress made it seem molded around me. I picked up the mink stole and tried it in various ways around my shoulders and arms. Feeling the very soul of glamour, I hoped everyone who saw it would think so too when I swept across the room.

I managed to get into the elevator in my high heels and my dress. I didn't quite trust the stairs. Then I made my entrance and caught Jenny Mae's eye across the room. Now, she, married lady though she was, could easily manage the movie star image, I thought, looking at her elegant way of commanding the room. She and Winston hustled over to me. Winston, without saying a word, pulled the vial from his pocket and slid it into my small clutch purse, alongside my hanky and sen-sen. Jenny Mae put her arms around me and gave me a big hug. Out of the corner of my eye, I saw Jimmy Lee hurrying over to greet us. He gave my shoulder a brief squeeze, gave Jenny Mae a quick kiss on the cheek, and turned enthusiastically to speak to Winston.

Mr. Lowenston and his men were drinking cocktails in the corner. Jimmy Lee excused himself to go speak with them. Mr. Barbee was nowhere to be seen. I felt a pang of remorse that Mrs. Barbee hadn't located him, and no one had mentioned him again.

Jenny Mae, Winston, and I caught on the news from home. Who had gotten married, who had had babies, who died. I think Jenny Mae used this babble of conversation to help calm my nerves. She had always been able to read me like a book. Jenny Mae had gone to the cemetery to attend to Momma and Poppa's graves since I hadn't been able to get home for Christmas. She assured me that the graves had been taken care of, and that she and Winston had taken some extra greenery to place on the graves. Jenny Mae told me she placed the boughs on the graves and told them I hadn't forgotten them but would be coming home after the Gala was over.

Soon, Jimmy Lee returned, and we had drinks and hors d'oeuvres before dinner. The appetizers and drinks were beautifully presented and delectable according to Jenny Mae. To me, even though everything looked bright and shiny, I could hardly taste a thing. My stomach was tied in knots. Dinner was wonderful as well. Many of the regular customers who knew me from my hostess duties came up to our party and introduced themselves or allowed me to introduce them to my friends. All of them seemed quite friendly. They were gracious and glad to be invited to the special affair.

Mr. Lowenston and his friends stayed in their separate group like a murder of crows. Curious name for a group of crows, I thought. It occurred to me to find the origin of the name. Still, they huddled in their little black group, seated at the table, eating, drinking, but not seeming a bit joyous.

When the tables cleared for dancing, we all stretched and moved about, greeting friends or business associates we hadn't had the opportunity to greet earlier. Most of the women went in to powder their noses and apply additional lip polish, and maybe to sneak a quick cigarette. I thought about doing the same, but since my hands were shaking, I decided it wasn't such a great idea. With my clumsiness, who knew where the lip polish would end up. And even if I did smoke, there was the possibility I'd burn the place down or catch something on fire. It would be better for me if I went back to work out my nerves with a little dancing.

Sure enough, when the dancing started, I loosened up quite a bit. I took off my heels so I could dance in my bare feet. At last, I felt like myself. I was more at ease than I had been all day. We had a few slower dances, and I used these to catch my breath and slow the emotional roaring in my brain. Still, these slow dances made me feel as if Jimmy Lee was covering me like a second skin. On one of the slow dances, I felt Jimmy Lee pull slightly away, and then realized Winston had tapped him on the shoulder to ask to break in so that I could have the dance with him. Jimmy Lee gave a smile and a shrug, and went on back to the bar, to get himself something more to drink. I'm sure he would have danced with Jenny Mae, but she hadn't stayed alone for but a few seconds.

"Everything okay with you?" Winston asked. "Keep your purse close."

"I will. I think I will be fine," I assured him. I wasn't certain I was fine, but I was going to give it my best.

"Good, then I will give you back into the arms of my best man," Winston said trying to control the smirk on his face as he looked at Jimmy Lee coming back to claim me.

The music broke into a series of fast rhythmic tunes. We all swayed and moved and bounced all over that dance floor. If I hadn't been worried about later, I would have been having a wonderful time. When the clock struck 10:45, the music slowed down again. Many of the couples were leaning into each other, some very drunk, some loud and shrill. Still, everyone seemed to be having a good time. Food had been set up at the bar, for those who needed an extra bit of food after all the dancing.

Jimmy Lee pulled me closer and closer to him. I tucked my face into his shirt so that I could be close but not too close. Once again, I felt him pull away, so I assumed it was Winston again. When I raised my head, I found it was Graham. Jimmy Lee was not happy at all. He gave me a sharp look with a scowl on his face but took my hand and handed me over to Graham who looked smug and self-assured, as usual. Graham leaned toward me almost wrapping me in his arms and whispered in my ear, "We got this covered. Try to leave as soon as you can." He turned and walked with me to where Jimmy Lee stood against the bar, and said to him, "Thank you for lending me this lovely lady." Then, he backed away from us with a quick grin, and a salute before disappearing.

"Here, Jimmy Lee, let me wear my heels. I want to look more lady-like as we get closer to midnight." I made my way to our table and rescued my lovely strapless heels from under the table where I had shoved them. Leaning against Jimmy Lee, I put one on and then the other. "Now, I'm ready to try some nice romantic dancing," I said, cuddled up to him. We danced a nice, gentle dance as I snuggled into his arms. We made a truly elegant turn, and I pitched forward as the doctored heel of my left shoe broke off. "Oh, how witless of me to be so clumsy. I'll need to go upstairs to get another pair. Give me a few minutes to find others, and then maybe you can join me?" I tried to raise one eyebrow but since that didn't work, I gave him a wink, "I do think Mrs. Florene has some lovely champagne we could sample while we are there."

Jimmy Lee gave me a long, slow smile, and said, "Sure thing, we can have a personal New Year's celebration."

With my shoes in hand, I trotted upstairs quickly as I could without being too obvious. On the landing of the second floor, I saw a movement in the shadows of the business section. Duncan stepped out of the gloom and grabbed me by both arms before I could process what was happening. My breath caught in my throat, and I felt a terrible sinking feeling throughout my body. He shook me so hard, I thought I heard my teeth rattle. My head snapped back as he snarled into my face. I could see his yellowed teeth in front of me and spittle flew out of his mouth as he spoke.

"I want to know what Mrs. Florene has been up to," he said. "We know Jimmy Lee has been blackmailing our clients, but we're sure now that Mrs. Florene is the one skimming funds off the top. Her and her damned girls, that nasty whore. I can't believe she's run off and taken everything with her. Where's she gone with it? If she told anyone, she told you. We figured she wasn't turning in all the cash from the girls, taking more than her portion for sure. Lots of cash missing. Boss thought Mr. Barbee was taking the money or at least informing your G-man friend about our business. Don't know about that, never told the likes of me and the guys, anyway, just that we had to take care of him."

He shook me so hard I fell backwards, landing on top of me pinning me to the floor. I couldn't breathe. I thought for sure I would smother to death with his massive weight grinding down. Just as I felt the room begin to darken and my vision start to fade, I heard a loud crunch. The weight which had pinned me down now rolled to one side. Looking up, I saw Lila holding the large table lamp from the hallway. The slag glass dome was buried in the side of Duncan's head. I gasped in shock. Not knowing whether Duncan was dead or alive, I pushed the rest of him off me and struggled to my feet.

"We need to push him back down the hall," Lila said. "No, not you. You go. Some of the other girls are coming down. They'll help me. We'll take care of him. Since the hall is darker without the lamp, we should have a bit of time. You, Josie, go!" She stabbed her finger toward the stairs.

I hurried on up the steps knowing my time was now more limited than before. When I opened the door, I noticed that the valise was still in the middle of the room where I had pushed it out of the way when I took Lila's down for her. I thought it best to move it over to the side of the armoire.

Even though I knew I shouldn't take the extra time, as I pushed the valise, I felt my curiosity getting the best of me. Maybe I had a few minutes to open my valise. I simply couldn't help myself. I lifted it. It felt heavy, but not excessively so. When I pushed the valise toward the armoire, the straps burst open and the top gaped wide. There were stacks and stacks of banded dollar bills. On top lay a velvet bag. When I opened it, there was Mrs. Florene's beautiful pear-shaped amethyst and diamond necklace. Even in the dark of the armoire, it glittered and glowed. There was a note attached.

Dear Girl,

I don't know when you will decide to open this. You can wear the necklace to the Gala if you open it in time. You shouldn't mention this gift to anyone. This is your dowry, so to speak. Follow your dreams.

Love Always,
Florene

All I could do was gasp. I had to get the valise back into the armoire and conceal these bills. I was short on time, but convinced myself I could do this. Breathlessly, I struggled, pushing and jerking the valise, until it was hidden. Then, I hurried to get ready. Taking the champagne from the icebox, I struggled to pop the cork. Earlier, I had planned to have Jimmy Lee open it, but thought he might have noticed the powder when I put it in his glass. When the bottle was finally opened, I poured the bubbly liquid into two tall crystal glasses and dissolved the Mickey Finn into it just as he came up the steps. I made certain that his glass was in the same hand on which I wore Mrs. Florene's purplish-red beryl ring.

"Hey there, sweet thing," he said. It was all I could do not to gag, but I smiled and managed to sit on the edge of the bed, pushing my garnet dress up over my knees, letting my bare feet swing back and forth. Handing him his glass of champagne, I retrieved mine from the bedside table. Immediately, he started kissing the side of my neck. Gently pushing him away, I said, "Let's toast with this champagne."

"Oh, the celebration libation," he said. How stupid, I thought. Still, I smiled and sipped and crossed my legs toward him. He did the same as he leaned closer toward me, encircling my waist with his arm, "Let's get this down, so we can start our personal celebration." He took several long swallows of his drink, and I simply held mine. When he was finished, he placed his empty glass on the table next to the champagne bottle with a gentle thump. He reached out and took my glass from me, placing it on the table as well.

Putting both his hands around my waist, he pulled me closer. His fingers slipped from my waist to my shoulders and upward so that his fingers ran through my hair. Rubbing his thumbs along my neck, he lightly grasped my neck in his hands and began squeezing. "You are serious about this, aren't you? Not hiding any guilty secrets," he said, rubbing his fingers up my neck and down along my collar bones. I felt the edge of a nail digging into my skin. "I'm not as dumb as you might think I am. Seems you're a little too cozy with Mrs. Florene, and I am beginning to wonder about the smell of this whole situation." His fingers gripped a bit more firmly, pressing so hard into the tops of my shoulders, I wondered if he would leave bruises. "Mrs. Florene seems to have jumped ship. I'm wondering just what it is you do know."

My stomach tightened with fear and anxiety. I had thought I would be fighting off his romantic intentions, not his murderous ones. "What a wild imagination you have!" I reached up and caressed his thumb with one hand. "I don't have a clue as to what you're talking about. Would you like more champagne? There seems to be more left in the bottle." I reached across him, picked up the bottle, and emptied it into his glass. "We can finish this lovely champagne and go on with our celebration," I said with a breathy sigh.

With a bemused look on his face, he took the wrist of my left hand, gripping it in his fist. His other hand still encircling my neck, pulled me closer to him. "This ring gives you away," he said, running his hand over my ring finger. "You know more than you're telling me, and I am getting it out of you one way or the other," menace smeared his voice and with an icy look, his tiger eyes were hard and unyielding.

I glanced up with what I hoped was an innocent look, eyes wide, lips pouting, "I don't know what you are talking about. You have had way too much to drink. Mrs. Florene loaned me this ring to wear tonight. She'll be back to get it after she and her sister have had their fun at the casinos in Havana." I needed to distract him away from Mrs. Florene's actual destination.

He tipped back his glass and drained his champagne with his left hand still around my neck. I looked at him for a moment and then asked him for my drink. He loosened his left hand around my neck to steady himself while he reached for my glass with his right. "Drink up sweetie, my party is about to begin," he slurred. I took my drink and managed a single sip while pulling away from him. "Where are you going? You seem to be the guest of honor, and you have the information I need. I don't believe Mrs. Florene is in Cuba, but I'm sure you know where she is. Unlike you, I didn't just fall off the turnip cart. I've been at this for a long time. I'm not about to be taken in by your innocent naivete. I know all about Graham, your G-man boyfriend. You are going to give me some details and some fun."

Grabbing me again, he began to unhook the beautiful buttons on the front of my dress. I tried hard not to resist, even though I wanted to. I was scared of what he would do if I did. I hoped that the Mickey Finn would save my honor and my life. As he worked his way down the buttons, it became more of an effort for him. I thought it was the way the buttons were designed. Just as he was about to get the last one undone, he began to slide down the satin sheets and onto the lovely, oversized rag rug I had made for Mrs. Florene. I had to slide with him, sloshing my drink a bit, since he was holding me tightly. At least, I didn't have to pull him down. He'd done it by himself.

I watched him lying there on the floor as I shrugged my dress back around my shoulders, buttoned the more strategic buttons, set my drink aside, and reached for my sewing basket. Jimmy Lee looked motionless as he lay there on the carpet, his skin as pale as buttermilk. The only movement was the soft lift of his copper-colored mustache. I couldn't help but notice tiny flecks of dandruff nestled in the shiny pomade of his hair. His hands with their long slender fingers and trimmed nails looked so dainty. Too bad they would have to be covered. I patted him gently on the face with a feeling of total satisfaction. Outside, I heard the bells and fireworks announcing that this new year was about to begin. Now, I could start sewing the lovely rag rug around him as Jenny Mae and I had imagined. The colors were so brilliant. What a contrast to his pasty flesh. The brilliant blues like velvet, the brownish yellow, the color of perfect fried chicken, yet with a deep pure texture.

I couldn't continue to sit and stare. I would have to continue to weave my carpet needles in and out as I provided the perfect spider's nest of entrapment until Graham and his men arrived. Jenny Mae would come in to check on me in a bit, so we could celebrate the arrival of the New Year. I told myself I couldn't wallow on the 'what might have beens' I'd had with my first dreams of Jimmy Lee. Funny how time and maturity change you. I continued to stitch on. Humming and stitching. The rug covering nicely binding feet, arms, and hands. Almost as if I had synchronized the stitches to the timing, I finished the last one just as I heard rushing footsteps on the floor outside. I put my sewing things back into my basket and stood to open the door.

"Oh, Graham, here you are," I said as I held the door open for him and the men behind him. His gaze darted from me and then over to Jimmy Lee.

"What do we have here?" he asked. His men stood snickering as they waited for a signal as to what to do next. They were alert and ready but perplexed as to how to make their next move.

I looked at Jimmy Lee lying still and immobile in his colorful cocoon. "This is where you put handcuffs on him, isn't it?" I asked.

Graham looked down at Jimmy Lee's prostrate form. "Now, Josie, how do you propose I do that?" he said, shaking his head in wonder. Tilting his head in my direction, he gave me a genuinely warm smile. "Seems like he will have to be carried out like a corpse. A living, breathing corpse to be sure, but you did manage to catch an interesting bit of prey in your design. Not a bug, not a fly, so I guess I'll just have to call him a louse."

Chapter Twelve

A Dream Come True

1940

Dear Journal:

My Name is Josie Kassemier, and I am 24 years old, almost. I think the time has come when I need to set you aside for a while. 1939 was a tumultuous year. Graham and I are working on sending Jimmy Lee to prison. After the raid, the Hey Ho was shuttered. I lost track of Lila and the rest of the girls. None of us has heard from Mrs. Florene. Someone may look at this and see things they needn't see. I will wait until the time comes when no one knows or cares what it is I do or have done. So, I suppose I will say it is time to close the curtain.

Chapter Thirteen

Those Old Journals

2010

Those old journals, how much it means to look over them once more. My clothing business in Cincinnati is now in the hands of Helga's capable granddaughter, Stella. Her sister, Louisa, manages the showroom downtown that showcases the wonderful gowns. Always in the front is the dress I made and wore for the competition when I was fifteen. I can hardly imagine myself at that age, although my portrait remains beside it.

I never saw Mrs. Florene again, but I put her money to good use. My designs, Josie's Jewels, have been used in several theater and movie productions. We process orders and see customers and socialites from New York to California, and all over the world. Graham never asked me directly about the money. He hinted, both before and after we married. I hesitated a moment before answering, knowing that Mrs. Florene had become my ideal of what a lady should be in that day and time. Then, I simply told him that Mrs. Florene had saved her money for years and gave it to me as her daughter-in-love. Which was true in a sense. The Raisch family became my family. Helga and Bertha helped with the start up of my business, Jenny Mae, being in the newspaper business helped to design advertisements and brochures. Albert, Helga's boyfriend and later Helga's husband, became my best salesman. He became as knowledgeable about women's fashions as he had been for men.

The money I put in Poppa's account as Jimmy Lee's 'layoff bank' person was used to indict Jimmy Lee for partial evidence in the extortion scheme. Mr. DeMarco and other customers appeared in court to testify to the demands Jimmy Lee had made. Mr. Barbee turned up in the spring of 1940. During the spring thaw, his body washed up and became entrapped in a downed tree limb on the riverbank. Even though his body was damaged by time and water, it seemed his death had been caused by a blow to the head. On his right wrist dangled a jade cufflink. Now I knew in my heart what happened to Mr. Barbee. The thought of reporting who I thought was responsible for his death crossed my mind, but I knew it would be useless. I never saw Mrs. Barbee again.

As I am sitting here reminiscing about the past, my beautiful young granddaughter comes to me and admires my necklace. "I have never seen anything so beautiful," she said with a wistful gaze. "I know that it's fake, but I think it is lovely. It makes me feel like a real lady, just like you."

"Here, dear," I said. "Please unhook it for me." She did, and I laid it gently in her hand. "Can you keep a secret?"

"Well, of course, Grandma," she answered.

"First of all, please call me Josie," I said. "Grandma makes me feel like an old biddy. I know I seem ancient to you, but I don't like the reminders. The secret is this necklace is not fake. It's probably worth a small fortune. The real story of the necklace lies in my journals and tells of the days when I was hardly a lady. I want you to keep them and discover the truth when I'm gone." I handed her the necklace, "you shouldn't mention this gift to anyone. This is your dowry, so to speak. Follow your dreams."

Acknowledgments

Special thanks to my mother-in-law, Goldie Strickler, for recording her memories and dreams into journals during the years mentioned in this book. She was indeed awarded honors for her sewing abilities by her local 4H chapter and the University of Kentucky. She also took the trip to Chicago and visited the places in Hardly a Lady. Special thanks to her good friend and neighbor Ollie Mae Boyers on whom the character, Jenny Mae was based. These two girls didn't do all the things written, but I could see them trying. I know Ollie Mae was a beautiful, smart and successful newspaperwoman.

Thanks to Liz Carey for spending countless hours helping me bring these characters to life. She is a wonderful and talented writer, and I am so grateful she took the time away from her own work to help. I don't know many who would be as generous with their time and encouragement. The Carnegie Center in Lexington is fortunate to have her as one of their mentors.

Much appreciation to the Newport Gangster Tour which fueled my imagination. Sin City was what they called Newport, Kentucky in the Prohibition era (1919-1932), and the years of efforts to reform it through the 1960's. The Newport Gangster Tour was named by Southern Living as one of the 10 best things to do in Kentucky.

My husband, Dewey Strickler, was a tremendous help in reading and rereading pages over and over again. He is so knowledgeable about the facts of farm life and financial details. This book would have been fifty pages without his memories and information.

My niece, Candace Diaz, helped enormously with fashion details, and other details. Thanks to my two Beta readers, Dawn Strickler and Mary Lou Mathews. My reading group was the best and Janeen, Krystol, and Tonya helped through tough spots.

Finally, to Erin Chandler for her edits and the whole team at Rabbit House Press.

About The Author

    Hardly a Lady is Frances Strickler's second novel dealing with the broad range of Kentucky history. She is from Franklin, Kentucky and holds a bachelor's degree in English from the University of Kentucky as well as a minor in history. In addition, she has a master's degree in Counselor Education from Western Kentucky University and additional graduate hours in psychology and counseling. She is also licensed in mental health counseling from the state of Kentucky.

    In addition to writing, Frances teaches yoga and mental health/ yoga workshops to both adult students and other teachers.

References

Drake, C. C., & Wigginton, E. (1976). The Foxfire Book: hog dressing, log cabin building, mountain crafts and foods, Planting by the signs, snake lore, hunting tales, faith healing, moonshining, and other affairs of plain living. Western Folklore, 35(4), 281. https://doi.org/10.2307/1499309

Strickler, G. (1930-1940) Journals.

Williams, M. (2008). Sin city Kentucky: Newport, Kentucky's vice heritage and its legal extinction, 1920-1991. https://doi.org/10.18297/etd/1574

Wigginton, E. (1973). Foxfire 2: ghost stories, spring wild plant foods, spinning and weaving, midwifing, burial customs, corn shuckin's, wagon making and more affairs of plain living. In Anchor Press/Doubleday eBooks. http://ci.nii.ac.jp/ncid/BA21180480